HELENE
novel f
publish
in 2001   o
acclaim   k
which '1   l-
time w   d
continu   e
time she   r
educatic   l
upon wl   e
beste bl

KARI D   n
Britain a   d
then late   a
number   1

Edinburg.., ... works as a part-time tutor at the university.

Some other books from Norvik Press

Victoria Benedictsson: *Money* (translated by Sarah Death)

Hjalmar Bergman: *Memoirs of a Dead Man* (translated by Neil Smith)

Jens Bjørneboe: *Moment of Freedom* (translated by Esther Greenleaf Mürer)

Jens Bjørneboe: *Powderhouse* (translated by Esther Greenleaf Mürer)

Jens Bjørneboe: *The Silence* (translated by Esther Greenleaf Mürer)

Johan Borgen: *The Scapegoat* (translated by Elizabeth Rokkan)

Fredrika Bremer: *The Colonel's Family* (translated by Sarah Death)

Suzanne Brøgger: *A Fighting Pig's Too Tough to Eat* (translated by Marina Allemano)

Camilla Collett: *The District Governor's Daughters* (translated by Kirsten Seaver)

Kerstin Ekman: *Witches' Rings* (translated by Linda Schenck)

Kerstin Ekman: *The Spring* (translated by Linda Schenck)

Kerstin Ekman: *The Angel House* (translated by Sarah Death)

Kerstin Ekman: *City of Light* (translated by Linda Schenck)

Knut Hamsun: *Selected Letters* (2 vols.) (edited and translated by James McFarlane and Harald Næss)

P. C. Jersild: *A Living Soul* (translated by Rika Lesser)

Viivi Luik: *The Beauty of History* (translated by Hildi Hawkins)

Runar Schildt: *The Meat-Grinder and Other Stories* (translated by Anna-Liisa and Martin Murrell)

Amalie Skram: *Lucie* (translated by Katherine Hanson and Judith Messick)

Amalie and Erik Skram: *Caught in the Enchanter's Net: Selected Letters* (edited and translated by Janet Garton)

August Strindberg: *Tschandala* (translated by Peter Graves)

Hanne Marie Svendsen: *Under the Sun* (translated by Marina Allemano)

Hjalmar Söderberg: *Martin Birck's Youth* (translated by Tom Ellett)

Hjalmar Söderberg: *Selected Stories* (translated by Carl Lofmark)

Edith Södergran: *The Poet Who Created Herself: Selected Letters* (edited and translated by Silvester Mazzarella)

Ellen Wägner: *Penwoman* (translated by Sarah Death) (2007)

HONEY TONGUES

A Novel

by

Helene Uri

Translated from the Norwegian by

Kari Dickson

Norvik Press
2007

Originally published in Norwegian by Gyldendal Norsk Forlag under the title *Honningtunger* in 2002.

Translation © Kari Dickson 2007.

The translator has asserted her moral right to be identified as the translator of the work.

A catalogue record for this book is available from the British Library.
ISBN 13: 978-1-870041-72-0
First published in 2007 by Norvik Press, University of East Anglia, Norwich NR4 7TJ.

Norvik Press gratefully acknowledges the financial assistance given by NORLA (Norwegian Literature Abroad), and the Arts Council (England) towards publication of this book.

Website: www.norvikpress.com
E-mail address: norvik.press@uea.ac.uk

Managing editors: Janet Garton, Neil Smith, C. Claire Thomson.

Cover photograph: © Laura Scott

Cover design: Richard Johnson

Printed in the UK by Page Bros. (Norwich) Ltd, Norwich, UK

SEWING CIRCLE

LISS, 36, homemaker
Good friends! Good food! Chat. Lots of laughter.
Wine. Often too much wine! We don't actually sew
anything. Our sewing circle evenings are an oasis in
the humdrum of daily life.

WOMAN, 74, retired bus driver
I've been in a sewing circle since I was in class two.
We used to do more actual sewing, but we still stitch
our grandchildren's names onto clothes and things
like that, you know. And we have a good time, drink
coffee and sometimes a little sherry. It's sad, you
know, when one of us dies. Magda died last year.
Cancer. And Olaug's husband passed away two years
ago now. We're all heading the same way. I guess I'm
just at that age now, you know. I always start at the
back of the paper and read the obituaries first.

MAN, 42, engineer and journalist
Sewing club, right. Isn't it the same as what we boys
mean when we say we're going on a fishing trip?

WOMAN, 31, bar tender
That's kind of old fashioned, isn't it?
Nowadays, I think it's more usual to have cultural
groups, gourmet clubs, dinner clubs and book groups,
things like that. I think sewing circles are more a
thing of the past. I associate them with middle-aged,
married women who are nice to each other on the
surface. Doilies, back stabbing and intrigue.

MAN, 76, retired warehouse worker
A flock of squawking gossipmongers! Every Thursday. They talk and talk, but I'm not sure that they actually say anything.

EVA, 36, (recently promoted) senior teacher
I'm just so grateful to be part of my sewing circle. It's something I've always wanted, ever since I was a girl. I've always wanted sisters and now I've got some. The sewing circle is one of the most important things in my life now. Sewing circles are often quite cliquey and hard to get into. It's actually quite difficult to make new friends at my age. But I managed.

WOMAN, 28, student
MAN, 31, nursery school teacher
'You have the opportunity to engage in crafts at quite a high level on the one hand and on the other, you engage with each other on a deeper level. As human beings, I mean.'
'Oh, come on, you don't do either at a stitch and bitch.'
'Remember, women can actually do two things at once. Unlike you men. You can't even chew gum and drive a car at the same time. There's a reason why there's no equivalent for men.'

TAMARA, 36, journalist
I've been in the same sewing circle since I was in primary school. To begin with there were only two of us, then three and now we're four. Sara and I, then Liss and more recently, Eva. Sewing circle, stitch and bitch, bitch and banter, banter and spew...

MAN, 27, student
They talk about us, don't they? I don't think much

sewing gets done. I'd love to be a fly on the wall at one. My girlfriend's in a sewing circle.

SARA, 36, translator

My sewing circle is a forum where I can discuss things that are important to me that I might not necessarily discuss with my husband. The bond between us is utterly unique. We can talk about anything and everything – and do. It is where I meet my very closest friends.

This book is dedicated to all my girlfriends,
to those in the dinner club, those in the book group and
those who are more free-range. Any similarities between any of
you and the characters in *Honey Tongues* are purely coincidental,
and can only be ascribed to all your inspiration over many years...
Thank you to all of you.

SEWING CIRCLE EVENINGS

It's probably relatively dark outside. Maybe late summer, or perhaps winter. Possibly early autumn. Or April. It could well be raining. Heavy, warm summer rain. Or a light spring drizzle. Perhaps even big, soft snowflakes. If there's any wind at all, it's only a gentle breeze. Because it's quite quiet. Quite quiet and quite dark.

Picture a newly-painted, light grey terraced house, or a red kit house with a balcony and bay windows. A classic yellow wooden villa. Or a spacious modernist flat with big windows. An occasional car drives past the grey terraced house, the red or yellow house, or the spacious flat. But there aren't many cars around this evening. They drive slowly past and perhaps the headlamps reflect in a puddle. Or the car skids a bit on the newly fallen snow, or the yellow maple leaves lying on the cold, black asphalt. In one of the houses, in the light grey terraced house, in the red kit house, in the yellow villa or the modernist flat, four women sit eating at a table. The interior is warm and light. Their voices are raised and happy. There is laughter and soft music. The smell of ginger and garlic or maybe chilli, fresh rosemary and dry sherry mingles with the scent of the four perfumes. The women are warm and their cheeks glow. Their mouths open and shut. They eat, they lift their wine glasses to their mouths and drink. And they talk. If we move closer, we can hear what the women are saying:

'Lovely food! Delicious and that slightly tangy aftertaste, is it lemon?'

'Have you heard about my neighbour's sister-in-law?'

'No, do tell! Nice jacket, by the way.'

'Who's your neighbour's sister-in-law? Is she the fat one?'

'Is it coriander?'

'Thanks. I got it in the sale just the other day. No, no, not the fat one. My neighbour's sister-in-law is the one with the long, red hair and beautiful clothes. The one that works in that advertising agency, you know...'

'Yes, I know who you mean.'

'So do I. What has she done?'

'Coriander seeds? Is that what you've got in it?'

'She's left her husband and children.'

'Has she? I have to admit the idea is incredibly tempting sometimes.'

'It's not sage, is it?'

'Yes, yes, with a musician in a Bulgarian dance band!'

'No! Really? The kind with Brylcreem and a green tuxedo?'

'Sky blue, I think, actually. And sequins. They eloped on Friday night, took the boat to Denmark. No, it's not sage either. It's actually Kaffir lime leaves.'

'Lime leaves, of course. That's just what I thought.'

'How much did you pay for it?'

'800. It was in the sale, like I said.'

'Hungarian, did you say?'

On one side of the table sit two dark-haired women. Their two dark heads move. They lean in, turn their faces towards each other and smile. The table is bedecked with plates, cutlery and wine bottles, a jug of water and a bunch of flowers in a low vase. On the other side of the table sit two other women. They look about the same age as the first couple. One has lighter hair and brown eyes. The other has a round face and blonde hair. Together, they make up the sewing circle. But can we see the flash of sewing needles? Do we hear the clicking of knitting needles? No, we hear the clinking of glasses. We see the sparkle of green wine bottles. Loud laughter. And chatter. At least two women's voices at once, all the time.

'Do you know what? I was at one of those home parties last week.'

'Tupperware, or something else?'

'I finally managed to get an appointment with the doctor yesterday. I've been getting such terrible headaches recently.'

'Which doctor do you use?'

'The one down at the health centre. The young one, new.'

'Right, him, yes! The good-looking one?'

'Exactly!'

'What did he say about your headaches, then?'

'He said: "Madam, please lie down on my gynaecologist's couch and spread your legs. I think a thorough investigation of your private parts is what is needed, more than anything."'

'Did he really say that?! But wasn't it a headache?'

'No. Of course he didn't. He gave me a prescription for some painkillers and said I should take it easy. Who said something about a Tupperware home party?'

'No, umm. It wasn't exactly Tupperware. What would you call it? I guess sex toys is the best description.'

'Wow! Did you buy anything?'

'Yes, well, there's quite a lot of pressure on you to buy. So I felt I had to.'

'Aha!'

'Um, I got one of those...'

'A two-headed? A three-headed?'

'What?'

'No, no, a completely straight one. Black.'

'And what does your so-called better half have to say about that? Grateful for some respite?'

'Maybe I could get your doctor's number?'

Laughing loudly, or perhaps talking in quiet, intimate voices, the women move away from the dining table. Dessert bowls displaying the remains of coconut parfait with bright yellow mango sauce, or maybe green kiwi sauce with the seeds floating in it like black commas, or the empty skins of baked bananas and white chocolate, are forsaken on the table along with the crumpled serviettes, the empty water jug and a wine bottle. The four ladies sit down and curl up in the armchairs and sofa. One of them holds an unlit cigarette in her slim, pale hand. High-heeled shoes lie in a pile on the carpet, which is an exclusive Persian carpet in soft crimson red, or a fluffy white sheep's fleece. On the coffee table stand one half-full bottle of white wine and an unopened one, and a bowl of rice cakes, with practically no calories, or for that matter, taste, smell or weight. In the background, music that no one is listening to. More laughter, intoxicating wine, giggling.

'Shall I put on some other music?'
　'And then I said I'd never heard anything like it.'
　'You said that? I can't believe you dared!'
　'Do you want to hear something else?'
　'Umm, yes, maybe. What have you got?'
　'A new CD. I...'
　'Let's have a look. Oh God! I hate that wrinkle between my eyebrows.'
　'Stop looking at yourself in my CD case then. Give it back and let me put it on instead. And anyway, you look fantastic. And you know it.'
　'Did any of you notice that I've lost a couple of kilos? But now I want to lose more. Give me another calorie-free rice cake! And more wine. Cheers, girls!'
　'Yes, I know. But I still like to hear it. Can't you say it again? "You look fan..."'
　'Oh do be quiet, sweetie! And cheers!'
　'Here's to Lancôme's new night cream. It works miracles.'
　'Miracles? The new night cream by Lancôme? What's it called?'
　'Cheers everyone!'

They talk. They eat. They drink. The bottles of wine and bowl of rice cakes are consumed. They carry on talking, they laugh. The ashtray fills up with a small mound of cigarette stubs, all marked with the same carefree, red lipstick. But now it looks as if it is time to go. The women get up. They are a bit unsteady. Even more laughter, smiles and nudges. They put on their shoes again, fix their hair, one of them takes a powder compact out of her bag.

Another puts her arm round one of the others' waists for a moment, it is the two dark-haired women. They all hug each other, move towards the door and three of them go out. Out into the autumn rain, the snow or the summer night. Out into the dark spring evening. Or the cold October night. The one who lives in the light grey terraced house, or the red kit house, or the yellow villa or the 1930s flat, stands at the door and waves to the other three, as they head for home. Then she closes the door behind her and we lose sight of the four women.

Chapter 1

Sewing Circle at Eva's,
Tuesday 22 August

Menu
Red and green sweet pepper mousse
Filet of lamb with peas and pommes Anna
Ice-cream with chocolate sauce

An enlarged copy of a class photo, probably from the late 70s, is lying on the table. Girls with lip-gloss, long pageboy haircuts and pert breasts under pastel-coloured sweatshirts and narrow-shouldered, flat-footed boys in faded Levis. Three of the faces have been circled with a thin, black felt pen. Two attractive girls with dark eyes and dark hair in the front row. And right behind them, a blonde girl with a round face. Eva bends down to get a closer look at the copy on the table, her face only a few centimetres from the photograph. One by one, she looks into the three pairs of eyes that are a bit grainy but still clear. First she looks at the girl with the round, smooth face and then at the two dark girls in the front row. She studies them until they start to squirm with discomfort on the hard wooden chairs and though they try to turn away, their eyes remain locked into Eva's, whether they like or not. But Eva doesn't want to bother them. Not at all. That's the last thing she wants to do. She tilts her head to one side and smiles at them. Her smile is slow and kind, like a mother smiling at her baby, or one sister smiling to another. Protective and reassuring. Then she folds the class photo carefully along the well-worn creases and carries it tenderly upstairs where she puts it away in the wardrobe in the biggest bedroom. As she shuts the wardrobe door, she starts to laugh. A quiet, contented laugh.

It is a quarter to seven on a mild, late August Tuesday evening. In quarter of an hour the sewing circle will be here. Eva has just wiped the coffee table with a damp cloth. The dinner table is set with colourful paper serviettes, gleaming wine glasses, silver cutlery and four pewter cover plates. Some sweet-peas from the small, well-tended garden outside Eva's house stand in a ceramic vase on the table.

Eva's house is red with white sills, white mock astragals on the windows and red and white railings on the veranda. Eva and Erik have lived there for one year and eight months, and Eva loves her red kit house. She loves the three bay windows, the archway from the kitchen to the sitting room, the colourful tiles in the bathroom and the ubiquitous profiled skirting boards. She knows what the girls think. Tamara and Sara, that is, but she loves her red house all the same. The cool, calm ivory walls of Sara's flat with its large, minimalist rooms and the shiny steel surfaces and highly polished oak herringbone parquet in Tamara's old, yellow wooden house bore Eva, even though she admires them. In fact, she positively reveres them, from a distance, but not for a second would she want to live there. Her attitude to Liss' slightly shabby terraced house, with children's fingerprints on the windows and dustballs behind the doors, is one of cheerful tolerance and understanding. Perhaps a little more understanding than she would care to admit.

Eva is aware of her own limitations. She admires Tamara and Sara's consistently elegant style, the beautifully made-up eyes, the neat, immaculate clothes, but she knows that she will never be like them. She will never be like Tamara and Sara. It's just not possible. But she can be their friend. She will be even closer to them than Liss. She will be Tamara and Sara's confidante. More than that. She will be one of them. Her head will lean forward between their two dark heads. She wants them to come to her for advice, to confide in her and to laugh quietly in her ear. And she's so close. She has worked hard at it for some time, but now she's nearly there. Just a little more patience and then she will be where she wants to be. With Sara and Tamara. With Tamara.

Eva sings an old Frank Sinatra song to herself as she opens the fridge to take out the starter. She has made a marbled sweet pepper mousse, with red and green swirls. A relatively complicated and time-consuming recipe. But the girls will be impressed. First she had to boil the peppers, red and green separately. Then she had to mash them and sieve the pulp, followed by a long, convoluted process that involved a lot of whisking and a lot of gelatine (which Eva had never used before) and cream and egg-whites. Eva got all hot and bothered, but thankfully, the recipe book had a detailed, precise, step-by-step description of what to do. She had to win the girls over. Tamara and Sara would love Eva's sweet pepper mousse. And no doubt Liss would like it too. Eva takes hold of the first two plates. Full of pride and anticipation she lifts them carefully out of the fridge, but the minute the mousse is exposed to daylight, she sees it. The surface is lumpy and bumpy! Just like my thighs, she giggles, but then stops abruptly. Quickly checks her watch. Rather nice. Calvin Klein in brushed steel with a blue face. A present from Erik. Tamara had nodded approvingly when she showed it off the last time they met. And it has remained clasped round her wrist ever since. Already ten to. Shit! And she still has to change her tights. They've got a ladder in them. She could of course not wear any, it's warm enough for that, but then she would have to shave her legs, and that would take just as long. And she cannot serve a sweet pepper mousse that is anything less than perfect. Not that anyone would say anything. But she knows what they'd be thinking. At least, Tamara and Sara. The hoover has to be taken down into the cellar. And the welcome drink. A tray and some glasses. Where's the sherry? She asked Erik to buy Tio Pepe. One of the girls had said it was the best, last time. Was it Tamara?

Seven minutes to go. The Hoover is in its place in the cellar, but she still hasn't changed her tights. Another coat of mascara wouldn't go amiss either, as long as it doesn't go lumpy too. The others are always so well turned out. Nubbly mousse just isn't acceptable. It simply won't do. Eva sticks her right-hand index finger in her mouth and then brushes her wet finger lightly over the edge of one of the sweet pepper mousses. It works. The mousse is smooth. She licks her finger again and spreads her saliva over the three remaining mousses. There. Eva tilts her head. One still looks a bit uneven. She bends down quickly and licks over the surface of the mousse to even it out. That's better. She hums as she carries the starter into the dining room. Marbled, smooth sweet pepper mousse and a small pile of rocket on a glass plate. An appetising sight. Eva knows that the girls will be impressed. Eva knows that she will have them where she wants them. Soon.

Out in the hall in front of the mirror, Eva smiles at her reflection. It cost more than 950 kroner to have her hair highlighted. But it was worth it. She suits being blonder, it sets off her brown eyes. And she looks younger. More summery. But she still has to change her tights. She runs upstairs. Off with the old, laddered pair. In the cupboard, under a pile of expensive, unopened packs of tights lies the class photo, neatly folded. In a moment of self-indulgence, she takes it out, unfolds it and looks at the faces again. She looks at the two dark-haired girls in the front row for some time, particularly one of them. Tamara. I see you, Eva thinks. But even when you look straight at me, you don't see me. Eva smiles as she folds the picture again and takes out some ridiculously expensive tights, the type that she only wears when she's going to meet the ladies. Tamara and Sara are always so beautiful and well dressed.

Eva sits on the edge of the bed with the tights in her hand. She never tires of thinking about them. Imagining what they're like. What they do. How they feel.

Eva imagines that Tamara's life is hectic and exciting. She meets new people every day. Asks them questions, gets answers, maybe even teases a secret out of them. Writes it all down quickly in a succinct style that is read by thousands. Then Tamara's work is thrown away, put into boxes in kitchens or halls, carried out and dumped in enormous paper recycling bins. But a new day dawns, with more people to meet and more questions to ask. That's Tamara, quick and efficient. No hesitation, no doubt. Confident. Tamara. With her bright red car. Cassette recorder, notebook and pen lying on the front seat beside her. Loud music. Maybe she toots impatiently at someone who's in the wrong lane and doesn't move fast enough. Glances up in the mirror. Her dark brown hair gleams in the sun and Tamara smiles. Sexy, successful. And satisfied with herself.

Eva turns her mind to Sara, sitting deep in concentration in front of her computer, in her airy, spacious sitting room (nearly sterile was how Eva had described it to Erik, overwhelmed by her first visit to Sara). Dictionaries and other reference books, some grammar books perhaps, piled up on the walnut desk beside her. Eva can't be sure, but she imagines that Sara reads the words and long, complex German sentences out loud to herself, in a slightly questioning voice and that her hands respond swiftly, moving silently across the keyboard as the Norwegian translation mushrooms on the screen. Eva imagines that Sara sometimes stops to look up a word and nods. Pushing her glasses back onto her nearly black hair, she makes herself a cup of tea, lights a cigarette. Of course she can't be certain, but Eva is good at piecing things together, and she's usually right. The atmosphere is quiet and intense. The beautiful Sara alone in front of her computer. But Sara is tense. Eva can feel it, see it through Sara's perfect, pale golden skin. Sara is frightened and Eva doesn't know why. But she intends to find out.

As for Eva herself, it will be two years in January since she walked into the new classroom. She stood by the desk at the front and looked at the 23 smooth, unfinished, gum-chewing faces. Blank with boredom. 23 pairs of eyes looking at each other or out of the window. Eva looked at them and knew that she would win them over. She would manage, she knew she would. And now she's nearly done it. This autumn, she will work on those last few difficult ones. And then she'll have won. Then the whole class will trust her, respect her and admire her. Eva works slowly, methodically, doggedly. She is never pushy, seldom enthusiastic. Says the right thing at the right time. An unobtrusive, hard worker.

Tamara and Sara. So different from her. And yet so alike. More like her than they think.

Eva looks at her legs as she pulls on the new tights, Wolford, 15 denier. Before she only used the cheapest brands. They all ladder the minute you put them on, no matter what make. Are her thighs a bit slimmer? Hasn't she lost some weight? She must remember to weigh herself before she goes to bed. No, not after everything she'll eat tonight. She'll weigh herself tomorrow morning. Or maybe tomorrow evening. If she only eats rice cakes and carrots all day? A spray of White Diamonds on each wrist (she had found it difficult to hide her surprise when she went to pay for it, but Tamara had recommended that perfume in particular and said it would suit Eva perfectly). A hand through the unfamiliar blonde hair. A brush of mascara (the cheapest sort, two for the price of one in Cubus, but it does the job). And everything's fine, it doesn't get all claggy. The doorbell rings. It is exactly seven o'clock. Looking out the bathroom window, she sees that it's Liss. Eva sits down on the toilet seat and in her head sings what she can remember of the Sinatra lyrics. If I can make it there, I'll make it anywhere. It's up to you. The doorbell rings again. New York, New York. She slowly descends the stairs and walks over to the door and opens:

'Liss, it's you! How lovely to see you. And you're looking so well! Come in!'

Eva gives Liss a hug. Eva feels a slight hint of middle-age softness in Liss' cheeks. And L'air du Temps as always. Why on earth doesn't she change to another perfume? It's far too young for her, far too sweet. Eva is certain that Tamara and Sara would say the same. Yes, now that she thinks about it, one of them did say something like that once when Liss was out of the room. And Liss really does look exhausted. Her fair hair frames her round, cheerful face like a colourless, thin curtain. Did she have those lines on her forehead before? Maybe it's the outside light, which she strictly speaking didn't need to switch on today. But sharp downward lighting can be quite interesting, as long as Eva is out of the light herself. Eva decides not to turn it off. Liss' high, happy voice rings clear in her ear:

'Your hair is beautiful, Eva. Did you go to the hairdresser's today?'

'Yes, can you tell? Do you like it?'

'Really suits you. It looks good when you have it like that round your ears. Have you highlighted it as well? I'm sure it looks lighter?'

'No, no, I've just had it cut. This is my natural colour. I always get blonder in summer,' replies Eva, without knowing why she's lying about the colour of her hair. Eva admires dark hair. But she does not want to have their dark hair.

'Come into the sitting room and I'll get you an aperitif,' Eva says to Liss.

'Mmm, how nice to have sherry,' Liss says. 'Tamara loves sherry.'

'Does she?' Eva says lightly.

Nearly quarter of an hour later, the bell rings again and Eva hears the door being opened from outside. Eva gets up and goes out into the hall.

'Hallo, we're here,' calls Tamara.

'So sorry, we're a bit late. Tamara came by so we could get a cab together, and then...' starts Sara.

They've come together, thinks Eva, and does not listen to the end of Sara's explanation, but it is undoubtedly elegant and well formulated, as is everything that Sara says. Tamara and Sara came together. Twice the joy, twice the challenge. The two dark heads close together on Eva's tiny porch. Tamara lets Sara go in first. A sharp, brief stab of jealousy in Eva's heart. Eva stops in the doorway to the hall. She leans against the doorframe and looks at them. It's as if their intimacy prevents her from going any nearer. Their closeness demands that others keep their distance. Years of secrets, warm friendly whispers in each other's ears, arms round each other's waists. Sleepovers, picture scraps, desks always side by side in the classroom, telephone calls every night, notes in the class, sharing the last cigarette in the smoking corner at lunch break, being chief bridesmaid, holding the bride's bouquet, straightening her veil, knowing all there is to know about each other. Eva stands there smiling at them, while Sara looks in the mirror and Tamara hangs her thin, burgundy silk blazer on a hanger. Eva feels only kindness towards these two women, deep gratitude for knowing them and wishes she could step closer, in between the two dark heads, be one of them, be even stronger, even closer. Swapping scraps, arms round her waist, secrets about Fredrik in the parallel class and the smell of Sweetmint, liquorice and dark, sun-warm hair. Steaming cups of tea and a comforting hand on hers. Eva looks down, frightened in case Tamara and Sara see the longing in her eyes and get alarmed, not now when she's so nearly there. But Tamara and Sara are only concerned with themselves and each other and pay no attention to Eva in the doorway.

'Come in,' Eva says with subdued warmth. 'We've been waiting for you. Food is served.'

At twenty-five past seven, four ladies sit down at a cherrywood table. Tamara and Sara. Two dark heads leaning in to each other. Liss' blonde hair against the beige back of the dining chair, she taps her wineglass with her wedding ring. Eva can't see the three glittering jewels (are they diamonds?), but she knows that they're there. Liss told her that Paul has given her one for every child. Quite touching, thinks Eva. Liss has stood up:

'I just want to say a few words.'

Of course you do, Eva thinks to herself. And what will we hear now? Eva makes a silent bet with herself that Liss will say something about her children or tell one of her many juicy, erotic stories, which always seem to surprise Tamara and Sara, despite their frequency.

'Well, then,' Eva says, smiling encouragingly at Liss. Eva appreciates Liss. Eva likes Liss.
    'I don't like to be over the top,' starts Liss.

Oh yes you do, Eva thinks. You love things like that, terrible films and books that are one of seventy-four in a series. But I like you all the same. Eva edges her bottom forward on the chair and stretches her legs out under the table. Liss talks. Eva has no idea about what. Liss' voice has already almost disappeared. Tamara's slim, sun-tanned arm reaches lazily for her wineglass. Sara leans back her head and laughs at something. Her hair is almost black and curls slightly behind the ears and at the neck. Both Tamara and Sara's eyes are focused on Liss. Eva turns her head so she can just see Liss, who is sitting on the chair beside her. Liss is also laughing. It's obvious that she's enjoying the attention that Tamara and Sara are giving her. Her round face is pink with laughter, whereas otherwise she is pale and nearly transparent. Her hair blends in with the beige upholstery of the chair. Eva can't see her any more. Liss disappears. Her chair is empty. Tamara nods and says something quietly to Sara, who is sitting more or less sideways on her chair, with her long, bare legs stretched out across the floor and her torso twisted towards Tamara. One leg crossing the other. The skin on her legs is golden and shiny. She's wearing sandals and her toenails are deep red and perfect. Then Tamara lifts her glass to her mouth. Her lips close round the thin rim of glass and the wine, dark and shiny, runs in between the red lips, white teeth and thin glass. Tamara is so beautiful, with her dark brown hair and slanting eyes. Eva hears Tamara say something. Out loud this time. She hears Sara laughing, but she does not hear what they are talking about, she has no idea what they are laughing at. But it doesn't matter. Eva is glowing and happy. I see them, Eva thinks. They don't know who I am. I see her and she doesn't see me. She doesn't know that we belong together, her and me. Eva nearly jumps when Sara leans over towards her. She has a white cigarette in one hand and her smiling mouth is saying something.

'Yes of course, just smoke. That's fine,' Eva answers and guesses right, at least, Sara lights up her cigarette and doesn't say any more.

Eva looks at Liss, who has raised both her hands. Liss is gesticulating with big, happy movements, and trying to wave away the cigarette smoke at the same time. Her voice is high, happy and penetrating:

'And imagine, in only a few weeks, it's our 25th anniversary!'

'Is that so?' exclaims Sara.

'Yes,' replies Liss. 'It is exactly twenty-five years since you and Tamara and I started having sewing circle meetings. The autumn we turned eleven.'

'Where should we go then?' Tamara asks.

'Oh, Tamara, that's exactly what I was about to suggest. How strange! Great minds think alike,' Liss says. 'Because we have to go somewhere, to celebrate and all that! Don't you agree?'

'Yes, of course we must. Paris? Rome?' Tamara says.

'Down the road? Paul and I haven't got much to spare at the moment,' laughs Liss.

'Jesus, Liss, you must be able to afford a weekend break in a European capital.'

'Yes, of course. I'll talk to Paul. So that's decided then. A girls' weekend away. Delicious food, Eva!'

'Yes, this is super. You really have surpassed yourself today,' Sara says.

'Thank you. I'm glad you like it. What about Copenhagen? I'll back the suggestion for Copenhagen,' Eva says.

'Who suggested Copenhagen? Not such a bad idea. Not far to travel, not too expensive,' Tamara concedes.

'By the way, how did you manage to get the paprika mousse so smooth and perfect, Eva?'

Chapter 2

SEWING CIRCLE AT TAMARA'S, TUESDAY 12 SEPTEMBER

Menu
Russian appetiser
Langoustine with saffron sauce
Grapefruit sorbet
Seared tuna steak on a bed of Puy lentils and wild rice, avocado and apricot salad with sunflower seeds
Chocolate truffles with home-made honey parfait

Sara, Tamara thinks, my best friend. My beautiful best friend. She's slim and sophisticated and has tiny feet with a high instep. The skin on her temples is so delicate and transparent that the blood vessels show through as an intricate pattern, like a faded tattoo. And when she's frightened or annoyed by something, one of the veins on her left temple throbs and Tamara can see the blood pumping through it. Tamara's best friend has dark hair and big, shining eyes. Sara and Tamara have known each other ever since they were born. Sara's mother and Tamara's mother knew each other from the sewing circle and decided to have children at the same time. So when Tamara's mother modestly whispered her joyful news into Sara's mother's ear, the latter turned triumphantly and welcomed her to the club. And at the top of her voice, too. According to Tamara's mother. And Tamara's family never lies. Lying is not in our blood, Tamara often says. As it turned out, Tamara's mother was due just a few weeks before Sara's, so Tamara is exactly seven weeks – to the day – older than Sara. But that didn't stop Sara getting teeth before Tamara, or taking her first steps before Tamara, or saying Mummy before Tamara, or making her sexual debut before Tamara. Tamara knows that Sara has always been a very determined young lady.
Sara has fine, fine down on her cheeks. Her thighs are slim and free of cellulite and when she holds a cigarette, the angle of her

wrist drives men wild. Sara has beautiful, brown, helpless eyes. Sara needs Tamara. Sara is innocent. White like an angel.

The book is quite small, but very thick. It has white, unlined paper and a black velvet cover. Tamara has been sitting bent over the book, which lies open at the first page, almost at right angles to the edge of the table. She straightens up, chews on the end of her pen and closes her eyes. Before they did everything together. Sara and her. Every day. With their mothers to begin with. Side by side in their prams in Frogner Park and by the lake at Bogstad. In the sandpit in Tamara's garden. Then on their own, just the two of them. In the park. At school. Their desks side by side. Sara and Tamara in the same class, where they learned to read and write, and later to solve quadratic equations and smoke. Sara and Tamara skiing in Nordmarka. On cycling trips with their matching bikes – Sara's was blue and Tamara's was red. Sara and Tamara on the beach. Sara and Tamara at the cinema with Jan Tore. Sara is frightened, so Tamara has to hold her hand. Sara and Tamara. Always together. Tamara stands up, fetches the watering can and starts to water the plants. She thinks best when she's doing something. Tamara doesn't like sitting still. She'll write more later. The book with the black velvet cover can wait.

Sara and Tamara don't see each other every day any more. They both have work and families now. Sara has Jakob and Julia. Tamara has Thomas and Emma. Emma and Julia are about the same age. Same age, same dark eyes. And both of them have dark hair. Just like their mothers. Emma and Julia are best friends too, just like their mothers.

Sara works from home. In front of the computer with her dictionaries. Tamara is sure that she thinks about her every now and then. Just as Tamara thinks of Sara several times a day at work. They meet as often as they can and speak to each other on the phone every day. Tamara loves ringing Sara, she loves hearing Sara's dulcet tones on the end of the line, dripping into her ear.

Sometimes Tamara phones Sara just to listen to her voice and then quietly puts down the receiver.

When they started the sewing circle, it was just Sara and Tamara. I liked it best when it was just us, Sara told Tamara and looked at her with her big, shining, vulnerable eyes. We rhyme, she said. Sara and Tamara. No one else rhymes with us. And it's a good sign when things rhyme.

Sara and Tamara meet as often as they can, at the very least whenever the sewing circle meets. Sara and Tamara. Liss and Eva. And today it's Tamara's turn to entertain. Today Sara will come to Tamara's house. Sara will sit on one of Tamara's dining chairs and eat the food that Tamara has prepared for her. Sara loves seafood, so naturally, she will have seafood. And sweet puddings, Tamara thinks. My best friend simply adores sweet puddings. I'm kind to Sara. I support her and I'm there when she needs me. I helped her when she was pregnant and suffered from pelvic dysfunction. I still make sure that she doesn't strain her pelvis. And I make sure that she doesn't eat anything with nuts in it. I call her every day. I give her presents – she still has that picture of a cat that we gave her one Christmas up on her kitchen wall.

Tamara passes by the mirror in the hall and throws a short, admiring glance. Tamara loves clothes, particularly red clothes and she likes shopping. But she only shops with Sara when she has to. It's one of the few things that Tamara does not like doing with Sara. Tamara is, quite frankly, frightened of what Sara might make her do. With her big eyes. Shoplifting, for example. Tamara was caught shoplifting once, when they were in secondary school. Sara and Tamara were in the cosmetics department when three serious-looking men came over to them. Sara and Tamara had just been looking at the make-up, lipstick and some gorgeous eyeshadows. Tamara remembers it well, but she doesn't like to think about it. Just before the suited men came over, Sara had looked at Tamara with her big, shining eyes. Do it, Sara's eyes said.

The three men caught them roughly by the arm and dug deep into their pockets. The men upset Sara. Do something, her eyes cried out. Sara was frightened. Sara is as white as an angel. In the end Tamara was forced to tell them. I took the eye shadow, she said, and put it in my friend's pocket. Thank goodness for that, sighed Sara's downcast eyes. Tamara was marched into an office. The men wrote her name down in a book and she had to promise never to do it again. The men said that the worst thing was that she had betrayed her friend. Tamara agreed. At least, she said she did. Sara was waiting for her outside the door. Tamara's best friend.

Tamara has to look after Sara. It's so awful when Liss starts humming 'If you go down to the woods today'. Tamara doesn't know anyone else who sings that stupid song in the same way. Liss seems relish the fact that 'you're sure of a big surprise'. Liss loves the song, but Sara and Tamara hate it. Tamara can see that it puts Sara on edge. And Tamara can't bear it when anyone upsets Sara. Sara's so vulnerable.

Tamara goes over to the sofa and plumps the cushions. The sitting room is immaculate. She took half a day off and came home at two. Tamara misses her job when she's not there. She misses the deadlines and the stress, and she's terrified she'll miss something big, miss the next big scoop, miss exposing the scandalous truth. And today she even had to drop an interview that she'd been looking forward to. Tamara's new colleague snapped it up greedily. What's his name? Tom or something like that. Would certainly suit him, thinks Tamara, like a tomcat, all inflated with male pride and ambition. Ambition as huge and formless as his fat arms and legs. He knows he wants something, just doesn't know what. Tamara doesn't have much time for people like that. She doesn't like Tom. She knows she doesn't, even though she's barely spoken to him. But I'm a good judge of character, Tamara thinks. I don't need to spend much time with someone before I've got them sussed. What they think and feel. Their weaknesses and strengths, I see it all. Straightaway. Tamara is glad that she is such a good judge of character.

But now she must make the food. The sewing circle and Sara are more important than her job. At least right now they are. The Puy lentils are soaking. The tuna fish is marinating in a plastic bag. But there's still plenty to do. Living up to expectations can be time-consuming. Tamara is the sewing circle's undisputed gourmet queen. Which means at least four courses. Which means that everything has to be home-made. From scratch. Needless to say there are no soup packets, ready sauces or half-baked rolls in Tamara's kitchen. Far from it. And Tamara is not going to put her reputation on the line by cheating and using a stock cube, say, instead of home-made stock. Tamara takes no short cuts. Not in the kitchen. She never uses dried yeast or slabs of Findus frozen puff pastry. There is only one person in the sewing club who would be able to expose Tamara and reveal all the short cuts she doesn't take, only one who is anywhere near her level. The other two couldn't taste the difference between fresh and tinned tomatoes, let alone vine tomatoes and plum tomatoes. And they have never owned a zest grater or an asparagus steamer. Sara is very good at making food. Personally, Tamara thinks that she is that little bit better, more creative, not so rigid. I reckon most people would agree with me, Tamara thinks to herself as she carefully unpacks the langoustine she bought earlier. Sara is good, but I am the best. As for Liss and Eva! OK, Eva turned up trumps last time with her sweet pepper mousse. Marbled and delightfully smooth. But then she served supermarket ice cream and chocolate sauce (from a bottle, no doubt) for dessert and spoiled the whole impression. And they're not ashamed of what they serve up, either. Eva always plonks down her stew from a packet that she's spiced up with some paprika and extra vegetables, on the table with a smile, not a humiliated, slightly apologetic smile, but a great, satisfied grin. Tamara is astonished by the complete lack of shame, in the same way that she is still astonished by the fact that small children are not bothered by food dribbling down their chin from their mouth.

Tamara's kitchen now smells of fresh langoustine, the faint scent of a woman's genitals. Tamara breathes in through her nose and looks forward to serving Sara shellfish. She sears the langoustine pink in olive oil and carefully takes off the shell. She'll wait until later to make the saffron sauce, so that it's fresh and newly made when they eat, and of course, she won't do the tuna steaks until the guests have finished the starter. She made the honey parfait yesterday, with lots of egg yolks and cream and nearly a decilitre of Scottish heather honey. Sara prefers heather honey. The ice cream is in the freezer now, but she must remember to take it up in good time so that it's just the right softness. She can make the chocolate truffles now and leave them in the coolness of the cellar. Icing sugar, butter and dark, bitter chocolate with a ridiculously high cocoa content (86% to be precise), a couple of generous tablespoons of cognac from Thomas' bottle of Hennessy XO. Tamara stirs the dark mass. Sara will love Tamara's truffles. Tamara shapes them into the size of a small golf ball and rolls them in cocoa. She makes them extra big for Sara. Then she stands there for a minute, thinking, before fishing out a packet of walnuts from the cupboard. Tamara can't help smiling as she presses half a walnut on the top of each truffle. Sara loves sweet desserts. Tamara closes her eyes and plans the surprise she will feel when Sara gets her dessert. Golden yellow, home-made honey ice cream. Two chocolate truffles, as big as golf balls, decorated with walnuts. Oh sweetheart, how silly of me. I completely forgot that you were allergic to nuts. And now you won't be able to eat that, will you? How could I forget. And you who love dessert so much, Sara.

Tamara also prepares the basis of the evening's palate cleanser, a grapefruit sorbet. Then all she needs to do is mix in the whipped egg whites before putting it all into the sorbet machine the minute the girls have finished eating their langoustine. Tamara boils the sugar water, and squeezes the grapefruits and a lemon. She pops her finger in and tastes. Sweet and sharp at the same time. The one perfectly balancing the other. This is Tamara's kind of dish. Just the way Tamara likes it. Tamara smiles. Sweeten the sour taste so that it's palatable, so that my friends think it tastes sweet and good.

*

Four women in two white sofas arranged opposite each other. Tamara's new sofa cushions are filled with real eiderdown and the tension in the springs alone should be a give-away to anyone who sits on the sofas that they cost more than a translator would be paid for two novels and a pathetic essay collection, or more than half the annual salary of a lower secondary school teacher, and more than a woman receiving child benefit could save in a whole year. And if the eiderdown cushions and tension do not say it all to her friends, Tamara is more than happy to tell them. Sara sits directly opposite Tamara. Eva is beside Tamara. And cutting through Eva's White Diamonds (which doesn't suit flabby, shabby Eva – Tamara suddenly remembers once joking that White Diamonds would suit Eva and this makes her smile), through Liss' sickly L'air du Temps, through the food smells from the kitchen, Tamara recognises Sara's smell. The scent of Sara's perfume, of Sara's body, intermingled with the spiral of blue smoke from her cigarette. From over the table she recognises the smell of Sara. Tamara knows that she could distinguish Sara's smell from all other smells in the world.

Sitting next to Sara is Liss, but you don't notice her. Liss is unimportant, insignificant, but absolutely necessary. She has to be here. She is part of the sewing circle, too. Tamara tries to ignore her, Tamara tries not to hear what she is saying, but listens just enough not to offend her. She mustn't annoy Liss. But she has to be kept in her place. She can't be allowed to forget who she once was, Pissy Lissy. She has to be reminded that for Tamara and Sara she will never be anything else. Dizzy Pissy Lissy. It rhymes, Sara said. It's a sign. Then that's how it's meant to be, Sara said.

Sometimes Tamara wonders if everything would have been different if Sara and Tamara hadn't rhymed and if Sara and Tamara's mothers hadn't been best friends. Sara's mother was small and fragile like a doll with enormous, blue eyes. And quite different from Tamara's tall, statuesque mother. It's strange that they were such good friends. Evidently they have no contact now.

Liss leans towards Sara, says something and giggles. There is a silver dish with some pickled gherkins, honey and sour cream on the table. Tamara has made a Russian appetiser for the girls. And Sara really loves honey. They are all sitting with an ice-cold glass of vodka. Liss has already had two. Now she puts down her empty glass and picks up a pickled gherkin that Tamara bottled earlier in the autumn. She fingers the gherkin, licks the tip and sniggers quietly. She looks up, nibbles the gherkin and laughs again. Eva and Sara are leaning towards each other over the table. They're talking about a TV programme they both watched, which Eva's husband was in, and about Sara and Jakob's bathroom, which is being done up. Neither Sara nor Eva pay any attention to Liss. Liss giggles again and Tamara decides not to hear her either. Liss looks around, laughs again and catches Tamara's eye, before looking over at Sara and Eva. Finally, Liss can't bear it any longer and says:

'I remember I went through a phase when I was obsessed with the male organ.'

Eva's head swings round to face Liss:

'Good grief! What are you saying, girl? Obsessed with what?'

Liss giggles happily and answers as she breathes in:

'Yes, I inspected every man's groin. The postman. The aerobics teacher. Men on the bus. Colleagues. The cashier at the supermarket. The prime minister.'

'Right... and?' Tamara says. 'You looked at their groin and...? That's not so strange. I usually look at their backsides.'

And it's true. Tamara does. Men's bums, the blue sea and her daughter's dark eyes that remind her of Sara's, are what Tamara likes to look at most.

'Oh, stop it, Tamara,' Sara says.

'No, seriously. You looked them in the crotch and then what?' Tamara inquires, with the politeness of a hostess.

'Well, then I got a real urge to see it,' Liss explains.

'It?'

'Yes.'

'And?'

'Well, I was completely obsessed with the different shapes and sizes and colours and widths, smells and tastes. I stared at men's groins and tried to picture their penises. Pink, thin and pointy, but quite long, is what I thought when I looked at the finance director's fly. Deep purplish-red, powerful and short with two great, throbbing veins twisting down the shaft. That's what I imagined the postman's was like. Quite a large, well-shaped foreskin...'

Tamara waved her hand at Liss:
  'OK, OK, we get the picture.'

Tamara believes that as hostess, you have to be polite. Look after your guests. And you can show curiosity. But there are limits. Liss is not exactly an exciting person, even though she sometimes comes out with some pretty outrageous comments. And that's fine, as long as what she says amuses the girls. Eva has said several times that she thinks Liss is sweet and funny. Well, she can think what she likes. Tamara and Sara know who Liss once was and it can never be any different. Right now, Liss is a housewife receiving child-benefit. Married to the pedant Paul. Three snotty children. As many zircons as she has children. A zircon for each child. Three tiny, pathetic zircons bought by Paul, mounted in her wedding ring one after the other, that were given to her with tears and smiles three times in the hospital. Liss. A person who has bored Tamara from the moment she set eyes on her, with her wispy fair hair and red satchel on the first day at school, and who hasn't changed in the slightest since. She scuttled alongside the school wall like a small, frightened smelly mouse.

'And did you do anything about your urges?' Eva asks.
  'A little more vodka?' Tamara asks Sara.
  'In some cases, yes,' Liss replies and giggles again.
  'In some cases?' Eva repeats and leans over to Liss.
  'No thank you,' Sara says and smiles at Tamara.
  'Well, quite often actually. If it agreed with my stars and that sort of thing. It was before I met Paul, of course.'
  'Of course!' says Tamara. 'No one likes unfaithful wives.'

'But once the package was opened, as it were, I lost interest. I didn't want sex, I just wanted to see it.'

'How exciting,' Eva says.

Sara rolls her eyes. Sara is bored. Her big, brown eyes. Tamara gets up immediately.

'Time for food, girls! Come and sit down. The starter is ready. Langoustine in saffron sauce.'

'Shellfish! Delicious!' Sara says. 'I just need to pop to the bathroom. Will you excuse me a moment, girls?'

'She's lost a lot of weight recently, hasn't she?' remarks Liss, the minute Sara leaves the sitting room. 'Being that thin is not attractive.'

'Yes it is,' Tamara retorts. 'But she should be careful not get any thinner.'

'She looks so pale and drawn,' Eva joins in.

'Let's sit down now,' says Tamara. Tamara can't bear it when anyone upsets Sara.

The sewing circle meets every third week. And then Sara is mine, Tamara thinks to herself. Her eyes in my eyes. My words in her ears. And every fourth time, they all come to Tamara's. And then Sara is even more Tamara's. Today Sara belongs to Tamara. She is mine. She is sitting in my dining room. She is eating my food. Now she is looking at me. Can she read my thoughts? Can she tell that I'm thinking about her, right now?

It must have been in the middle of the summer holidays. Liss was at her grandmother's in Trysil. It's so boring when Liss isn't here, Sara said. Sara has big, dark eyes that can easily look sad. It was a warm, dry day. Go out and play in this lovely weather, said their mothers. They were sitting on the terrace at Sara's house, drinking iced tea. Sara and Tamara went out. They knew very well that their mothers wouldn't approve, so they headed straight for the graveyard. Sara is wearing a white dress with small, blue flowers. Under the material, her breasts are flat. Tamara hunches her shoulders to hide her small breasts. Now no one can see them.

Tamara wants to be like Sara. Sara's hair is blue-black when the sun shines on it. The churchyard is quiet. An old lady is kneeling in front of a gravestone. She's pulling thin, green weeds out of the dark earth. Sara and Tamara look at the gravestones. The ones with small, white angels and marble birds on top are the prettiest. Sara and Tamara work out the age of the people who are buried there. Some were only children when they died. Then Sara wants to go. But Tamara wants to stay. Sara looks at her with her big dark eyes. Liss always thinks of something to do, Sara says. Tamara knows that it's not true. Liss never thinks of anything to do. Liss is one of the most boring people she knows. That's just the way it is, but both Sara and Tamara know that they can never talk about it. And they never do talk about it either. Liss is in the sewing circle. She has to be. Sara and Tamara asked her if she wanted to join ages ago now. Last year, at the end of summer. Nearly a whole year ago. Gosh, nearly a year since that day. Tamara tilts back her head, the sky is blue, bluer than the flowers on Sara's dress. Tamara looks up at the church spire. The windows are not proper windows, just painted, black squares high up above her head. She gets dizzy and quickly bends forwards. I'm going home, Sara says. Wait, shouts Tamara. Lying in the gravel in the shadow of the spire is a pile of brilliant white down and feathers. Look, says Tamara. Sara turns round and comes back to her. It's a sign, Tamara says, as Sara often says. It's feathers from an angel, Tamara says. Sara smiles. Sara is so beautiful when she smiles. They gather the angel feathers. A bouquet of angel feathers. The white feathers against Sara's dark hair. This is a sign from Heaven. What does it mean? Sara asks. That you will definitely be an angel when you die, answers Tamara. You will be the most beautiful angel, Sara. Yes, Sara says and helps Tamara to stick the feathers in her hair. Sara is an angel. White and fragile and without shame.

Sara looks at Tamara and smiles. They have got as far as the palate cleanser. The grapefruit sorbet is served in tall glasses, garnished with a double lemon balm leaf. A cool pause in the middle of the meal. And Tamara has added enough sugar. Sara has eaten the lot.

Tamara likes to remember that day in the graveyard. Tamara likes to think of Sara as an angel. And Tamara's memory is like a well-read, well-used book. It more or less opens by itself, without her even wanting it to, at the same place that it has been opened so many times before.

The book opened by itself. The brown stripy book. It was September, about a year before she adorned Sara with the angel feathers. Tamara came home from school, opened the door and shouted hallo. All was silent. Mummy and Daddy weren't home from work yet and Philip wasn't home either. The silence in the house reminded Tamara of another day. A day she did not want to remember. A day not so long ago. The 28th of August. But it was somewhere else. At Sara's house.

That afternoon, in Tamara's house, marked the end of Tamara's childhood. At least, that's what she wrote in her diary in bed that night. In between the starched, white sheets that Mummy had just put on, which had been hanging out to dry all day and smelt of late summer and sun. A mosquito bashed against the lamp on the bedside table. Her yellow plastic diary, shaped like a flower – a sunflower no doubt – with a worn, red, varnished heart-shaped lock. A new page. Oslo, 5 September. Dear Diary. Today I became a woman. I am eleven and will be twelve in March. Tamara wrote in neat schoolgirl handwriting. With an ink pen that used blue cartridges. Possibly she wrote it because she thought it was the sort of thing you should write in your diary, but also because she had become a woman earlier on that afternoon, when she was alone in the house. But she didn't write any more. She didn't write that the afternoon would probably have been different if it weren't for that day not long ago. The day at Sara's house. Tamara had kept a diary ever since she learned to write, but she had also learned early on to filter what she experienced. So Tamara just wrote something else about a hopeless teacher on the 5th of September. And something about Rune Dahl-Arnesen in the parallel class. Sara and I are going to the cinema tonight. We should ask Liss as well, she wrote. Love Tamara. But she didn't write why they should ask Liss. There are so many things that you don't write in your diary. Even ones with padlocks. But it wasn't other people that Tamara was afraid of. On the 28th of August, she wrote nothing in the yellow diary.

*

Tamara still has all her diaries. Somewhere or other in a box with lots of old photos and papers. School books and a collection of serviettes.

She shouted hallo and no one answered. She dropped her bag and went into the sitting room. It was stuffy and warm. Unusually warm for September. But she couldn't face opening the window. Couldn't be bothered, her body felt too heavy. And she was angry. Angry with her dad. Tamara was angry with her father. Angry and disappointed, perhaps. Or a bit frightened? She went over to the bookcase. Tamara's parents had lots of books and they were kept in order. Separated into author's nationality, Norway first, then the other countries in alphabetical order. And then within each country, the authors were shelved alphabetically. There were most books in the Norwegian section. She let her fingers run over the green, red and blue spines as she said the authors' names in her head. Everything was in place. No mistakes. Tamara's parents knew their alphabet. She wished she could discover a mistake that Daddy had made, so she could show him that she was angry. That she despised him. That she knew what he was like. Not that a small error in the alphabet would really have helped, but all the same. Alnæs, Borgen, Boyer. C, D, E, F, G. Hamsun, Haslund, Hoel, Holberg. And then suddenly she saw a book where it didn't belong. Right at the top, on the second set of shelves, in the section for Norwegian authors with surnames beginning with S, between Scott and Skram, was a book with an M-surname. Tamara eased the book out with her right hand and took it down to have a look. And as she held the spine, with the pages closed against each other, the book opened. Almost of its own accord, without her wanting it to, at a place quite near the start. The words 'pressed his face between her legs and lapped up her wine' jumped out at Tamara, then the words dissolved into black, meaningless symbols on a white page, before joining together again and falling into place in the sentence, the words and their improbable meaning. Tamara could feel she was getting even hotter and she sat down on the sofa with the book open in her hand. She sits right in a pool of sunlight. Tamara finishes reading about Ask and the Rubens girl on the boat, and leafs on to find more. The pages are blindingly white. Tamara can barely see the letters any more. She is hot all over and she can feel the sofa fabric through her thin summer blouse. The muscles in her thighs are tense even though she is sitting still. She is wet behind the knees with sweat and the woollen sofa cover is itchy through her blouse and against the back of her legs. She breathes fast and silently. She is constantly listening for noises in the hall. She holds the book up to her nose, because she wants to know what this kind of book smells like. And then she makes a discovery. The book opens of its own accord again. The first time was not a coincidence. The book opens at the pages when Ask is with Wilhelmine, when he is with Constance, under the apple tree and at the Christmas ball when he puts his hands between a girl's legs and 'pushes his index finger far up into her vagina'. Tamara tries again. Is it because she wants it to happen? Is it because the book knows what sort of a person she is? Is it because the book knows who she is, but doesn't want to be?

But she knows that's not true. Of course Tamara understands why. The book makes it absolutely clear. But she's not like that, is she? I don't want to be like my dad, Tamara says so loudly that she nearly jumps at the sound of her own voice. I want to be an angel. White and without shame.

Tamara doesn't like the fact that the book is like that, because it's Mummy and Daddy's book, and Tamara realises that it must be him who has made the book open on its own at certain places. Tamara knows what her father is like. She has seen him. She saw what he was doing. She knows what he's like. She has just discovered what he's like. Now, not so long ago. That day. The

28th of August. That day at Sara's house. The day that Tamara wrote nothing in her diary. But she wrote the date and then left the page blank. So that it never happened? So that she could fill it in with things she wished had happened instead? Tamara wasn't sure.

Suddenly noises from that day flood her mind. And images. The half-open mouth. The white teeth and the red tongue. The smell from that day blends with the sentences in the book that she is still holding in her lap. Tamara starts to see people she knows. Teachers. The parents of girls in the class. Uncles and aunts. They're all naked. Just like that day. The bodies tumble all over each other inside Tamara's head. They are hairy and sweaty and warm. Aunty's fat white thighs with blue veins don't stop where her swimming costume starts. Aunty and Uncle. Liss' mother and father. It's like Vigeland's Monolith. A mass of bodies. Almost the same as the Monolith. Only soft, with winter-white skin. With hair and veins. Some with rolls of fat. Others thin. They writhe around like maggots. And Tamara herself with Rune Dahl-Arnesen from the parallel class. Tamara feels dizzy. She feels sick. She finds it difficult to breathe. She pushes away Rune Dahl-Arnesen. And she sees her own body. Thankfully. It is flat, dry, smooth and hairless. No rolls of fat, no moles, not a single hair. I don't want to be like them. Tamara does not want to be like her father.

But that is when it happens. There on the sofa, she sees her nipples getting darker and starting to grow, and under them her breasts swell. Does she like it? Tamara is not sure. But she knows that she doesn't want to like it. She sees hair growing in a triangle just below her navel. At first light and soft, and then darker and stiffer, and it is difficult to breathe normally and her body is nice and soft to touch. Rune Dahl-Arnesen and Tamara. Naked. Hot. And by the time she hears her mum's key in the door, the hair has even started to curl.

She shoved the book under the sofa. And to her great surprise, her mother didn't even notice that Tamara looked different. Mummy didn't see her breasts, she didn't see her hair. But Mummy doesn't know anything. She doesn't know anything about that day. Mummy is not guilty in any way for what happened. Tamara knows that. Gosh, it's warm in here! We need some air in here, Mummy said and opened the window. Cold air soothed Tamara's face. She could get up again. And in the evening she wrote in her yellow sunflower diary that she had become a woman. Nothing more. Tamara wrote nothing more.

But now everything would be different. The thick book with the black velvet cover would be different. Because this time Tamara would write in red ink.

Not long after, it actually started to happen. She pulled out the first hairs and when Tamara's breasts started to grow, she got rounded shoulders. Sara, on the other hand, was smooth, white and hairless for a while longer. Tamara envied her as she walked around with a straight back. Tamara wished she was as white and without shame as Sara. But it wasn't long before Tamara realised that she was like her father in more ways than one. Not only had she got his colouring and strong hands. The images and sounds from that day and the sentences from the book often came into Tamara's mind. She kissed Rune Dahl-Arnesen in the bicycle shed. She let Andreas in the second year kiss her at a party. She learned to French kiss from Geir. Tamara kissed with passion, curiosity and shame. She was sure that Sara never thought about that day. And if she ever did, behind the lily-white skin of her forehead, she did so with embarrassment and anger. Tamara was certain of that.

*

As soon as Sara developed small, pointed breasts, a slim roundness over her thighs and an angle in her wrist, she had more conquests than Tamara. Sara is a determined lady. And Tamara has always found it difficult to keep hold of the boys. Things have always ended with Tamara's boyfriends. Particularly those she liked the most. Unfortunately. Tamara has never been much good at choosing the right men.

But then she has Sara. And now Sara is at Tamara's and it's a sewing circle evening.

They are all in Tamara's dining room. Tamara's dove grey dining room, which is three metres from floor to ceiling, with an enormous crystal chandelier and original stencilled wallpaper. Sara and Tamara. Liss and Eva. And Sara has Jakob and Tamara has her Thomas.

Liss looks up from her tuna steak, which is of course perfectly done. Hard and crispy on the outside, with a thin layer of browny-pink flesh and then red in the centre. Tamara has served it with lentils and wild rice and an avocado and apricot salad with roasted sunflower seeds. A sophisticated salad mix that none of the other sewing circle members would have the culinary flair to come up with.

'Delicious fish, Tamara,' Sara says. 'And what an amazing salad.'
    'Thank you,' Tamara says.
    'I'm so glad that we've got each other, girls. I really appreciate you all,' says Liss with a sincerity that is typical of her. 'You're like an oasis in my humdrum daily life.'
    'Poetic, Liss,' Sara says. 'But I'm very grateful too. You are my time out.'
    'Yes, and I'm glad that we've stayed together for so long. It's incredibly valuable to have good, close friends,' Tamara says. Sara is after all her closest friend. It is important to have good friends. Friends you can trust. Friends you can talk to about anything. Friends who support you.
    'And we mustn't forget our anniversary. Was it Paris we agreed on? Paris, on y va,' Sara mimics. 'Or was it Berlin? Berlin ist ja eine schöne Stadt, nicht war, meine Damen?'
    'No. We agreed to go to Copenhagen,' Eva says. Her voice is surprisingly loud and they all look at her. Then she coughs and says in a terribly serious voice: 'Am I allowed to come too? I know I'm not a part of your past, when the sewing circle really was a sewing circle with bad cross-stitch and crocheted oven

41

gloves. When you had plaits and braces...'

'Spots!'

'Sara, that was later!'

'...and puppy fat...'

'I rather liked my puppy fat. It was better than the extra fat I've got on my hips now. Old bitch fat,' Tamara says, secure in the knowledge that someone will tell her that she has slim thighs, because she does.

'That's enough, Tamara, you who are so slim, trim and beautiful. Yes, of course you must come with us, Eva. You can celebrate your second anniversary. In April it will be two years since you phoned me and asked if we wanted to come for dinner, you said that you had just moved into the area and didn't know many people yet,' Sara says.

'...and at some point in the evening you – I think it was you, Liss – asked if I wanted to join you the next time you had the sewing circle. Here's to that!'

'Cheers!'

'And here's to the chef! Cheers to us! Nothing can separate us,' Liss says, looking around with her serious, light blue eyes.

'Yesss! New men have come and gone, and no doubt will continue to do so in the future,' Sara says. 'But we four, we will stick together. Always!'

Tamara looks at her friends. Sara. Liss and Eva. Rubbish, she thinks and raises her glass to eternal friendship.

It is past midnight. The girls have left. Thomas has come home from Jakob's. Evidently they've been doing some tiling. Sara has wanted to do up the bathroom for a long time, so they made a start. Thomas is helping to do up Sara and Jakob's bathroom. That's good. You should help your friends. Just as you should be loyal to your friends. Thomas is in the sitting room. Tamara can hear the TV. From where she is standing in the doorway to the kitchen, she can see him but he can't see her. The sports programme on the screen is reflected on his forehead, which Tamara suddenly notices is longer than it was a few years ago. Thomas cannot see

Tamara. Which is unusual. Usually Thomas always sees Tamara. She decides to forgive him this once and goes up to the bathroom.

She's meeting him tomorrow morning. Tomorrow morning when Sara is at some translators' seminar, Tamara will lie on Sara's sheets. Tamara immediately feels an excited vibration low down in her stomach. But she also feels something that is even stronger and even sweeter than the anticipation in her loins. Jakob is no great lover. But tomorrow he will be Tamara's man. He will be mine alone, Tamara thinks, and smiles at her reflection. Tomorrow, Jakob's body is mine. And I am Sara. She squints at her reflection. Yes, I am Sara. Then she epilates her legs and rubs them with body lotion. She is smooth and shiny. She shaves her pubic hair with Thomas' razor, leaving only a thin stripe. She dry brushes her arms, thighs, behind and back. Tamara wants to be smooth and soft. And she is smooth and soft. Tamara often gets what she wants. But not always. It's not always easy to be Tamara. And Sara can be a very determined lady.

Tamara strokes over her skin. She is smooth, but she wants to be even smoother, even softer. As smooth and as soft as Sara. She wants to be Sara. Helpless, pure and without shame. She knows what she'll do.

Tamara puts on the white silk nightie that she got from Thomas for Christmas (which she doesn't really like) and she takes the massage oil he gave her for her birthday (which they have never used) in her hand and she goes down to her partner and stands in front of the TV. Tamara moves towards Thomas. Now Thomas can see her. Tamara doesn't need to say a word. She just smiles, shows him what she's got in her hand and starts to walk towards the bedroom. Thomas switches off the TV and follows her.

She pulls off the shoulder straps and lets the nightie fall to the floor, then she lies down on her stomach on the bed. Tamara lets Thomas massage the back of her body, with long deep strokes. She can hear his breathing. Then she turns over. Thomas warms some more oil in his palms and massages the front of Tamara. She opens her legs so he can get to the inside of her thighs as well.

'Thank you,' she says and sits up. 'I have to go over to Sara's tomorrow morning. Can you give me a lift?'

'Yes of course I can,' Thomas says. His hands are glistening with massage oil. 'But isn't she going to some seminar tomorrow morning? Something about translation? I thought Jakob mentioned something like that.'

'Yes, she's going to a translation seminar on metaphors, organised by the Goethe Institute,' Tamara answers.

'That's it,' Thomas says and leans his body in towards her.

'I'm going to water their plants,' Tamara says and slides her hand down over her hip bone. Thomas follows her hand with his eyes and leans even closer.

Then Tamara wraps herself up in the duvet, turns her back to her partner, wishes him goodnight and closes her eyes. My skin is smooth and soft, Tamara thinks. It is no longer my skin, but Sara's. Sara is so pure and white and without shame. Sara is an angel.

Tamara keeps the thick book with the black velvet cover in the drawer of her bedside table. Perhaps it would have been different if they hadn't rhymed. And if Dizzy Pissy Lissy hadn't rhymed with herself. It was Sara who had made up that name. Of course it was Sara. I'm not as inventive as she is. The veins on Sara's temples look like a half-faded tattoo. I love watching them fill with blood, grow and swell. Like Sara's husband between my soft thighs. Sara, my best friend. My best friend, who had to watch us while we ate chocolate truffles with home-made honey parfait. What a shame I forgot that Sara can't eat nuts.

Chapter 3

SEWING CIRCLE AT LISS', TUESDAY 3 OCTOBER

Menu
Melon with parma ham
Cod au gratin with white wine sauce and mussels
Divine sherry cream

'You may not control the external environment as much as you would like, but you are in control of the internal one. You can tune your own brain into any channel you want, at any time.' Liss must have been in her mid-twenties when she first read those lines and they didn't make much impression on her at the time. At least, they didn't seem to. And later she couldn't even remember where she'd read them or in what connection she'd come across them. But exactly one week after her 27th birthday, she woke up beside Paul with the two sentences in her head. She remembered them word for word. Paul was lying on his side, with half his back and the lower half of one of his legs sticking out from under the duvet. Liss was absolutely certain that Paul was the man in her life. He was steady and reliable and so far he had given her two beautiful children. Mona and Martin. Liss had named them after the hero and heroine in one of Barbara Sandeland's best court romances (the rich merchant's daughter, Ramona Dupret, finally gets her Martin Bos, who was the victim of a terrible mix up when he was born and on the last page discovers he is not the poor servant that everyone thinks he is). Liss stared at Paul's foot, his big toe with a sharp edge of hard, yellow skin. Ah well, the duvet cover was almost new, in glowing matt Thai silk. Very expensive, impractical and a lot of work. At least three times through the mangle. But she had set her heart on these bedclothes. Thought that they would make all the difference. Change everything. But they hadn't. Just as the new, white fitted kitchen and the holiday in Florida last year hadn't changed anything either. Liss was constantly trying to escape her past. To draw the veil of forgetfulness over it, as Ramona would say. Liss did not want to hear the clicking heels and see the red, shiny lips. Liss wanted to lead an exciting life. Her gaze moved up from Paul's foot to Paul's rather thin, February white leg.

Liss sat up in bed, stretched her arms above her head and yawned, with the English sentences still echoing in her mind. According to her horoscope in the magazine that was still lying open on the bedside table, today would be a favourable day for Pisces, a day of good fortune, particularly for those born at the beginning of March, like Liss. You seem to be at an important crossroads in your life and Wednesday is the day to make the change, Liss had read last night. Liss turns away from her sleeping husband, puts her feet down on the Chinese carpet (which hadn't met her expectations, dramatically changing her life and marriage, either) and walks into a world that is exactly how she wants it.

It was not as easy to achieve absolute control of your inner world as the quote had promised, as she had fully believed when she put her feet down on the soft Chinese carpet made from almost real silk thread and had sworn that from now on everything would be different. But since that day, a few years ago now, Liss has generally been satisfied with her life. Because although she does not have absolute control, she at least controls the greater part of her inner universe. And it's an exciting world, where Liss plays a sensitive and sensual leading role.

Liss is at home at the moment with the little one, so five days a week she sends Paul and the two eldest children off to work, school and nursery with their packed lunches. Brown bread with Gouda or liverpaté for the kids and two slices of white bread with fish pudding for Paul, who has a delicate stomach and a tendency to wind. The children wave goodbye and disappear through the gate with their tartan satchels and Paul kisses her, picks up his briefcase and runs to the car after Mona and Martin. And then only she and Maja are left in the light grey terraced house. Maja is about one and she's a placid child, just as dreamy as her mother. Liss deeply appreciates Maja's good nature. She is happy to spend the greater part of the day playing on her blanket. Maja can sit with some building blocks for hours, banging them gently together, staring out into mid-air daydreaming. And over Maja's soft head, Liss smiles flirtatiously at an Italian count in an Armani suit, with a three-day shadow.

Liss is a woman whom men desire. A woman surrounded by men fighting for her favour. In medieval Norway, with thick, wavy flaxen hair, in a long scarlet red dress with a wide silver belt. In Paris with racks of Chanel suits and Dior underwear, a chestnut bob and glittering, dark eyes. A modern, cosmopolitan demimonde. Or in 1920s New York, with the Charleston and sequin dresses. An English chambermaid with a bound, corseted wasp waist and high buttoned boots in foggy Victorian London. Liss changes Maja's nappy and breastfeeds her. She keeps the house in reasonable order, does a bit of hoovering, waters the plants when she remembers, washes clothes and cleans the windows in spring, she goes food shopping and serves her family relatively healthy, nutritious meals, she even sews new curtains sometimes, and decorates the house at Christmas and Easter. Liss is happy with her life. She turns on the kitchen tap to rinse a cloth and hears a waterfall in Hawaii. She runs her finger over the floury surface of the bread dough and knows that it is the smooth inside of her lover's underarm. She scrubs the worktops until even the most stubborn yoghurt stains disappear, and she does it with pleasure, for it is the broad, tanned, muscular back of her favourite client, who pays a fortune every week for her massage, so she scrubs. She admires her own milk-filled breast in Maja's mouth, and the mouth that closes around her nipple belongs to an Arab prince with black eyes, baggy trousers and a sickle-shaped sword in one hand.

Liss paints the light grey terraced house with adjectives like golden yellow, ruby red, ebony black, pearl white, sky blue, emerald green. She fills the living room with its downtrodden parquet with phrases like burning passion, heavenly lovemaking, undying love, until it's stuffed to the rafters, until there is nearly no room for the furniture, for the rather worn sofa, the two armchairs, the bookcase, the artists' posters in thin, pine frames. When she opens the cupboard doors in the bedroom, clichés, platitudes and well-used phrases tumble down around her ears. The words pour out of the cupboard, hitting her softly and pleasantly on the head.

Liss is just about to open the post box. She didn't hear him coming, but suddenly he's there. Breathing heavily on her neck, his body against hers. She can feel his cock pressing against her behind. His hands grasp her waist, her slim waist, then slide up and close on her breasts. She leans back against him. Her keys fall to the ground. She straightens up before bending down to pick them up again. Has anyone seen her? She looks around, none of the neighbours are out, but maybe someone has seen her from a window? Liss opens the post box and looks inside. It's empty apart from the usual advertising bumpf. Or is it? At the bottom of the post box is an ice blue envelope with her name written on it. Handwritten in careful, but very masculine, joined-up writing. The stamp is foreign. French perhaps. No, it's definitely Italian. On the back of the envelope is something that looks like a coat of arms. Two crossed swords over two lions, or are they leopards? She turns and walks back towards the door. From an unknown, Italian admirer. Or perhaps the count with the three-day shadow.

The sewing circle are coming tonight. Paul has taken the children, including Maja, to his mother's. The food is ready. The starter is in the fridge. The fish gratin is on the worktop, ready to be put in the oven. She made the dessert yesterday and added enough sherry to make it taste right, then decorated it with glacé cherries. Now she has to tidy the living room and set the table. As Liss wipes the table before starting to set it, she notices that it needs to be oiled. She goes into the kitchen to get the oil and some rags and then she leans over the table – a ten-year-old, rickety IKEA pine table – and starts to rub in the furniture oil. And as she rubs, the IKEA table disappears.

In the middle of the room is a wavy-grained birchwood table, polished and huge. A woman is crouching in the middle of the table. It is Liss. She is the Famous Leopard Woman. A man is sitting on the sofa, looking at the woman on the table. Liss is squatting on the table. She is not wearing any underwear and her dress (leopard skin pattern of course) is crumpled around her waist. Her deep red vagina stares at the man on the sofa. Just to the left of Liss is a plate of eggs. She moves the dish into position between her legs. Then she rests her elbows on her knees, and folds her hands. The dish with the eggs is right in the middle, between her legs. She lifts her backside ever so slightly, adjusts her position and starts to suck in the first egg. Slowly the clean white egg disappears between her brownish labia. Liss looks up at the ceiling, it is obvious that she is focusing hard. She lowers herself a bit more and breathes in before starting on egg number two. Soon that has also disappeared. Now? she asks the man in the sofa, who nods. The Famous Leopard Woman lowers her backside to the table, puts her hands down behind her, opens her legs even wider and pumps out the egg whites, yolks and shells.

Rich Arabs could pay up to twice the normal price for a kabbazah slave. The magazine article said that the literal translation of 'kabbazah' was one who holds. A woman with strong, well-trained and supple vaginal muscles. She should be able to sit astride a man and make him come without moving anything more than her vaginal muscles. There are stories of women with such strong muscles that they could crush the organ of their lover if he did not please them. The Famous Leopard Woman is just such a woman. She is both dangerous and desirable. She hides a rose and a predator between her thighs.

The table is done. Liss feels that her muscles are tired after all her exertions but at least the table looks good. She decides to hoover a bit until seven o'clock. She has plenty of time and she is sure to fit in the hoovering and a wealthy, virile Frenchman who is interested in philosophy, before the fish has to be put in the oven. She has made fish gratin with cod and mussels – frozen cod and tinned mussels in white sauce. Liss nearly always makes simple dishes that don't require much preparation and only minimal effort in the kitchen. It's not that Liss isn't interested in food. Liss loves reading the food columns in the Saturday papers, she always picks up the free food magazines in supermarkets and she studies the menu carefully when she goes to restaurants. Her favourite toilet reading material is cookbooks. She sits on the loo with her mouth watering and her trousers round her ankles like a pretzel, reading about the most tempting dishes while the smell of her excrement oozes out and fills the small, tiled room. She can sit like this for hours, planning sumptuous banquets. But then Liss is not particularly keen on making food. She's too impatient, too slapdash and possibly too scared of failing.

Liss hoovers the living room carpet, which is a deep-pile carpet and home to unbelievable amounts of dust and biscuit crumbs. It used to be white. Over the noise of the hoover and a tinkling sound that means it has sucked up something more than just dust, Liss hears the telephone. It's one of Liss' clients. She must leave immediately. It's urgent. It's one of her regulars, a shipowner with dark hair, shot with silver over the temples. He can't live without her, and now, right now, he needs Liss and her unique services.

Liss is on her way home after a job well done and it won't be long now until the sewing circle girls arrive. She opens the gate and sees the back of a dark-haired Sara or Tamara walking up the path, nearly at the front door. Liss runs as fast and as silently as she can, sprints past, her jacket grazing the dark-haired woman. She turns around and sees that it's Sara, opens the door, pulls off her fishnets and black silk corset, throws the whip into a trunk with the children's rainclothes, puts on a nice, newish dress and just manages to pull up the zip and nonchalantly open the door when

Sara rings the bell. Sara notices nothing. Tamara and Eva arrive shortly after.

The melon and ham tasted good, the fish gratin was a success. Sara talked about the bathroom she and Jakob are doing up, and about hopeless mother-in-laws, Eva was interested in Sara's sister and Tamara talked about her work. Liss apologised for the unsophisticated food and said that she had had a busy day. She could see that none of the girls believed her, but she realised it was pointless to tell them about the French count, the letter in the post box or the Famous Leopard Woman. What would a woman like Eva know about kabbazah women? And what would Sara and Tamara know about satisfying the demands of shipowners, for that matter? Liss said nothing. And she just smiled and shook her head when Tamara discovered some eggshell on the dinner table and asked, somewhat surprised, if she had been making waffles or scrambled eggs in the dining room.

'Lovely food, Liss,' Eva says. 'So, what do you think of my new skirt, girls?'

Eva stands up, slightly unsteadily as you do when you have been drinking wine with girlfriends. She giggles: 'I'm obviously a bit tipsy. But what do you think? Am I too fat to wear it?'

Yes, Liss thinks and says: 'No, of course not. You're not too fat. You look lovely and slim.'

'Yes, but doesn't my bum look a bit big?' Eva asks.

'No,' Sara reassures her.

'Oh, come on,' Liss says.

Liss looks at the grey-blue skirt in shiny stretch material that is glued to Eva's solid backside, hips and thighs. She can see quite clearly where her knickers are digging into her thighs. Incredible that Eva doesn't realise that she should at least wear a thong with clothes like that! Somebody should say something to her. Tamara is usually good at things like that. Tamara isn't exactly diplomatic, her tongue can be a bit sharp for that, she is an Aries after all, but at least she manages to say what she thinks clearly. Eva's skirt follows the contours of her bulging upper thighs, it's as if the slightest cellulite, flab and bump is pressing through the shiny material. Liss imagines Eva standing at the blackboard writing up the homework and Please Leave! while the small movements that her right hand makes as she moves the chalk ripple down her body, making her behind shimmer and shake. Suddenly Liss can clearly see all the pupils reflected in their teacher's behind. They're sitting at their desks, stifling their laughter and watching their wobbly, grey-blue reflections moving across their teacher's shiny, undulating arse.

'Great skirt,' Sara and Tamara say at almost the same time.

'It's DNKY,' Eva informs them.

'DKNY,' Liss corrects automatically. 'The shiny material is lovely,' she adds and thinks that, after all, it's nice that Eva is showing more interest in how she looks. When they got to know her just under two years ago, she was barely presentable. Now she turns up in a strange mixture of her own not-interested-in-clothes-period clothes chosen for their high utility factor and low price, and some impractical, expensive, but chic new designer outfits. A strange mixture, true enough, but definitely an improvement, thinks Liss, who likes Eva a lot. Liss likes Eva. It's a good thing that she's joined the sewing circle, because Eva can help Liss.

'Was it in the sale?' asks Tamara.

'No,' Eva replies.

'Lovely colour,' Sara says.

The colour reminds Liss of her old teddy bear, Bamse. Bamse was the same grey-blue colour. He had worn, grey-blue nylon fur and huge dark blue eyes with friendly black pupils. A sewn-on black nose. The fur on his ears is nearly worn off. Bamse is soft and kind. He is always with Liss. She got him from Daddy when she was little. Daddy had bought him in Rio de Janeiro. That's such a nice word to say. Rio de Janeiro. Bamse never lets her down. He's in her bed at night and sits waiting for her on the sofa when she comes home from school. He is always kind. The eyes that look at her are always the same. Always happy and kind.

'Some more wine?' Sara is holding the newly opened bottle of Chardonnay that she brought with her.

'Yes, thanks. Just pour,' Tamara says.

'I'll have a bit more as well, thanks. I slept so badly last night,' Eva says.

'La vie est dure,' Sara says.

'Yes, girls, real life is hard. That's the way it is. Life's a bitch,' Liss says.

'You're all so wrong,' Tamara teases. 'It's quite the opposite. In real life it's never hard enough. Dreams are hard, stiff and last for hours. Whereas real life is often half erect and prone to premature ejaculation.'

'Good God, Tamara! You are always so vulgar,' Sara says.

'Excuse me, I won't be a moment,' Liss says. 'Sorry.'

Almost as soon as Liss has locked the door of her tiled guest toilet, the long legs with high-heeled court shoes click-clack towards her. This is when I could do with a knight in shining armour, Liss thinks, or at least some fiery, broad-shouldered Spaniard. She looks up the legs, but she can't see the face because it's too high up. The shoes are black with tiny decorative holes in a border along the edge of the instep, which is white and slightly swollen. She sees the knees and some flesh folds just above. She tilts her head back and now she can see the red, shiny lips. They're moving, opening and closing. If you don't behave properly, I won't want to be your mummy anymore. I'll leave you.

*

It's summer. Sunshine in the sitting room. It smells of floor polish. The door to the garden is ajar and the curtains are rising and falling on the breeze. Liss is sitting on Mummy's lap. They're sitting on the green velvet sofa. The smell of freshly baked bread wafts in from the kitchen and mingles with the floor polish.

Mummy hugs Liss close. Darling little girl, she says. Liss feels her lips against her crown, moving, whispering pet names. Little Liss, my treasure. Mummy's little girl. But Liss knows that it's coming, no matter what. She gets scared. She looks around the room. It looks quite normal. The sun streams in through the newly cleaned windows, marking out squares on the parquet. Liss is frightened. Liss doesn't dare to turn round and look at Mummy. Because what if it isn't Mummy? What if it's the woman with the red, angry mouth and the black shoes? She feels her heart starting to pound in her chest. She's cold. The sweet talk continues to float in through her ears. Little Liss, Mummy's little girl, Mummy's only comfort. You and me, Liss. You and me. And she can't turn round.

Liss has fallen and hurt herself. Fallen on the asphalt and grazed her knee badly. It's bleeding and there's small stones and dirt in the wound. Mummy, cries Liss. Mummy, where are you? Mummy is sitting on the green sofa with a book on her lap. She doesn't look up. Mummy, I've hurt myself. Liss is crying. Mummy doesn't answer. Bamse goes with her to the bathroom. Liss hums and Bamse helps her to put disinfectant on some cotton wool and clean her knee. Mummy is reading, her lipstick red mouth is moving, but Liss can't hear the words.

It must have been in class three, because the teacher was Tilde Smith-Larsen. Liss, you're so good at learning things by heart, I thought you could do 'At the bottom of the sea all the old ships lie' by Inger Hagerup, the teacher had said. Liss is happy, but she sees Sara and Tamara whispering something to Lillian. Lillian is the chosen one. Lillian is lucky. Sara and Tamara are terribly bossy, they decide everything in the class and all the girls are frightened of them. Tamara decides most. Pissy Lissy, Sara and Tamara shout at her. Dizzy Pissy Lissy. Liss, you smell, they say and turn their backs. Sometimes Lillian is allowed to play with Sara and Tamara, but then they fall out again and Sara and Tamara disappear arm in arm. The one darker than the other. Sara is prettiest, thinks Liss. Sara has starry eyes.

At the end-of-term assembly, Liss stands alone on the stage. She has ribbons in her newly plaited hair. A white and light blue striped dress, white knee socks and sandals. Her voice is loud and clear. You were very good! What a lovely reading! You must be proud of her, Mrs Krogh. Mummy smiles, nods and strokes Liss' hair. Then she takes her by the hand and they go home. When they get out on to the pavement, Mummy lets go of Liss' hand. At home in the sitting room. Mummy sits on the sofa with a cup of coffee. No one says anything. At the bottom of the sea all the old ships lie, with great black sails, Liss repeats inside herself. Again and again. It's wet and windy in the sea's red trees. Does she think I was good? Mummy's soft, slightly flabby upper arm on the arm of the sofa. Liss sits down on the sofa, the arm does not move. Liss snuggles in to it, rubs her cheek against the warm skin. Mummy takes her arm away, looks at Liss, stands up and walks away. Her heels click clack on the parquet floor.

Liss, darling? Where are you? Liss and Bamse are in the cupboard. They say nothing and Mummy continues to shout. Sweetie? Liss love, little Liss, where are you? Liss comes out and Mummy hugs her. Little Liss. Liss' head between Mummy's breasts. Loose and soft. Mummy hugs her tighter. Liss' nose presses into Mummy's prickly woollen sweater. She squirms, can't breathe. She hears Mummy laughing. From above and inside, inside Mummy's body. She loosens her grip. My baby, Mummy says. Don't ever leave your Mummy, Liss.

Liss sits on the toilet seat. The tiles on the walls are shiny. Far too shiny. Like the back of Eva's skirt. Eva's grey-blue DKNY skirt. Kind, well-meaning Eva. Liss smiles spontaneously, but then Mummy's big, shiny, red mouth leers towards her again. The lips are opening and closing and Liss remembers how she ran after her mother, because her mother had said she was going to leave Liss. But Bamse was always there. Soft and worn. Almost bald in some places. Bamse smelt lovely. And his big, dark blue eyes understood everything. Liss pulls herself together, flushes (in case anyone is waiting outside) and goes back to the others in the living room. They are in the middle of a conversation about the value of friendship and the importance of having female friends. 'Just listen to all those beautiful words,' Sara says. 'We are so lucky to have someone we can tell everything to, to have friends we trust absolutely,' says Eva. The others nod in agreement. Tamara tells them that women cope better than men in many ways, because they have a social network, someone to discuss their personal problems with. Tamara wrote quite a long feature article about it for last week's Saturday paper and she talked to both men and women and even interviewed a psychologist working at the university who usually likes to have his say about most things. But of course, you read it...? 'Yes,' Liss says, sitting down beside Sara. Sara called her Pissy Lissy when they were little. Dizzy Pissy Lissy, you stink. I don't want to sit next to you, Liss. You smell.

But Liss is different now. Liss wants Sara and Tamara to see that. And Eva will help. Sara still has starry eyes.

Liss comes home from school. But where is Bamse? He's not on the sofa, where he usually is. Liss goes into her bedroom. Bamse's back is sticking out between the duvet and the pillow. Liss picks Bamse up. Bamse's eyes have been cut off, only two tangles of black thread stick out from the light blue material. Bamse has a big hole in his tummy. It looks like somone has stabbed him and some stuffing is spewing out of the wound.

'More wine, Liss?'
    'Yes please.'

A glass of wine and everything will be fine. A small glass of wine and it will all disappear. Then another glass of wine and he will come riding in on his white horse and save her. A Montenegrian aristocrat, who says Liss has a mouth like a ripe berry, cherry-coloured lips, eyes like starflowers and a forehead of white alabaster. Unbridled passion. Eternal friendship. Burning love. Till death us do part.

It's a long time now since Liss has been like this, a long time since she has seen the shiny lips. The magic formula usually works. 'You can tune your own brain into any channel you want, at any time.' Tune out the boredom of everyday life, the making of sandwiches, the husband with a fuzzy naval and wind, the crying children and half-dirty house. It always works. But not against Mummy's red, shiny lips and hard, high heels.

Liss sews up the hole in Bamse's tummy as well as she can, humming loudly. She'll give Bamse new eyes. Oh Liss, what happened? And Bamse, who you love so much? Come here, let Mummy make it better. Come and sit on my lap! Liss sits on Mummy's lap, Mummy whispers sweet nothings into her hair. Little Liss. Mummy says she can help Liss, that she can sew on new eyes for Bamse. Mummy chooses a couple of metal buttons from the box in her sewing basket. Bamse's new eyes stare at Liss in the dark, the metal shines out. Liss doesn't dare to take Bamse to bed. She puts him in a drawer, but then after a few days feels sorry for him. Poor Bamse, having to lie all alone in the dark. And it's not Bamse's fault that he's got eyes like that. Bamse is allowed to sleep in her bed again. Everything is as it was. But then one day Liss comes home from school and Bamse has disappeared. They never find him again. Well, maybe you were a bit too old to have a teddy in bed, Mummy comforts her. You are eleven, after all.

'Are you alright, Liss?' Sara asks in a quiet voice and strokes Liss' arm. 'You seem a bit distant. Is something wrong?'

'No, no,' Liss whispers back. 'I'm just a bit tired, worn out. I'm still breastfeeding, you see. And today I had to express and Maja is away from me for the first time. I think I'm just a bit nervous, that's all.'

And then out loud she says: 'Now it's time for coffee and dessert on the sofa, girls. Please excuse the dust in the corners!'

'Everything looks fine to me,' Eva says.

'Don't worry about that,' Sara says at the same time.

'It's such a relief to meet a housewife who's not bothered about her house being a bit mucky,' Tamara says after a brief pause. She gets up from the chair where she's been sitting, smiles at Liss, and brushes off the back of her skirt.

When the girls have left and Liss has tidied everything away, she sits down on the sofa in her empty house. She is the Amazon queen, Penthesileia. She gallops across the plains on her white mare. Her long, blonde hair flutters in the wind beneath her engraved silver helmet. She swings her sword above her head, turns round and shouts a sharp command. Just behind her, on either side, ride her two dark-haired servants, the one darker than the other. They obey her every word. Now they ride up alongside Penthesileia and ask what they can do for her. The voices of the two dark-haired women are full of awe and wonder. Penthesileia smiles. And falls asleep on the sofa.

Chapter 4

Sewing Circle at Sara's, Tuesday 24 October

Menu
Scallops
Cream of mussel soup with aioli
Lamb en croute with balsamic and port sauce
Grilled chèvre
Chocolate and orange semifreddo

Sara really wants a cup of tea, the second of the day, but then she would first have to collect the post. It is imperative. And it is far too early for the postman to have been, but in order to have cup of tea number two, she has to check the post. Those are the rules and they are absolute.

The post box is, of course, empty. There are sixteen steps from the green post boxes on the ground floor up to Sara's flat. Sara knows this perfectly well, but she cannot start counting until she has reached the ninth step. On the tenth step, she starts counting. Always and without exception. Only in this way is she able to say seven as her left foot touches down on her floor, not far from the charcoal grey, dust-free doormat in front of the smooth door with her, Jakob's and Julia's names on it.

*

Sara's sitting room is always tidy, always clean. And today is no exception. But the moment that Sara walks into her sitting room, where some defiant dust particles dance joyfully and audaciously in a strip of sun that has slipped into the room through the opaque, light ivory curtains, the inner peace that she felt only a short while ago evaporates. Sara does not feel happy any more. A fragile Wedgewood cup balances on Sara's right palm, which is cupped to hold it. It is filled with freshly brewed, steaming Earl Grey that will never be drunk. The tea leaves are bought by the hectogram from a well-stocked tea and coffee merchant on one of Bogstadveien's quieter side streets. A silver spoon, designed like an elongated rose, which Sara inherited from an unmarried great aunt, who passed on relatively recently from Parkveien to Paradise (that is as long as her own beliefs held true), stands heating in the sepia-coloured fluid. The spoon is newly polished, shining and poised for action in an upright, pert position. Sara does not feel that she is shaking, but she hears it. The silver spoon is clinking against the thin porcelain.

Behind the sunbathed dust particles, Sara sees the vibrating computer screen. The screen saver's star storm races towards her in a relentless, unstoppable stream, reflected upside down on Sara's retina, but is immediately perceived, without a second's hesitation, by Sara's cerebral cells as being the right way round all the same, just as they have turned round every impression received for more than thirty years now. The sight of the computer swiftly confirms for her what she must do next, which has an immediate calming effect. Sara puts the Wedgewood cup with the warm teaspoon down on the rough surface of the oakwood coffee table, where it will be forgotten beside the sugar bowl that looks remarkably similar, and left to get colder, bitterer and more and more undrinkable. As soon as she has put down the cup, Sara feels her pulse by placing the index and middle fingers of her right hand over the inside of her left wrist. Her pulse is high, but regular. Thank goodness. Reassured, Sara sits down in front of the computer, turns her attention to the screen and lets her fingers move quickly and confidently over the keyboard. She feels far better already.

About halfway through her seventh and therefore most significant attempt, Sara's intense concentration in front of the screen is interrupted when the telephone on the small sideboard with a bevelled glass plate that stands close to the white sofa, starts to ring. Sara hesitates. She oscillates between the need to see if she will succeed this time – because she must, the seventh attempt –

and the need to pick up the phone, to find out who it is, what this person who has chosen to call her at precisely this moment wants. Her curiosity wins. Sara gets up and walks towards the increasingly insistent ringing of the phone. The aces from the computer screen, in the order of spade, heart, diamond and club, are burnt onto the inside of her eyelids. Sara can feel her mascara-heavy lids blinking several times in rapid succession over her smooth eyeballs. The cards, in black, white and red against the pleasant moss-green background, are reflected in a blur of colour and the image remains intact as Sara approaches the telephone, even when her eyes are open. But when her hand reaches out for the surprisingly cold, white telephone receiver, when part of her body comes into contact with what is essentially the world outside her fish-bowl silent sitting room, the image vanishes in an instant. It disappears. Sara sees only her own dark eyes in the mirror, which hangs in its heavy gold frame with bunches of grapes, chubby cherubs and vines, yet another reminder of the great aunt who relatively recently passed away from her spacious, but somewhat impractical and old-fashioned three-bedroomed flat in Parkveien. Sara presses the cool white receiver to her ear. Her aural faculties are wide open, like a funnel, to capture the telephonic message from the world outside. Her lips part from their pursed position with a small, nearly inaudible pop. She says her name and immediately knows that no voice other than her own will be heard during the course of this telephone conversation. Sara is scared. She leans closer to her reflection in the mirror, her lower ribs touching the bunches of gilded grapes, cherubs and vine leaves, and she sees the fear dilating her pupils to black, frightened holes. Because this is not the first time this has happened. In recent weeks, Sara has been an unwilling participant in a number of telephone conversations that have been as one-sided and short as this. Too many for it to be a wrong number. Who is it who keeps calling Sara and then putting down the phone without saying a word?

Her nose looks just as abnormal in the mirror as usual, big with a very unattractive break in the line just above the middle, where the nose bone changes into softer cartilage. And her sorrow over this deformed nose, a sorrow that is in fact chronic and ever present, but which at this precise moment, on seeing her reflection in the mirror, is manifest, amplified and at the forefront of her mind, actually overshadows her fear. Sara is nearly no longer afraid. She turns her head, her huge pupils trained on the face in the mirror, and looks at her profile, so with her nose casting a shadow over the right side of her face and the silent telephone receiver still pressed to her ear, Sara counts to seven and knows, without a shadow of doubt, that she will not succeed at Patience this time either.

Lisa in 4b says that Tamara and Sara are so alike. Sara looks at Tamara in the changing room after gym. She is tall and thin and very beautiful. Everyone says that Tamara is beautiful. Sara looks at Tamara in class. Her brown hair is parted so you can see her white neck when she bends forwards. The skin on the rest of her body is darker, golden brown in summer and sallow in winter like now, but Tamara's neck is always white. Lisa says that Sara is beautiful. No one else in the three parallel class fours has hair as dark as Tamara and Sara. Tamara says that they are both beautiful. I have bigger eyes and you have whiter teeth, says Tamara to Sara. But your nose is quite big. You've got a big nose, says Tamara.

Of course. Not even the seventh attempt at Patience is successful. (Sorry, you have no tricks left). Even though the triumph of being right acts as a mollifying soft down cushion between her and the blow of failing, it is still a heavy burden for Sara to bear. Ever since she was a little girl, Sara has been drawn to solving things, making things right. When she was young, she loved jigsaw puzzles and riddles to which she already knew the answer. In later life, she preferred Patience, maths, Agatha Christie and the German language. She, Sara, has the key to people who seem incomprehensible to others.

Sara has to punish herself. Having thought for a while, she decides on her punishment: she has to wash her hands seven times and she is not allowed to eat dessert this evening with the sewing circle. This last part of the punishment in particular will be hard. Sara adores her own semifreddo, especially with orange and chocolate, which is exactly what she is serving tonight and she knows it will please the girls and she has been looking forward to feeling it lying uppermost in her stomach, which has been deliciously filled with layers of scallops, creamed mussel soup, lamb en croute with balsamic and port sauce and ratatouille in just the right amounts. But now, balanced atop these other dishes that have been chewed until they are unrecognisable, half digested by Sara's stomach juices, there will unfortunately be no semifreddo, but instead, a piece of toast with chèvre, which will be Sara's last course for the evening. It's a mean punishment.

*

Having washed her hands thoroughly with soap seven times and moisturised them with a good nourishing hand cream (bought in the duty-free shop at Gardermoen airport en route to a meeting with a publisher in Düsseldorf) between each wash, Sara ascertains with a quick glance at her watch that it is high time she started to make the food. Sara enjoys making food. She feels better already. Her pulse is no longer abnormally high.

Once she is in the kitchen, which is done out in black, white, turquoise and shiny metal, once she has breathed in the faint but distinct smell of chlorine, let her gaze rest contentedly on the white, spotless worktops, once she has stood there for a few seconds with her clean hands folded and surveyed her gleaming kitchen kingdom, waves of transient pleasure pulse through Sara. She starts to whistle quietly. Sara gets out a plastic chopping board, covers it with greaseproof paper and starts, still whistling, to cut up the vegetables for the ratatouille. The work is done quickly and precisely and in a remarkably short time, remarkably short taking into account the fact that she changes the greaseproof paper on the board between each type of vegetable, like the good and extremely hygienic vegetable cutter that she is. Very soon, each vegetable sort has been cut up into exactly the same sized portions. Just as she is about to tip the result of her work into the spitting pan, which is gaping in anticipation on the front hotplate – a small plate of chopped garlic, a plate of greenish white, tear-inducing onion rings, another of cream coloured chopped aubergine with shiny purple skin, one with strips of red pepper and another with green and light yellow courgette – she discovers a forgotten red pepper behind the old, but only yesterday carefully disinfected Dutch crock (Sara shudders at the thought of food prepared in kitchens that are full of old, dried flowers, dusty ribbons and greasy knick-knacks). It shines out at her like a reproachful red alarm. Sara does not like it, as she at this point sees vegetable chopping as a closed chapter. But she is neither unreasonable nor hysterical, so she reaches out her hand and lets the red pepper roll onto the chopping board. While she changes the greaseproof paper for what is definitely the last time, the pepper lies and rocks cheerfully like a bright red buoy on the white worktop, and it is then, once the paper has been carefully folded around the chopping board and Sara has raised her newly-sharpened Sabatier knife with a dark wooden handle, bought at Rafens for just under one thousand kroner, that she discovers a small, black fleck on the shiny pepper skin. An exceptionally disgusting, black spot that grows and spreads with alarming speed. In the few seconds that Sara has stood with her knife raised, the fleck has multiplied and spread all over the red pepper, which is now spotted like a ladybird. Sara stands there, transfixed, but when the telephone starts to ring, she makes a quick decision and with obvious and demonstrative disgust, as if she had an audience, she stabs the ladybird that has just started to drag itself across the worktop on its belly, and throws it into the bin on the inside of – praise be to God – the nearest cupboard door, so near in fact, that the whole time she has been chopping she has been touching it with her left kneecap. Then she scrapes the contents off each plate, letting it tumble bit by bit into the bin, where it lands on top of the still feebly struggling insect. Sara watches the torrent of vegetables with a pinched mouth. As if it were half-chewed food, as if it were vomit, ruined, contaminated and rotten. The cascading vegetables land on top of the black spotted ladybird's back: chopped, stinking garlic, pieces of onion the colour of sun-deficient shoots under a stone with scurrying beetles and squirming worms, sick-looking aubergine (who would want to eat purple food?), menstruation-coloured peppers and gall green, snakeskin-patterned courgette. The telephone is still ringing when she turns off the cooker and lets the olive oil settle in the pan. Sara notes with some satisfaction that the fact that the sewing circle girls will not be served ratatouille does not particularly bother her, in fact, it bothers her about as much as the knowledge that she will not reach the phone before it stops ringing. Sara counts to seven, sinks down onto a kitchen stool, in surprisingly good spirits, puckers her mouth and starts to whistle again, softly this time, and the phone goes quiet.

In Liss' kitchen and Eva's kitchen there are pictures everywhere, great swarms of pictures all over the walls, big and small, cheap reproductions from IKEA in clip frames, children's drawings with names and dates ('Giraffe', Mona, September '94 and 'My family', Martin, 5 years), wedding photos, photos of children. Even Tamara has pictures in her kitchen, sharply delineated and clearly defined into a carefully composed row, tasteful and original, just like Tamara. Tamara, my best friend, Sara thinks, standing in the middle of her kitchen floor, which is black and white squared like a chess board in Indonesian marble tiles that cost an extortionate amount (Sara, there must be a zero too many here, Jakob had said when they got the quote from the tiler that a colleague had warmly recommended to Sara). Tamara, my dearest friend, successful, beautiful, with a lovely, perfectly shaped nose with narrow nostrils that are just the right size. Tamara. A slow wave of gratitude washes over Sara, who puts out her hand and holds on to the edge of the white worktop, she has to hold on to something so that she's not pulled back by the undertow, so that she doesn't drown. I couldn't cope without Tamara, Sara thinks as she clings on to the worktop, standing on her toes, with her chin held high so she doesn't get water in her mouth. Tamara has always been there, always helped me. The wave ebbs away, but Sara stays standing by the worktop.

*

Sara's kitchen walls, in contrast, are bare. She does, on the other hand, have quite a substantial collection of kitchen utensils in stainless steel, predominantly Italian made, but otherwise the walls are empty, with the exception of one rather small picture, which hangs on the wall directly above the high-backed chair with a light-coloured cover, where Sara normally sits when the family eats together on weekdays, meals that are meticulously and lovingly prepared by Sara herself; on Sundays, the small family, which comprises only three members, eats in the dining room. Despite the fact that both Jakob and Sara's twelve-year old daughter, Julia, and several other guests have praised the rather unremarkable watercolour in shades of blue, Sara never looks at the picture herself. Never. In fact, Sara often feels uncomfortable, sometimes just a dull, vague feeling, and at other times quite a strong discomfort, about having the picture on the wall above and behind her when she sits down to eat with her small family. All the same, Sara chooses to let the picture hang there, because then it is at least in a place where it is barely visible to Sara when she is making the meals, and it would not be appropriate, in fact it would be impossible, to remove the watercolour from Sara's kitchen.

Sara got the small picture, which is of a cat, nearly three years ago for Christmas, from Tamara's daughter, Emma. As soon as Jakob, dressed for the occasion in a bright red Santa costume, had put the present, which was beautifully and meticulously wrapped (winter night blue shiny paper, strewn with silver stars and tied with a broad ribbon in white silk), in Sara's lap, it made her feel slightly unwell; unwell in a way that she knew was not due to overindulgence in roast pork, chipolatas and red cabbage. A faint, but irrepressible feeling of discomfort. Even now, long after, Sara can clearly remember, even evoke, right now where she is standing in the kitchen with her heels raised and one hand on the worktop and the picture of the cat behind her, the vague feeling of discomfort she had felt on that Christmas Eve nearly three years ago, as she sat with the present in her hands. Who is it from, Mummy? Julia had asked. Having read the small gift tag in thick cream-coloured paper with elegant calligraphy, Sara could tell her daughter that this exceptionally beautifully wrapped present was from Tamara's daughter, Emma. Emma, who at that point was exactly nine (she was born a few months, three to be precise, after Sara's own daughter, Julia). Julia stood close to her mother, though probably not driven by love, but rather a burning curiosity. A curiosity that was soon accompanied by a smidgen of jealousy. To you from Emma, Julia had repeated, that's nice, but a bit strange. She certainly didn't write that herself, she had added, running her index finger over the elegant letters. The faint feeling of unease evaporated, it's a present from Emma. Sara is touched. She has always felt very attached to Tamara's only child and she knows that Tamara, Sara's best friend, Sara's dearest friend from childhood, also has a warm and close relationship with her daughter, Sara's only child. It's just such a shame that Emma and Julia do not seem to get on particularly well. Dearest friends' daughters should also become close friends – it would have been so lovely, so symmetrical, so right, but it was just not meant to be. Emma and Julia can't stand each other. Next Christmas, or maybe now, before New Year, she must make sure that Tamara gets a little something from Julia, Sara thinks to herself and looks down at the present in her lap. She starts to open it, carefully, trying not to ruin the wrapping paper. The size and shape of the present – it is quite small and flat – makes Sara guess it is a book, a delightful, slim collection of poetry, no doubt, or one of those thin, modern novels. Sara's fingers have reached the innermost layer of rustling tissue paper and under it they feel, not the slightly rough cover of a poetry collection or the even dust jacket of a modern novel, but something smooth and cold, with raised edges. A picture. Sara's fingers recognise a picture. Still smiling, still deeply touched by her best friend's little daughter, she takes the picture out of the paper and holds it up to see, up to her unprepared eyes. What is it, Mummy? asks Julia, but Sara is unable to answer her nine-year old daughter. Instead, Sara gets up suddenly and the paper, ribbon and present all fall to the floor, where they land in a heaving, evil, staring pile on the light blue, hand-knotted carpet, and when the pile starts to purr softly, she can no longer suppress her screams, which are forced, rather loudly, from her mouth. Surprisingly unaffected by her mother's screams, Julia kneels down and picks up the picture from the rustling pile of paper. Oh, look, Mummy, Julia says, obviously delighted that the present from the arrogant, unbearable Emma is for some reason a fiasco. Look, Mummy, it's a little pussy. It's called Purring Cat, Mummy, and here's a little note. On the note it says, this time in clumsy childish letters: Dear 'Aunty', this is for your kitchen so you can look at it when you are making food.

Sara hates cats. She has hated cats since she was a young girl. Sara has hated cats since she was eleven. Sara shudders when she thinks about, sees a picture of or even hears a cat, not to mention when she meets a real, live cat. She immediately feels the disgusting, soft cat body twisting between her legs, wrapping itself round her legs, warm fur against naked skin. Cats have untrustworthy, yellow eyes, with ellipse-shaped pupils that always stare right at you. Cats creep up to you without a sound, but behind those soft padded paws are razor-sharp claws that can dig in and rip open your cheeks, blind your eyes. And in the down-turned, sneering mouth with its pink tongue, which is soft and wet and rasping all at once, there are teeth that are as sharp as needles. Cats narrow their eyes, tense their muscles, prepare themselves, lash their tails and at any moment can jump right into your unprotected face.

Vulnerable, powerless. Kristian's eyes when she said it was over between them. Sad. Sara thinks about Kristian. She does so every now and then, and she always feels so sad when she thinks about Kristian. She remembers Kristian well. He had such a lovely smile and such kind, narrow eyes. Kristian had a sailing boat and he knew the names of all sorts of wild flowers. Kristian loved sweet desserts and fish and seafood. He was perfect. They were perfect for each other. It was a real shame it had to end that way. But they had to finish. It was absolutely necessary.

And Tamara agreed that he was quite jealous, possessive and domineering. Sara couldn't cope without Tamara. Sara knows that she is helpless without Tamara.

Suddenly Sara realises that she is angry with Tamara. A strong desire to scratch Tamara's soft skin, to claw out her eyes with her nails, to bite her so that the bones in her slim, but solid, strong hands snap between Sara's teeth and she tastes blood, surges through Sara. But no sooner has she felt it, than she uses every ounce of her being to repress it. And she succeeds. She uses both her hands to push the desire back down to where it belongs, where it slopes off back into its dark hiding-hole again, ashamed, with its tail between its legs and downcast eyes. Sara does not understand how she can have such thoughts, she does not want to have them and she does not have them either. Not at all. It is incomprehensible, it is inexplicable, and Tamara is Sara's best friend. She supports her and helps her. Sara needs Tamara.

*

And how could Emma know that 'Aunty' was afraid of cats?

Sara's normally quiet dining room is full of laughter and female voices. Right now it's Tamara who is praising the food. And the food is good, Sara knows that. The food that Sara prepares is always, without exception, very good. The second course is already on the table, steaming in front of Sara's closest friends, an almost yolk-yellow soup with big mussels, garnished with fresh basil and a dollop of home-made garlic mayonnaise, as soft and as supple as Dior's best face cream, in each bowl. Five courses, but if you include the gin beforehand and the espresso after, seven courses. Is laser hair removal a good investment? Compared with a timeless designer suit? Have I read his latest book? Yes, I've read everything he's written, since he started. He's getting worse and worse. Mother-in-law? No, not yet. Not at all, you just have to make sure you add the oil in small drops to begin with. Delicious. Yes, but we do need some calories if we're going to enjoy ourselves. Emma's now the editor for the school magazine. Oh, have I already said that?

Sara looks at her friends. In their mouths, and her mouth, their teeth are grinding up the pink, juicy roast lamb, mulching the crispy, golden brown puff pastry crust to a grey pulp, mixed with saliva, and rhythmical contractions are forcing the now papier-mâché-like lumps down through their digestive systems. In the course of a few hours it will have made its way to the intestinal villus' greedy, waving movements.

'Delicious,' Tamara says and Sara sees the bits of lamb in balsamic vinegar and port sauce sliding down Tamara's oesophagus, reaching her stomach where they are drenched in Tamara's digestive juices. Sara looks over at Eva and Liss, who are also chewing and digesting. Sara is sure that Eva's digestive juices are gentler and don't contain as much pepsin or have as high a hydrochloric acid content as Tamara's digestive juices do. Now the roast lamb has been sufficiently mulched and carefully divided up in Tamara's stomach, and is being transported on to her duodenum, where it will be sprayed with bile. Tamara's bile is sure to be a more intense green than say, Liss', which is lighter, more like a spring green. Sara smiles back at Tamara:
    'Yes, I hope it tastes all right,' she says. She is taking a small break at the moment, herself.

When the girls have eaten the last course before dessert, a thick slice of chèvre that Sara has put on a piece of melba toast (home-made), grilled for thirty seconds and then placed on a bed of salad on the thinnest, most delicate plates she has inherited, Tamara stands up. She excuses herself with a smile and announces in a loud and clear voice that accords demonstratively with her personality, that she is going to the loo. But did she not just nod imperceptibly in Liss' direction? Sara cannot be sure. Tamara's steps are silent on the parquet floor, even though she is, as always, wearing high-heeled shoes, and she glides up the stairs, elegant, slim and silent. Her tail could almost go unnoticed as it slips up the stairs behind her. No doubt Sara is the only one who sees it. After a while, Liss gets up as well and heads towards the bathroom upstairs. Sara's nose immediately starts to grow and in the space of a few seconds has grown from being gigantic to taking on cyclopean proportions, and she can feel her heart beating violently and her sinuses are sending out crazy signals making her heart flip like a Romanian gymnast, her heart valves are fluttering uncontrollably, and a galloping heart attack is on its way. But before an internal disaster has had a chance to develop in her chest, Tamara returns, bends down over Sara and for a brief moment, Sara feels Tamara's dark hair like warm tar against her cheek:

'What's wrong?'

'Nothing, I...' Sara starts.

'You didn't think that I'd... Sara! You know you can trust me. I would never do anything like that to you,' Tamara says, looking at Sara with a serious face.

Sara's eyes meet Tamara's. The knowledge that they are both thinking about exactly the same thing in that split second, the time the sewing circle was at Eva's and Tamara had taken Sara with her to Eva's bathroom, like a shared secret that only they know, pacifies Sara. And they both start to laugh, quietly so that Eva will not ask what caused the sudden laughter, but loudly enough to give her plenty of opportunity to see the intimacy that only Tamara and Sara share, right now, right in front of Eva and Liss, who has just returned. That time, in the bathroom, Tamara had mocked Eva's bad taste and Sara had gone weak at the knees with laughter, she had sunk to the floor and said that it was at least a relief that the toilet roll lady and seat cover were not in place. Probably just getting washed, Tamara suggested, pulling open one of Eva's bathroom drawers. Tamara rolls her eyes and inspects Eve's selection of make up. Oh my God, she's only got cheap stuff from H&M, Cubus or postal order. Tamara laughs when she finds an exclusive powder compact from Versace among all the cheap tat. But of course, the colour is completely wrong – the powder is nearly piggy pink. Sara laughs as well. She takes some light-blue eye shadow and holds it up to her eyes. Hideous! Blue Sky. And look, even worse, this one's glittery. Frosted Clouds. Tamara has now opened Eva's double bathroom cupboard doors. Sara sees packets of sanitary towels, boxes of Paracetamol and Disprin. Cough mixture. A thermometer. Tamara, really! Tamara has kneeled down and is looking systematically through the things in the cupboard. Oh my God, look. Eva's got haemorrhoids! And what's this? Canestan. Aha, a bit of fungal infection here and there, I see. Sleeping problems as well. Imovane, sleeping pills. Hmm. Eva always seems to be so hale and hearty, you would think she had no trouble sleeping. But still waters run deep. What d'you reckon, Sara?

Tamara, smiling that same good, confidential, knowing smile that she always smiles when she and Sara share a secret, big and small secrets for more than three decades, is still looming above Sara, who is sitting at the dining table. Sara looks straight up into Tamara's big, dark eyes. In the same moment that Sara decides that of course Tamara would never do anything like that to her, to Sara, to her best friend and a feeling of relief, tinged with a trace of guilt that she could think that of Tamara, washes over her, Tamara whispers:

'What d'you reckon, Sara?'

Tamara's comment takes Sara completely by surprise, she stumbles, nearly falls, but manages to clutch on to it, hanging in mid-air kicking her legs aimlessly, holding on with only her finger tips. She is terrified of falling down into the unknown, dark abyss below. Did Tamara actually say something, or was it just an echo of Sara's thoughts? Could Tamara see inside her head, read her thoughts? She felt the strength draining from her hands and her grasp slipping from the smooth branch, but then she hears Eva's voice across the table:

'Can you see that I've lost weight?'

'Yes, yes you can,' Tamara answers.

'Oh yes,' Liss says as well.

There is a slight pause before Sara manages to say anything appropriate:

'Yes, you're incredibly slim now,' Sara says to humour her, though she can't see anything to indicate that Eva is slimmer. In fact, she looks even more inflated and well-fed in her pastel pink sweater than the last time Sara saw her.

'Yes, I've actually lost four kilos, 4.3 kilos to be precise.'

'4300 grams! Wow! That's exactly what Martin weighed when he was born,' Liss informs them with the same intense enthusiasm she shows every time she succeeds in getting a new acquaintance's star sign right in less than three guesses.

'Goodness. Julia didn't weigh that much,' Sara says. 'She was 3550.'

'Emma was, of course, premature,' Tamara says. 'But fortunately everything went well. Touch wood. She's just become editor of the school magazine, did I tell you? Emma started to talk very early, as you no doubt remember.'

'Yes, Martin did as well,' interrupts Liss. 'He was barely one when he said Mummy, Daddy and cake clearly.'

'Ahh,' Eva sighs.

'Emma said, "Mummy give me cake" on her first birthday and she spoke fluently by the time she was three,' Tamara tells them with pride.

'Martin also started walking incredibly early. He was only eleven months old when he first tottered round the living room,' Liss says.

'Ahh,' Eva says.

'Julia actually walked some steps before she was nine months old.'

'Both Martin and Mona understood everything so early. And I don't think that Maja is far behind, even though it's a bit early to say, perhaps.'

'Yes, how old is Maja now?' Sara asks.

'She'll be exactly thirteen months on Wednesday,' Liss replies.

'Hmm, Emma...' Tamara starts.

Eva interrupts in a loud voice:

'Well... I have a second cousin who has a cousin who had a baby called Jens. And Jens, he could do backwards somersaults when he was only four months old, and then when he was two, his family were in a restaurant, and Jens read the menu and ordered his food in fluent French. Garçon, je voudrais bien...'

'OK, Eva, point taken,' Tamara says. 'Sorry. We should take our childless friends into consideration. Sorry that we got carried away by our maternal love, but it's an incredibly strong emotion, you know.'

'It was thoughtless of us,' Liss says.

Tamara pauses for a bit, before continuing:

'Or that's exactly what you don't know. Sorry again.'

Sara folds her hands in her lap. She presses her palms together as hard as she can and counts to seven, seven times. When she reaches the lucky number 49, Sara tentatively explores her emotions and makes the diagnosis that she has been struck by a mixture of sympathy for Eva (it can't be easy to be childless among so many mothers), anxiety that Tamara may have been hurt by the fact that Eva actually interrupted her (you simply never interrupt Tamara, you let her finish what she is saying) and bad conscience (Sara has neglected her duties as a hostess, she should have stopped the conversation rather than joining in with gusto). It is both a stroke of good fortune and a source of relief for Sara that she is to be punished shortly. Why is she thinking about Kristian now? His kind eyes. It's such a shame they had to split up.

*

'Let's talk about something else, something that we can all talk about. Let's talk about our trip to Copenhagen! Not many months to go now. I'm really looking forward to it,' Tamara says.

'Me too,' says Eva. 'A real girls' weekend! And it's great that it's Copenhagen. Not too far to go. And quite cheap, which is good for you, Liss.'

'Yes,' Liss responds.

'And for you, Sara,' Eva continues. 'You can finally go to Louisiana – you've talked about doing that for so long now.'

'Yes, it will be very nice,' Sara says, who usually claims that the word nice, particularly when preceded by an intensifier, is a sure sign of the user's limited vocabulary. Sara immediately starts to formulate silent, possible excuses that she can use when the time comes. Excuses that cannot fail to prevent her from going. Sara does not know why, but the very thought of a weekend with Eva, Liss and Tamara makes her hyperventilate, her heart starts pounding and she breaks out in a cold sweat, and Sara knows that she simply cannot go. Tamara will find a way for me, Sara thinks, then she counts to seven and tries to breathe normally:

'Time for dessert now, girls!'

When the semifreddo was on the table, a cold, but not freezing (hence the name), porous, white mass containing tiny specks of real vanilla, flakes of dark-brown chocolate and large pieces of orange, the evening's hostess had to refrain, in the face of heartfelt encouragement from her friends. No, I can't, girls, Sara said. Sara was unfortunately too full to fit in even the smallest spoonful, she assured them, several times, and each time she said it, it felt less true. But the bitter, lonely satisfaction that her punishment really hurt, took the edge off her greedy desire for the dessert and allowed Sara to lift her head, despite feeling miserable. Tamara narrowed her beautiful, slanted eyes that shone nearly yellow in the light from the lamp:

'You really have got an impressive profile, Sara,' Tamara said. 'You always have had.'

'Amazingly good dessert,' Eva said. 'I'm really looking forward to our anniversary trip.'

'You certainly have a healthy appetite,' Tamara said to Eva.

Chapter 5

SEWING CIRCLE AT EVA'S, TUESDAY 14 NOVEMBER

Menu
Pastry shell with prawns
Roast beef with potatoes dauphinois, broccoli and baby carrots
Chocolate pudding

They're so alike. Like sisters. As dark and beautiful as each other. Eva is sitting comfortably in the sofa, holding the enlarged class photo in her hands, close up to her eyes. She puts the photo down on the coffee table, then goes and gets a blue photo album. She turns to one of the last pages and finds a picture of herself at about the same age. She places it on top of the class photo, so that it covers the darkest of the two girls. Yes, there is definitely something about the eyes and maybe something about the broad, open forehead, isn't there? Eva finds her handbag and takes out a faded colour photo of two children. A dark-haired boy and a dark-haired girl. She studies the two children for a long time before putting the photo back in her bag with great care. Then suddenly she snaps the photo album shut and throws it down on the sofa. She puts her index finger in her mouth to wet it and then rubs her finger over the class photo, trying to erase the fair head in the row behind the two dark girls. She wets her finger again and rubs until the paper loosens in small, pointed pellets under her warm fingertip. Eva's movements are not violent or harsh. Quite the opposite, they are gentle and careful. There is no anger, or even irritation, underlying Eva's action. Only the wish to get rid of what is uninteresting, what is distracting. The two dark-haired girls look up at Eva. Oblivious to what she has just done. Their expressions remain unchanged, their smiles are the same. Just as beautiful, just as untouched, they look straight at Eva. Eva looks at them for a long time. The fact that there is a white patch in the row behind them doesn't seem to bother them in the slightest. Or do they actually look vaguely relieved? Slightly jubilant?

77

Eva settles down in the sofa. The food can wait. She's made it simple today. Or rather, it turned out simple today. She had more or less run home from school to start making the dessert, which she thought would impress the girls. A zabaglione she was going to serve with home-made orange biscuits. She had even managed to get hold of a bottle of Marsala wine. The dessert looked so elegant in the picture, light, cream-coloured zabaglione in small glasses with long, golden biscuits. But the zabaglione had separated and the orange biscuits (super easy – you can't go wrong, it said across the top of the recipe in the magazine) were burnt underneath and soft on top (she later discovered she had only turned on the bottom element in the oven). And now it was too late. No complicated dishes today. A bowl of mayonnaise (Denja low fat) with diced fish pudding and shelled prawns stands waiting in the fridge and the pastry cases are on the worktop in a box with a cellophane window. She'll fill them with the mayonnaise mixture just before her guests arrive, so that the pastry doesn't go soft. The roast is in the oven and she'll put the potatoes dauphinois (two packets mixed with cream and margarine) in later. She can just warm the frozen vegetables up in a little water with butter. And she needs to put the chocolate pudding (from Tine Dairies) on a plate. Thank goodness I had that! They'll just have to take me as I am, Eva thinks. They saw what I can do the last time they were here, the sweet pepper mousse will have to do for a while. I'm different from Tamara and Sara. I'm wasn't born with a silver spoon in my mouth, willowy and graceful. But I still belong, even if I sometimes wear a cream bra with white knickers or forget to put on earrings.

Eva picks up the album, but doesn't open it again, just sits with it in her lap. Then after a while, she starts to look through it. Black-and-white pictures of her as a baby. Every so often there are faded colour photos with a white border. All the pictures are of her on her own, or her and her mother. Never anyone else. Her darker blonde head against her mother's strawberry perm, her small fingers in her mother's hand. Her mother with both her hands on a low-slung pram, smiling at the camera. Who took the pictures? Eva in a high chair with bits of porridge on her chubby chin. Her and her mother in front of a small, brick house, a garden with a high hedge round it. It doesn't look Norwegian, it looks foreign. A childhood in another country. A childhood in another place, without the two of them. Without her.

Her pictures of Tamara and Sara are almost as clear as those in the photo album and Eva has looked at them many, many times before. To begin with, none of the pictures had faces. Then, when Eva was around ten, they got a face – the most important one. But it was really only a couple of years ago that the pictures were finally complete. And now they pop up in Eva's head one after the other. Slowly to begin with, then faster and faster, until the pictures just flood in, so that Eva barely has a chance to look at one before the next one is there. One continuous, slightly jumpy sequence. Just like the cartoons Eva and her mother made when Eva was little. Mummy holds a pile of thin cards with drawings on in one hand and with the other, she bends the pages back and then lets go. The pictures fly up to meet Eva. Tamara and Sara picking flowers in a meadow. Tamara and Sara in an inflatable paddling pool, naked and glistening with water, pot bellies and folds on their thighs. Tamara and her little brother in yellow t-shirts, Tamara with her arm round her brother's shoulders. Tamara and her brother in front of the Christmas tree. Tamara and Sara in front of a snowman. On skis. On a sledge. On a beach in bikinis. Tamara and Sara with new bikes. With an ice cream each. When they finished school. Close together, smiling, whispering. And in later pictures, only Tamara.

Eva is in the garden. It's summer. She's on her own. Mummy is in the kitchen. The window is open and Eva can hear her turning on the tap, humming as she does the washing up and tidies away the breakfast. The smell of fried egg and bacon lingers in the air outside the kitchen window. Eva hears voices and laughter from the next-door garden and suddenly Eva sees Lotte up in the air. Lotte flying high up in the air. Lotte is floating above the hedge. Lotte is the same age as Eva. They will be starting school together in the autumn. Lotte has a little sister and a big sister. Lotte has a father. Lotte has a red beach ball, but so does Eva, only hers is blue.

And Lotte has a yellow sundress and now the yellow sundress is up in the blue sky. Lotte laughs. Eva moves closer, she creeps into the hedge until eventually she is crouching right up by the picket fence and she can now see that it's Lotte's father who is lifting Lotte high above his head, with his arms stretched up. I'm flying, Lotte shouts. Yes, you are, Lotte's father says. Eva watches.

Eva squats in the hedge and imagines what is must be like to be Lotte. In Daddy's outstretched arms, high up in the blue sky. Daddy's arms carrying her through the air like she's flying. Like a bird. Other birds – all of them white – flutter around her head and twitter and sing. Eva is also singing. And she is eating the soft air, swallowing great mouthfuls. She uses her arms as wings, up and down through the warm, soft, light blue air. She flies between small, white clouds, light and fluffy as candyfloss. And Daddy's hands around her waist are firm and strong. Daddy looks after Eva.

*

Eva lies in bed. Mummy has just sung two lullabies for her and kissed her goodnight. It's night outside. Lotte's father, or maybe it's Eva's own father, carries her high on strong arms, high in the air. Eva is a fish. Her back is arched and her legs are pointing upwards, like a tail fin. She is swimming with her arms. As she swims, shining pointy stars fall away from her like phosphorescence. She swims through the soft, dark, warm night air. And under her, she feels Daddy's strong arms. She feels his hands around her waist, holding her tight, and she cannot fall. Daddy is holding her. Daddy is strong.

At the end of August, just after school has started, Lotte turns seven. And Eva is invited to a birthday party with all the other girls in Eva and Lotte's new class. They get sausages and cream cake. And yellow juice in small glasses. After they have watched the film, Father of Four, first forwards and then backwards, the girls go out to play in the garden. They throw balls and play bowls. Lotte's mother pins up a big piece of white paper with a donkey on it. The

80

girls are blindfolded, spun round in the sunshine, and then have to try to pin the tail on the donkey. Eva manages the best. You're clever, aren't you, say Lotte's mother and father. Eva smiles at Lotte's father, and feels proud and happy.

Now you can play a bit with the dolls, while we drink our coffee, Lotte's mother says. But Eva goes over to Lotte's father: 'I really want to fly.' Lotte's father smiles and lifts Eva up high, just like she wants him to. Just as she's imagined. His hands squeeze her waist. It hurts a little. Eva is flying high. Just as she has always dreamed. But there are no shining stars to swim in. Because it's not night. And there are no white birds singing around Eva's head either and the air is not as soft as she'd imagined. Lotte's father has stretched arms and stretched hands. His hands are firmly clasped round Eva's tummy, which is full of birthday food. And everything is so different from her dream when suddenly small bits of red sausage and sour cake in yellow juice spew out of her mouth on to Lotte's father's hair, on to his glasses, his white shirt.

Eva grew up alone with her mother, in a suburb of Copenhagen. Rows of small red-brick houses in well-kept gardens with flowerbeds and high hedges. Eva and her mother lived in a house like that. A friendly corner shop that always smelt of freshly-ground coffee. A duck pond and a big poplar tree, a warm bakery. Housewives on bicycles and fathers with hats and briefcases. Her sleeping doll, Sofie, with curly hair and painted-on shoes. Breakfast in the sun.

Eva's mother inherited the red-brick house from her younger sister, who was married to a Dane, when she and her husband were killed in a tragic car accident on Fyn, about a year before Eva was born. But why did you want to move away from Norway? Eva asked her mother, who just shook her head and smiled. When Eva was little, she didn't know what her father was called, who he was or where he lived. It was only when Eva grew up that she found out his name. The only thing that Eva knew, as a little girl, was that her mother sometimes received letters with Norwegian stamps on that were not from Granny or Auntie Bea, her mother's older sister, and that these letters in light yellow, long envelopes disappeared as soon as Mummy had read them. The first time that Eva asked about her father, her mother didn't answer. When Eva then repeated the question some weeks later, her mother closed her eyes so that all Eva could see was her soft eyelids and her long, fair lashes, and she still said nothing, just smiled a slow smile.

The girls in Eva's class at school teased her when they discovered that she didn't have a father, but soon stopped. It was no fun teasing Eva and besides, she told the other children that she did in fact have a father, only he lived in Norway. He was rich and quite famous and soon he would come and take them home to Norway. Because Eva was Norwegian, you see, even though she had been born in the main hospital in Copenhagen, and one day, in the not so distant future, she would move home again. Once when her mother was in an unusually good mood, she said to Eva, my happiest memories are from this house and I want to live here until I die. But when Eva climbed up onto her mother's lap and wanted to know more, wanted to know about her father, her mother just rocked her and started to sing quietly into Eva's hair. Eva was sure that her mother was sitting with her eyes closed and a small smile on her lips. Her mother's warm breath on her scalp was the sweetest caress and Eva knew that she and her mother belonged together and that they loved each other very much. Eva never asked her mother about her father again.

Eva was a lonely child, but it was perhaps through choice. She was happiest on her own, preferably close to other people, but on the edge of a group, the outskirts of a game. She generally watched what the others were doing and listened to what they said. Eva was an unusually attentive listener and a quick and keen observer. And she did take part in the game when she wanted to, so no one could say she didn't.

Eva had wanted to be part of the sewing circle ever since she heard about it. And she had wanted it long before she knew it existed. All her life she had dreamed about it. She had wanted to get to know Tamara and Sara. Liss had been a great help. And Eva had succeeded. As she always does. Sooner or later. It often takes time. It might take months, it might take years, but sooner or later, Eva always succeeds in what she sets out to do.

Eva has beautiful, dark eyes and dyed blonde hair. She has long, slim fingers with short, unmanicured nails. She knows that Tamara and Sara probably laugh at her, at her taste, her clothes, her extra kilos. Eva has never really bothered much about clothes or her appearance. But in the last few years she has bought a few designer garments. And she has discovered that she likes dressing up, but she really only does it to get closer to her sewing circle friends. First and foremost Tamara and Sara, but Liss as well. Liss is also part of the sewing circle. Liss also has nice clothes. It's just they get dirty so quickly, the buttons fall off. Her skirts get creased and her trousers don't fit as well around the hips as Tamara's and Sara's. Liss is different, but she is still part of the group. Eva wonders why.

Eva has never heard them laughing about her, but she has seen it in their eyes. Even Liss has laughed at Eva. Kind, sweet Liss. But Tamara and Sara like Eva. And that is what she wanted. She was nearly there now.

The roast is done and resting under a checked dishtowel. The potatoes are in the oven and the vegetables are heating on the cooker. The mayonnaise mix has been spooned into the pastry cases. Now she has to get the pudding ready. Eva takes the litre carton of chocolate pudding out of the fridge, cuts open the carton and turns the pudding onto a plate, where is lies like a quivering, brown brick. Ugh, that doesn't look very impressive. Shame about the zabaglione and the orange biscuits. This won't do much for me, Eva thinks, and regrets that she hasn't prepared something a bit more fancy. She would have had time, but it's definitely too late now. It's already half past six. They'll just have to take me as I am, but I'm not quite as bad as that brown quivering lump there.

Eva stretches up and takes down a small, round glass mould from the kitchen cupboard. She pushes the brick of Tine Dairy chocolate pudding into the mould, but there's only enough room for about half of it, and the rest lies in brown furrows over the worktop. She ploughs the remains into the rubbish bin on top of the burnt biscuits and then wipes the worktop with a yellow-stained dishcloth. There now, that doesn't look so bad! The pudding looks nearly home-made, but still has some tell-tale ridges and cracks on top. Eva carves off the top layer and then wipes over the chocolate pudding with the dishcloth. Then she stands there looking at the chocolate pudding. Shit! What has she done! Sometimes you just have to do things like that, she tries to reassure herself. A well-presented, nicely decorated meal is more palatable for everyone and could tempt even the most spoilt bon viveur. When you're tired and full, a big plate of rustic food is the last thing you want. Even though it tastes just as good, well, maybe even better, she philosophises to herself. The world wants to be deceived. And this is now home-made chocolate pudding. A complicated recipe with lots of eggs, cooked in a bain marie and... How on earth do you actually make chocolate pudding? She'll have to find out before her guests arrive. I'm almost there, Eva thinks and puts the cloth with chocolate pudding on it at the bottom of the laundry basket, before going up to the bedroom to put on her make up and her new top that was ridiculously expensive. White Diamonds on her wrists. Mascara on her lashes. The world wants to be deceived. Well-dressed comfort food.

Eva has to wait until the time is right. But I'm almost there. Eva smiles at her reflection. She knows exactly how she wants it to be. She has to choose the place carefully. A nice restaurant. Good food, happy people. In front of the mirror, Eva plans what she will say. She chooses her words, constructs sentences, tries out phrases. My home town. A man and a woman. The relationship had consequences. Absolutely adored. Two lithe girls. Longing.

The girls have arrived. They are talking and eating. Drinking wine and laughing loudly. They praise Eva's food, but it is obvious to her that at least Tamara and Sara don't mean what they say. They tilt their beautiful, dark heads and say that the food is excellent. Delicious, tender carrots and beautifully done, both the roast and the potatoes (Eva thought that the potatoes dauphinois tasted a bit burnt, but she's not sure). And now the glass mould with chocolate pudding is on the table. The dessert bowls have been passed around, but Tamara and Sara have requested a smoking break before dessert.

'Ooh, look at that lovely chocolate pudding,' Liss says. 'Did you make it yourself?'

'Mmmm,' Eva answers somewhat vaguely.

'I've never tried to make my own chocolate pudding,' Liss says.

Nor have I, Eva thinks to herself.

Sara stretches out her hand to get her packet of cigarettes and suddenly winces in her chair and lets out something akin to a small, quiet gasp of pain.

'What's wrong, Sara?' asks Liss.

Sara smiles at Tamara, who has lit her cigarette for her, inhales and then blows out the smoke before answering Liss:

'Oh, I just turned a bit too fast. It's my pelvis, you know. It still bothers me, I had pelvic dysfunction when I was pregnant,' Sara adds in explanation and looks over at Eva, as if she assumes that Eva doesn't know this detail from a time long before she joined the sewing circle.

'But it's a long time since Julia was born,' Eva says, in a questioning tone, careful to balance the sympathy in her voice. A feeling of genuine sympathy is mixed with relief that the subject of the chocolate pudding has been dropped, plus she is eager to learn more about Tamara and Sara. Sara too.

'Yes, I know, and generally it doesn't bother me much any more. Only very occasionally,' Sara replies. 'But sometimes it aches a little. Today, for example, I was sitting at my computer working for several hours and...'

'What are you working on at the moment?' Tamara asks.

'A novel.'

'By?'

'I can't even remember the name. She's young and unknown. North Germany, apparently.'

'Is it good?'

'No, not particularly. I have no idea why they have chosen to translate it. The heroine, who is blonde and beautiful, meets her dream prince, who is dark and handsome, in the first chapter and then...'

'Say no more,' says Tamara.

'I think it sounds good,' Liss says.

'Yes, you would,' Tamara says.

'And then afterwards I had to hoover the flat, as my mother-in-law is coming to visit tomorrow,' Sara continues. 'And hoovering is the worst thing I can do for my pelvis, apart from skiing.'

'Couldn't Jakob do the hoovering?'

'Yes, he normally does. And the skiing too. But there was something he had to do today. An important lunch meeting. To tell the truth, he has been behaving very oddly recently.'

'What do you mean by oddly?' Liss asks.

'You should have seen Sara when she was pregnant,' Tamara tells Eva. 'For a start, she looked like a medium-sized hippopotamus, with an enormous belly and water retention in her legs. Didn't you put on 19 kilos? And she was in a lot of pain, poor thing. She could barely move.'

'She had to lie down for the whole of the last month,' Liss adds.

'And that is when I really discovered what good and loyal friends I have,' Sara says.

'Well, it was mainly Tamara,' Liss says.

'Yes,' Sara agrees. 'Tamara was fantastic. She looked after me all the time. But you did a lot too, Liss.'

'Well,' Liss says.

'Tamara came to see me every day towards the end. She was pregnant herself, but she still came to see me every day after work and made dinner and tidied the house and talked to me. Do you remember we kept a pregnancy diary, Tamara? With a record of when the babies kicked and when they were asleep. Lists of possible names and weight charts.'

'Mmmm,' Tamara answers.

Tamara strokes Sara lightly on the neck. Plays with some of her black hair. Sara closes her eyes and smiles. Eva watches. She sits on one of her own dining chairs and imagines what it must be like to be Sara. What it is like to be stroked on the neck by feather light fingertips, what it is like to have such a close friend, someone you can tell everything, someone who looks after you and whom you look after, someone you have grown up with. Almost like a sister. It must be like swimming in stars and eating sweet honey clouds every day.

'But what about Jakob? Could he not help?' Eva asks.

'Jakob did a lot too, but he had just started a new job and had to travel a lot at the time. I do not know how I would have managed if Tamara had not been there. And Liss too. You were fantastic.'

'In the same way that you have always been there for me, Sara,' Tamara says. 'You were an amazing support to me when I got divorced. My divorce is one of the hardest things I've been through. And without Sara I think I would have broken down completely. In fact, I'm sure of it.'

'Ouch,' Eva responds. 'Was it that bad? Was that Emma's father then?'

'Yes,' Tamara replies. 'Yes, that was Håvard, Emma's father.'

'Tell me about it,' Eva encourages.

'No,' Tamara says.

After Tamara's rejection, Eva is not sure how much more she dare ask today. But once they have finished the chocolate pudding, she ventures all the same:

'Tamara and Sara, you're so alike. I don't think I've really noticed it before, but now that you both have your hair away from your face, I can see it.'

'Yes,' Liss says. 'It's true.'

'Were you very alike when you were small as well?' Eva

continues. 'Coffee anyone?'

'Yes please. Yes, no, I don't know,' Tamara says. 'Quite similar, perhaps.'

'Don't you think our eyes are quite similar as well, Tamara?' Eva asks.

'Mine and yours?' Tamara replies. 'No, I don't think they are.'

'Liss, what do you think?' Eva says and turns to face Liss.

'Umm, well, I guess you've both got brown eyes, but I'm not sure,' Liss hesitates.

'I wish we'd all been at school together, all four of us,' Eva says and looks at the other three. 'Was it fun? I bet you were popular, Liss.'

'I'd love some coffee if you're making it. Popular? Oh, I don't know,' Liss says. Her round face turns questioningly to Tamara and Sara.

Eva wants to know everything about the sewing circle, everything about Tamara and Sara. And Liss. Maybe Liss shouldn't be rubbed out after all, maybe that's exactly what Tamara and Sara want Eva to do. Liss is different. Liss is eclipsed so easily by the other two. She disappears, even though she's there. It's almost as if Tamara and Sara want her to disappear at the same time that they're frightened of her.

Eva goes to her very first sewing circle evening. At Liss'. Eva takes flowers with her. She is happy. She has managed to achieve her first goal. But she's also nervous. There's still a long way to go before she is where she wants to be. Liss has just discovered that she's pregnant with what will become Maja in nine months time. She's a bit nauseous and unwell, but Liss suits being pregnant. Blonde and rosy-cheeked, she sits on the sofa. She is already blooming. Swelling in an attractive way. She reminds me of freshly baked bread and red-checked kitchen curtains, Eva thinks. Liss is glowing. The day before, Liss gave a short talk at the local library. It was an Alternative Evening. The smell of incense hung heavy in the air. It was full of women in batik tunics and leggings. Hair put up with silver clasps. Big earrings. There were several talks in the programme. New Age. Healing. Tarot readings. Liss had been asked to talk about astrology. Tamara and Sara had come. And Eva too. She had met all three of them several times now and tomorrow would be her first sewing circle evening at Liss'.

Liss gave her talk. She was good and got a lot of praise from the organisers afterwards. Now she is sitting in her own sofa, in her own terraced house, which she and Paul will soon have paid off. She has served the girls a three-course meal, the new member has made her debut, she is pregnant with her third child and proud of what she did yesterday.

'Well, girls, did you learn anything from my talk yesterday?' she asks with great expectation in her high, happy voice.

'Absolutely,' Eva says. 'I know so little about astrology. Very interesting.'

'Yes, if you believe in all that rubbish,' Sara retorts. 'Sorry, I'm only teasing. It was exceptionally interesting and instructive.'

'Yes, you were very good,' Tamara says. 'I thought I'd just say one thing though. Since you're asking. Sara and I talked about it afterwards on the way home. Just so you're aware of it next time you give a talk...'

'Oh, of course,' Liss says, still smiling, still blushing.

'I'm sure you're already aware that you say 'like' a lot, but you might want to think about it next time. It just doesn't sound professional when there are too many 'likes'.'

'OK,' Liss says. 'I'll remember that. Anything else?'

'Well,' Sara starts. 'You kept wrapping your hair round your fingers.'

'Yes, and you danced around on your feet too much, it made it look like you needed the toilet. But we're not saying this to criticise, it's so you can do it better next time.'

'Yes,' Liss says. 'Thank you.'

'And don't forget to use a good deodorant. Sweat marks under your arms don't look good, do they?'

Both of them laugh so that everyone realises that they only mean well. Just some friendly advice. Liss seems somehow to look flatter and greyer. More like the other times when Eva has met her.

'But you were really very good,' Tamara says.

'Yes, you were excellent,' Sara says.

'Thank you,' Liss says and pauses. Eva feels sorry for her, but she says nothing, because it is Tamara and Sara that are important to Eva. The fear of offending them is greater than her wish to help Liss. And Eva is new and careful not to irritate anyone, to do anything wrong.

'I really wasn't looking forward to it,' Liss continues. 'So it's not that surprising that you could tell I was nervous, that I was sweating and things like that. I read in one of those relaxation technique books (Get to Know Yourself, 199 ways to relax), that I should think of the audience as a friendly forest of flowers. And I tried to, but it didn't help me relax, as I know there's not only flowers in the forest.'

Liss laughs. With some uncertainty. But Eva sees that Tamara and Sara immediately change. They tense in their chairs. The look in their eyes changes. They look almost frightened. Eva sees it, but she doesn't understand. And since then she has seen the same thing happen several times. Liss says something. Apparently harmless. Apparently as cheerful and inane as normal. Eva has no idea what it is that Liss says that frightens Tamara and Sara, but they suddenly change.

It's obvious that Liss bores Tamara and Sara and that they try to see through her, pretend that she's invisible, but they can't quite do it, they don't quite dare to. Liss has a power over them, but Eva can't quite work out what kind of power and why.

Eva can overlook Liss too, she is so insipid compared with the other two, who shine with such glory. Eva knows very well that Liss is sweet and funny, full of titillating stories and care. But Tamara and Sara can't see that. They don't want to see that. Or maybe they don't see it, because they have only seen Liss the way they want to, for too long. Eva wants to know more, she wants to be part of everything. Right from the start. She wants to be like the others. Because she is one of them.

'Were you friends, all three of you, right from the first day at school?' Eva wonders.

'My mother and Tamara's mother were best friends, so Tamara and I have known each other since before we were born,' Sara replies. 'The coffee is really good, by the way.'

'And what about Liss?'

'We got to know Liss when we started school and we knew straight away that she would be fun, that it would be worth getting to know her,' Tamara answers. Eva can tell that Tamara has given this explanation before. Many times. And then, without further ado, Tamara continues: 'Do you use cooking chocolate or cocoa powder when you make chocolate pudding?'

'Cocoa,' Eva answers quickly. 'And your parents, did they all know each other then? Were they friends?'

'Yes,' Tamara says. 'Friends. Did you cook it in a bain marie? That's what I usually do. That is, when I make crème caramel and crème brulée.'

Eva doesn't answer, just closes her eyes and smiles slowly. And when she opens them again, she sees that they're uneasy. All three of them. They don't like her questions. Eva sees them squirming on their chairs. And that is not what she wants. She doesn't want to frighten them. She doesn't want to scare Tamara. She wants to be one of them. That's all she wants. She wants to put her head between their two dark heads. Feel her hair tangling with theirs. She wants to know their secrets, confidences, fingers playing with the hair on her neck. She wants intimacy and friendship over steaming cups of tea. She wants to be in the pictures she was looking at earlier today. Tamara, Sara and Eva picking flowers in a meadow. Tamara, Sara and Eva in an inflatable paddling pool, naked, glistening wet, with pot bellies and chubby thighs. In front of a snowman. On skis. On a sledge. With new bikes. Each with an ice cream. When they finished school. Close together, smiling, whispering.

They don't know who I am, Eva thinks. They have no idea who I am. Eva doesn't want to frighten them. She doesn't want to frighten Tamara. She just wants her to understand.

*

Eva always carries a picture in her bag. It's a faded colour photo of two children. The older child has its arm round the younger child's shoulders.

The letters that came in the pale yellow envelopes with Norwegian stamps on disappeared immediately once her mother had read them. And it was almost as if her mother knew beforehand when the letters would come, because on those days she would always stand on the step waiting while Eva got the post, then she would go into the bedroom, close the door and read them and the letter would simply disappear. But one day, when Eva was taking a book down from the bookshelf in the sitting room, one of the pale yellow envelopes fell out of the book. Eva recognised the envelope straight away and she stuffed it under her sweater and went into her room. Here she opened it. There wasn't a letter in the envelope, just a photograph. Eva had found one of the pictures she had seen in her mind so many times before. She had found the first one. One of the pictures without faces. But now there is one. One of the faces is suddenly in place.

One of the pictures was in Eva's hand. A photograph of a girl and a boy. T and P summer -76 was scrawled across the back. The girl was Eva's age, the boy a bit younger. The girl had dark hair and big, dark eyes. She had her arm round the boy's shoulders. The boy was looking at the girl, but the girl was looking straight at Eva.

Chapter 6

SEWING CIRCLE AT TAMARA'S, TUESDAY 5 DECEMBER

Menu
Russian caviar with blinis
Terrine of Icelandic scallops with feta and dill
Monkfish with orange and ginger sauce, served with root vegetables à la julienne and bulgur wheat pilau
Rooibos tea ice cream

When Tamara was little, she was different from other children. Not outwardly, as she looked more or less like the others. More beautiful, perhaps. Sara and Tamara were more beautiful than the other girls. They were both quite small and thin and darker than the rest of the girls in their class. But inside, Tamara was different from everyone else, even Sara. And Tamara knew that. As early as six, she understood things that most girls don't understand until they are considerably older – and some never understand at all. Tamara knew that if anyone on the street at home teased her – not that there were many who dared – she should just smile at them and walk away. Tamara linked arms with Sara and walked away. Then, when Tamara was older, she knew perfectly well that if Karin said that Lill Inger had a horrible dress, it was basically because Karin's mother stayed at home all day drinking port. Tamara has always found it easy to discover other people's weaknesses. She could tell from the way the teacher tilted her head that she hated her double chin. She knew that Peter in the parallel class was in love with Randi, long before Peter realised himself. And by the time that she started in upper secondary, she could without any effort predict the plot of any film (particularly American ones) after watching the first five minutes. Tamara has always known how to get people where she wants them. But not Sara. Tamara likes Sara too much and Sara has such big, helpless eyes.

Yesterday, Tamara was Sara again. She lay on the crisp, clean sheets that Sara had told her were bought in Germany, with Sara's husband between her legs. Tamara is Sara. I was Sara, Tamara thinks to herself. I spread my dark hair over her pillows and it became hers. When Jakob bit my nipples, kneaded my breasts, licked the thin skin between them, they were no longer mine; it was Sara's small, pert breasts that hardened under Jakob's touch, Jakob's mouth and tongue. And when Sara's husband clumsily entered Tamara, it was no longer Tamara's vagina, it was Sara's. And when Tamara arched her neck and pushed her nose into the air in a display of pleasure, it was no longer Tamara's nose, but Sara's big, beautiful, hooked nose she lifted up to the ceiling. Sara is like an angel. White and without shame.

Tamara rang Sara again this morning. Tamara could feel her fear down the telephone line. Tamara could imagine the blood vessels on Sara's temples swelling, she could see them pulsing. Then she put the phone down.

A few days ago, Sara said to Tamara: 'Someone keeps phoning me, then hanging up.'

'Oh, sweetheart,' Tamara said and stroked her arm. Tamara could see that she was scared. She suggested that Sara should buy a phone where she could see the number of the incoming call.

'That's a good idea,' Sara said.

Tamara thought it was a good idea too. Tamara's telephone number is ex-directory.

Then Sara said: 'Tamara, I think Jakob is being unfaithful. He has been behaving so strangely recently.'

'Oh, sweetheart,' Tamara said again.

She put her hand on Sara's. Tamara felt very sorry for Sara. Tamara could never bear anyone upsetting Sara. Tamara looked her straight in the eye and realised how much she loved Sara. Then she felt real anger towards whoever it was who was upsetting Sara and she had to look away. Their hands were on the

94

table. Tamara's broad and strong, but beautifully slim right hand holding Sara's narrow hand, with her long elegant fingers helplessly splayed. Tamara has two rings on her right hand. One on her ring finger and one on her middle finger. The gold ring that Thomas gave her to celebrate the five years they have lived together and the smooth, wide ring in white gold that Jakob gave her a few months ago. Ever since she's worn these two rings side by side, Tamara has had great pleasure in moving her fingers so that the ring from Thomas rubs against the ring from Jakob. She does it quite often. In fact, it's become something of a habit. And when Tamara stroked Sara's narrow hand, Tamara's two rings touched Sara's wedding ring. She absentmindedly wondered whether the ring was inscribed with 'your Jakob', but then she realised that she should remember what is inscribed in Sara's wedding ring, as it was she who held the ring up in its little box so that Jakob could put it on Sara's finger. The little box with red velvet padding. The two gold rings. Sara's small one and Jakob's big one. That day in the church many years ago. Tamara had cried. And so had Sara. Tamara was, of course, Sara's chief bridesmaid when she and Jakob got married, just as Sara was, of course, Tamara's chief bridesmaid when Håvard and Tamara got married. Sara and Tamara are best friends.

'I don't know what I'll do if Jakob is having an affair,' Sara said. Tamara started to move her hand, she carefully stroked Sara's hand and tried to comfort her as best she could. Sara needs Tamara. Sara, who has always had such delicate hands and such big, fearful brown eyes. Tamara has a sudden urge to phone Jakob at work. 'I just need to call Thomas,' she explains to Sara. Sara nods and Tamara rings Jakob. He's surprised, as Tamara never usually calls him at work. Surprised, but happy. 'I'm just calling to say that I miss you,' Tamara says to Sara's husband, with her eyes still locked into Sara's. 'And to remind you about the meeting tomorrow.' 'I can hardly wait,' says Jakob in Tamara's ear. And with Sara's husband's voice in her ear and Sara's eyes looking straight at her, Tamara suddenly feels bizarrely happy.

Later that day, Tamara wrote something in the book with the black velvet cover. She sat down at the kitchen table with a cup of strong, black coffee and wrote. In red joined up letters, Tamara wrote that she was considerate. I am being considerate, she wrote. I never sleep with Jakob and Thomas on the same day. I never go straight from Sara's bed to my own. Thomas' and Jakob's sperm have never mixed in my vagina. When Jakob and I have been together, I never go straight home to Thomas. I have to wander around a bit, buy some clothes, do a stint at work, go jogging. But as soon as Jakob and I have parted, I need to talk to Sara, to hear her voice at least. I usually phone her. Sometimes I talk to her, ask how she is, what she's up to, if she's well. Sometimes I just listen to her voice and then hang up. Once when I phoned, Julia answered, so I spoke to her for a while, about her schoolwork and jazz ballet and all the time I felt the remains of Jakob seeping out of me, millions of Julia's half-siblings.

Sometimes Tamara wants to tell Sara everything, no, not to tell her, but to let her find out for herself. But the dark hairs on the pillow look like her own. Tamara's scent is Sara's scent. Tamara could of course do something as banal as to forget her bra under Sara's duvet, Tamara could bite Jakob's shoulder or neck hard, scratch his buttocks. Or scratch a blood-red T on his back. But she never does. Tamara loves Sara and Tamara gets angry if anyone tries to upset Sara. But Sara can be very determined.

When they were little, Sara and Tamara were always together. Tamara's earliest memories are of being together with Sara. Obviously, Tamara has a lot of memories of her mother, father and Philip too, but Sara is always there.

Our memory is like a well-read book. Sometimes it is like the thick, light brown striped book that Tamara found in the bookshelf at home. It was late summer, the year that she turned eleven in the spring. The thick book was standing in the wrong place between books by authors whose surname began with S.

Some pages open automatically. The book spine is worn thin, the pages have been opened so often. The book falls open at those very pages every time you rest it in your lap. What was it like when you were little? asks a young niece, a daughter, the son of a friend. And immediately the book opens at the pages from your childhood that you have looked at so many times before. This is what it was like when I was little, you say, and start to tell them. The same, fixed things. And you smile a bit. But there is always something that you don't tell. Something you see in your mind's eye, something that doesn't make you smile. You see the pages, the book opens at those pages as well, but you never tell anyone what's written there.

Or maybe it's not your niece or daughter who asks. Perhaps you see a photograph from that time. Hear a song. Or catch the smell of tyres on warm, summer-soft asphalt. And then they flood back. Memories. The same memories. Fruity ice lollies. The plastic tablecoth in the kitchen. Randi with her hair in bunches, who sat in front of you at school. The choir uniform. The pattern on milk cartons. Daddy's ears. His hair that fell in a wave. The nappies with plastic tape that your little brother used. And you yourself. You see yourself on a warm summer day. You've got your short blue dress and sandals on. You're on the way to the kiosk to buy some popsicles. Or you've got your woolly hat and mittens on, the ones your aunty gave you for Christmas. The red ones with a yellow and black border, you know. It's cold. The snow makes cornflour noises under your winter boots. You're on your way to the ice rink, you can feel the weight of your skates over your shoulder and they thump against your back with every step you take. You've got red cheeks and frozen eyelashes. You can see it clearly. But hang on! How's that possible? How can you see that your own cheeks are red like roses and your own eyelashes are covered in snowflakes? And your mother. You remember your Mummy when she was little, don't you? You have just as real and vivid pictures of her as little girl as you do of yourself. Just close your eyes and try. You see her with her fish-skin boots and a handful of ration cards. Swedish soup tins, paper clips on her lapel and a red knitted hat. Red? Yes, you know it was red, but the picture in your head is grey. Black and white. Like the first photograph ever taken of your mother when she was a little girl. Not wearing a red knitted hat. That must have come later. But otherwise, just like that picture. The picture that hangs out in the hall, or maybe stands on the piano.

*

But there are some pages you don't want to look at. Our memory is a bit like the book of fairytales you had when you were small. You know very well that certain pages are there, but you skip quickly past them. Like the page with the terrifying three-headed troll. The troll that will leap out of the book and eat you if it sees you. You were frightened even to touch the book at first, but gradually you became bolder. Eventually you could even look through it, taking great care to pass that particular page without looking at it.

Our memory is a book. But we don't know the full contents of our book of memories. Thick as a bible, a massive book with thin, thin pages, gold leaf and thick leather covers. A book with an elusive, mysterious content. There are pages in the book that we don't even know exist. They have never been opened, never been read since they were written. Perhaps whatever happened, whatever is written on these pages, happened a long, long time ago. Or maybe it was yesterday. Maybe terrible things are written there. Or maybe only harmless things. Things that mean nothing and therefore have never been looked at again. But they are there. All the pages are there and are a part of our lives.

We remember the same things. Over and over again. And the more often we think of them, the more easily the book opens of its own accord at the same place next time. But the pages you never open, never ever, are still there. Even though you perhaps aren't aware that they're there any more.

Tamara was going back to Sara's after school. Then the last three classes were cancelled because the teacher was sick. Sara unlocked the door and went in first. The flat was silent. 'Hallo?' Sara called out, all the same. Sara and Tamara went into the kitchen and then they heard something from the bedroom. A kind of thumping. Sara looks at Tamara. Tamara moves closer and the two girls open the door. The first thing that hits Tamara is the smell. A smell she has never smelt before. Sweat, warm bodies and something else, something unknown. Then she hears the noises. Noises from deep in the throat, purring. Low groans. Wet smacking sounds. Tamara sees the bodies. Naked bodies. The body on top is moving rhythmically, she sees the muscles tense and relax. The sound of thumping is louder. And now she can see what it is; it's an alarm clock that has fallen against the wall and is being banged backwards and forwards, backwards and forwards. Tamara sees Sara's mum. Her breasts falling out to each side. The brown nipples are staring at Tamara. And Sara's mother's mouth. Her mouth is half open. The white, sharp teeth, the red tongue. And even though Tamara can only see him from behind, she recognises him. She recognises his back and she recognises his pale backside with the big mole. Tamara has only seen the mole once before. A couple of years ago when she accidentally opened the bathroom door. She had closed it carefully again. Daddy hadn't even noticed her. And he didn't notice her now either.

Sara and Tamara said nothing to each other. Not a word. They left. They walked along the familiar roads, all the way to the kiosk by the woods. Then they went into the woods. They sat down on some logs. Behind them is a hut that the big boys in third year are building. A hammer is lying on the ground. Beside it, a box of nails and some pliers. The girls have still not said a word. They have not even looked at each other. There is a pile of dried old leaves from last year lying by the logs. Brown and dry. Tamara kicks the pile with her foot and the leaves underneath are damper and darker. A cat comes towards them, miaowing. Tamara recognises it. She has seen it before. It's quite small and thin, with black, slightly shabby fur, not yet fully grown. No one seems to own it. Earlier in the summer, she gave it a slice of bread with liverpaté from her lunchbox. The cat wraps its body around the girls' legs. They bend down and stroke it. It pushes its head against their hands and rubs against their legs. Stands up on its hind legs and thrusts its head into their hands. It miaows from somewhere deep in its throat. The miaowing of a cat on heat. Short, high miaows followed by a long, deep purr. It rubs and pushes against them. Against Sara and Tamara. Warm fur against bare legs. Its tail is standing straight up, quivering. Its arse shines bright pink against the dark fur. Tamara kicks the cat away with her leg. Carefully. The cat jumps back, but quickly returns. Tail quivering, guttural miaows. This time she kicks it a bit harder. The cat sits at a distance and licks itself. Then it rolls over onto its back and wriggles while it miaows. Tamara and Sara do not look at each other and they still have not said anything. The cat has sat up again and is licking itself between its legs. Then it comes back towards the girls again, miaowing and looking at them.

Tamara is not sure who started it. All she remembers is the cat writhing in their grasp and that they pulled its legs apart while they nailed it to the wall of the hut. Tamara remembers blood and screeching. Tamara remembers all the scratches on her hands felt good. It was good that they were stinging. Tamara doesn't remember who hammered the nail into the pink hole, but she can still see quite clearly the nail moving in and the blows of the hammer. Rhythmical blows. The cat's half open mouth. The white, sharp teeth, the red tongue.

Later that day, Tamara saw Sara's mum at the Coop. Sara's mum was wearing a turquoise dress. She was small and thin, and she pursed her lips together as she bent over the freezer. It looked like she was comparing the price of whale steak with fish fingers. And Daddy at the dinner table. Can you pass me the potatoes? Well, wife, how was your day? And you, children, have you been good today? Tamara? Philip? Any homework for tomorrow? And in the background, Tamara could make out the sound of hammer blows, the smell of sex, the half open mouth, the white teeth. But none of it can have happened. It's not possible. Not now. Not with meatballs, gravy and a salt shaker on the table. And Daddy isn't like that.

Sara and Tamara. Their faces in the mirror. Sara's big, dark eyes. Tamara's big, dark eyes. Tamara's brown hair, Sara's black hair. They were alike. Like sisters? Tamara looks at Daddy's dark hair at the table. Daddy? Yes, Tamara? Daddy reads the paper. His slippers are on the carpet. His eyes behind the paper are brown. What did you want to say? No, it was nothing, Daddy. Are we? Tamara and Sara. Sara and Tamara.

Tamara scrubs and cleans the scallops in cold, running water. Sara will be here soon. Her best friend. Her hands turn red and numb around the nails, but it doesn't matter. Tamara is doing this for Sara. Tamara cuts the monkfish into four pieces. Sara loves fish and shellfish. She will have Russian caviar as a starter. Tamara mixes the batter for the blinis: egg yolks, buckwheat flour, a little yeast and milk.

A few hours later, Tamara, Sara and Liss are standing in Tamara's sitting room. The three women stand in the middle of Tamara's newly polished, herringbone parquet. Tamara wonders if they have noticed the orchids in the expensive brass pots, Tamara wonders if Sara and Liss have noticed that the orchids are exactly the same shade of smoky blue as the main colour in the oil painting on the wall behind them, or whether she should point it out. Liss needs a bit of guidance, Tamara decides. So Tamara tells them about the orchids and the painting, about the lady in the shop who had praised Tamara's good taste. Then she says: 'Eva just rang. She'll be a bit late. She has a meeting with the parents of one of the boys in her class.'

'Yes, she mentioned that she had some boisterous boys, who ruin everything for the rest of the class,' said Sara.

'Hmm, it can be a real problem, I know. In Mona's class there's...'

'I actually bumped into Eva in a shop yesterday,' interrupts Tamara. 'She looks so tired these days. Pale and drawn in the face.'

'Yes, she has my deepest sympathies. It is not much fun being a teacher today,' says Sara.

'No, poor Eva,' Tamara agrees. 'She looked pretty exhausted.'

'And she is not the youthful type in the first place. I mean, she really has not aged very well,' says Sara.

'No, that's true,' agrees Liss. 'She hasn't really.'

'In fact, I think she's put on even more weight recently,' Tamara comments

'Strange you should say that. I was thinking the same,' Liss says, enthusiastically. 'Of course, it's typical for Taureans to put on weight when they get older. And she always eats so much.'

'How much do you reckon she weighs now? She's pretty wide over the hips,' says Tamara, and without thinking about it, she smoothes down her own svelte hips.

'And her dress sense certainly does her no favours,' comments Sara.

'Did you see the top she was wearing last time?' asks Liss.

'Yes, awful.'

'Could you taste that she had burnt the potatoes dauphinois?' asks Tamara.

'Yes,' Sara says. 'It was pretty obvious. But the worst thing was that she said the chocolate pudding was home-made.'

'Oh, wasn't it?' asks Liss.

'No, it was bought,' Tamara says. 'I don't like friends who lie. It's not good when friends lie to each other.'

Tamara is in the kitchen. Sara, Liss and Eva wait in Tamara's spacious sitting room, with real Persian carpets on the floor. A mixture of contemporary art in thin, brass frames and old, valuable paintings in heavy, gilded wooden frames hangs on the walls. Tamara's white sofas with the light cushions filled with eiderdown, the open fire, the shining glass table with the three smoky-blue orchids, everything looks just as it should, inviting. There is an understated, reserved luxury about Tamara's home. Sara, Tamara, Liss and Eva will sit there, in front of the fire, after their meal. Sit by the flames with their coffee and liquor (blue Parfait Amor for Liss and D.O.M cognac for the others). There will be a confidential and intimate tone to their conversation. But right now the girls are enjoying a glass of champagne (Tamara has explained in detail the difference between champagne and sparkling wine), by the door out to the conservatory. The double doors into the dining room are open and from where the guests are standing, they can – hopefully – see a blinding white damask tablecloth and silver candlesticks and old Meissen porcelain. Tamara can hear them laughing and talking. She has just welcomed Eva and poured them all some champagne in wide glasses, of the sort supposedly shaped like Marie Antoinette's breasts, which must have looked almost exactly like Sara's. Tamara carefully cuts the whipped eggwhites into the blini batter and fries four thick pancakes. She puts them on green glass plates, where they lie cooling while she whips the cream.

She gets the whisk and a steel bowl, pours in the cream and begins to whip. The whisk hits the side of the metal bowl. Over the sound of metal on metal, Tamara hears the girls chatting in the sitting room and above it all, she hears Sara's voice and Sara's laughter. Tamara likes whipping cream and she always uses a whisk, even though it takes a long time and she gets a sore wrist. Tamara likes watching the white liquid go through its metamorphosis, until it is just as she wants it. And it's just air. Tamara almost laughs. Just air! She whips in more and more air, until the cream is just right: thick, airy, light and white. But if it's overdone, the cream turns into a lumpy, fatty mass. The trick is to stop just in time. Not go on for too long. Tamara mixes the cream with sour cream (so that it's as close as possible to the mild-tasting Russian smetana) and spoons a small pile on to the plates beside the blinis. Then she opens a jar of caviar. Real Russian caviar. Bought at Place Madeleine in Paris. Nearly 400 francs for 30 grams. Small, grey-black, salty egg pearls. Only the best is good enough for Tamara's dearest friend. Tamara puts a particularly generous dollop on what will be Sara's plate.

'Lovely champagne, Tamara,' says Eva when Tamara comes back into the sitting room. Eva has on an unflattering, slightly too short dress. Tamara looks at Eva's dress from top to bottom, but finds no redeeming features.

'Glad you like it,' Tamara answers. 'Nice dress, by the way. And now, girls, the starter will be served. Warm blinis with caviar, plundered from the womb of a female sturgeon in the Caspian Sea. Bought in Paris. Come, let's sit down.'

'Ah, real Russian caviar. My absolute favourite!' says Sara and Tamara smiles at her. Sara, my best friend, thinks Tamara.

'Delicious! Tamara, you are incredible.'

'Thank you, Liss. Eva, pass over the champagne, I'm completely dehydrated after my stint in the kitchen.'

Eva. Tamara wonders who Eva is. Tamara knows that she is the same age as the others. That she was born in Denmark, that she lived there until she finished school. Tamara knows that Eva is slightly overweight. That she buys nine out of ten items of clothing from H & M or KappAhl, whereas the tenth is Nina Ricci or Versace. She's a teacher. She's married to Erik. They have no children. But there is something about Eva. Not that it means anything. Eva is friendly and nice. Perhaps not the most exciting woman in the world, but more exciting than Liss, at least. But Tamara sees Eva looking at her. And she's always asking so many questions.

They had been three for so long. Sara, Tamara and well, Liss. Ever since they were eleven. Tamara was surprised when Liss suddenly asked Eva if she wanted to join the sewing circle. Strictly speaking it was Sara and Tamara's sewing circle. They had started it. Maybe Liss asked Eva if she wanted to come because she had seen Eva's husband on TV. Erik is quite well known. Almost a celebrity, and Liss loves that kind of thing. Eva was invited to dinner at Sara's (she almost invited herself, Sara told Tamara afterwards). Liss just said that it was written in the stars, that Eva would fit in perfectly with the sewing circle. A Pisces, an Aries and a Gemini. All we need is a Taurus, the only sign missing from the sequence, Liss had said, her face deadly serious. Water, fire, earth, air. We're lacking earth, it will bring harmony. The sewing circle needs Eva. Tamara was about to laugh, she planned to be loud and scornful, but then Liss started to hum quietly. And Tamara was quiet. Both Sara and Tamara know very well what Liss' humming means.

All the girls, the sewing circle, are sitting round Tamara's dinner table. Tamara loves her grey dining room, with its original cornices, Finnish designer furniture in beechwood and crystal chandelier. In the same way that she loves her partner, Thomas. Journalists in medium-sized newspapers do not earn nearly enough to buy Finnish designer furniture, paintings and Persian carpets to fill an entire yellow villa. A yellow villa with a mansard roof and glazed Dutch roof tiles. Poets don't have enough money either. So when Tamara was married to Håvard, they lived in a terraced house. Just like the one Paul and Liss live in now. In the next street, in fact. Tamara smiles at her friends. All sitting round her beech table, eating and enjoying themselves. They are now on the second course. The scallops are perfect and Tamara delights in the combination of the half-melted, salty feta and sweet dill. Just as successful as she thought it would be and she hopes that Sara, at least, will recognise the stroke of genius in this simple dish. The girls talk about food, orgasms, holiday plans, good books, great films, the dream man, their men, their children, their jobs. Sara leans over to Tamara to whisper something about Liss in her ear. Tamara doesn't quite catch what Sara says, because Sara has a big piece of scallop stuck between her front teeth and Tamara can't take her eyes off it. It hangs there like a wet rag and covers nearly the whole of Sara's front tooth. Tamara says nothing. She just stares. Sara continues to talk and smile and the whole time, Tamara sees the golden-brown, slimy coating over the refrigerator-white teeth.

'But, Sara,' Liss says suddenly from the other side of the table. 'You've got something on your teeth.'

'Have I?'

'Yes, something brown and disgusting.'

'Uff, it's a piece of scallop,' says Sara, looking from the small, light brown strip on her index finger to Tamara. Tamara looks Sara right in the eye. Her dark, vulnerable eyes. Tamara has nothing to be ashamed of. Sara loves shellfish. But perhaps the piece of scallop reminds Sara of the time that Tamara let her walk around in her tight, white trousers with a seeping period stain at the back. Tamara didn't say anything for the whole morning, she just watched the red stain slowly blossoming from Sara's crotch. In fact, it was the same day that Lars and Tamara split up.

'Have you seen the new guy in the bookshop?' asks Liss. 'The bookshop down at the centre.'

'Is that the new one who took over from the fat one with the monkey arms?' asks Eva.

'Yes, the cute one,' Liss answers and licks her lips.

'Mmm, not bad,' Tamara nods.

'Have you seen him, Sara?' Eva asks.

'Yes,' Sara replies. 'If you mean the one with the longish, curly hair.'

'Yes,' Liss says. 'That's the one. He's cute, isn't he?'

'No, Liss,' Sara retorts. 'He is not. Do you really think he is worth looking at, Tamara?'

'Yes, he's sweet,' Tamara says. 'And very nice and helpful too. He checked something on the Internet for me and ordered a book that I really wanted to read. He seemed to be both well read and polite. Absolutely charming.'

'Sweet? Charming? Polite? Really, I do not understand how you can say that, Tamara,' continues Sara. 'Good God, the man looks like Louis the Fourteenth.'

'Oh come on, Sara,' Tamara says.

'He does,' insists Sara. 'Long, thin legs in tights...'

'Right.'

'OK, then, not tights, but certainly tight trousers. And he's got a paunch, a stoop and he is thinning on top so the mop of curly hair is obviously just compensation. And cowboy boots!'

'Did Louis the Fourteenth wear cowboy boots?' asks Tamara, and Eva and Liss laugh. But Sara doesn't even listen to what Tamara says, and continues: 'And so self-important and pompous.

Sometimes it seems that you are completely blind when it comes to men, Tamara.'

'Cheers,' says Tamara, laughing. 'That's fine by me. The new bookseller is not cute at all. No, you're absolutely right. He could easily be confused with Louis the Fourteenth. Eva, perhaps you should take your history class on a little outing?'

Everyone laughs. Including Sara. The subject is dropped and Eva starts to talk about a new current affairs programme on TV that Erik is going to present. But Tamara isn't able to listen properly. The man in the bookshop reminds her of something. He reminds Tamara of something that she doesn't let herself think about. He reminds her of one of those pages in her memory that she quickly flicks past. She knows the page is there, but she doesn't want to, dare to, can't bear to look at it. Because it doesn't fit in with the rest of the book. Because then it's not the book that Tamara wants. The man in the bookshop makes Tamara think about Håvard. Sometimes I think you must be blind, Tamara.

The split with Håvard was very painful for Tamara. They had only been married for three years and four months, Emma was barely two. Things started to go wrong between Tamara and Håvard quite early on. Things got worse and worse. Things they couldn't talk about. And eventually Tamara had to tell Håvard that she wanted to separate. Håvard nearly went to the wall. He was on sick leave for a whole year and Tamara knows that he still has not found anyone else. At least Tamara has Thomas and a yellow villa with a mansard roof and underground heating in the driveway. And Tamara has grown fond of Thomas. Tamara has Emma and her work. And Sara. Sara has always been there.

Tamara really liked Håvard. Tamara loved Håvard. I loved Håvard, Tamara has written in her book. The small, thick book with the black velvet cover. There was nothing I wanted more than for things to work out between us. Nothing has ever meant as much to me as Håvard. Except one person. I have never been so attached to anyone. Except one person. The only one.

Tamara loved Håvard. But there were too many suspicions and hurtful words. Neither of them could stand it any longer. It's the last evening with Håvard. It's been over between them for a long time. They have even stopped quarrelling. They know each other's arguments and retorts by heart. There's nothing left to say. They've packed nearly everything. Divided the wedding presents. Taken the pictures down from the walls. Tamara and Håvard are each sitting on a wooden chair. They have a thermos of coffee and nothing to look at other than brown cardboard boxes and light patches on the carpet. And each other. They look at each other. Håvard is sad. Tamara is even sadder. Emma is sleeping in her cot in her room. Tamara and Hårvard are downstairs in the terraced house they bought just after they got married. Neither of them says anything. Tamara feels so bad for him. And she wants to comfort him. And she feels so bad for herself. Tamara knows who can comfort her. She finally makes up her mind, goes over to him and puts her hand on his. Their wedding rings, which neither of them have taken off yet, clink against each other. My love, says Tamara.

Like all couples, Tamara and Håvard have their secret box. A box full of words and fantasies. Smiles and looks. Now Tamara puts on one of the smiles and one of the looks from the their secret box. A smile and look that can only be understood to mean one thing for Håvard and Tamara. And Tamara whispers something in his ear. Which cannot be misunderstood either. At first he doesn't move, then he starts to smile as well, he looks at her and his smile widens, then he gets up and goes upstairs to the bedroom. All couples have a secret box. Some only have a mental box, but in Tamara and Håvard's case, there is a rather small, metal box with a lock. Tamara has sent Håvard to get it. The box that they refer to as their P.E.B, Håvard and Tamara's Private Erotic Box. The box that they laugh about, are slightly embarrassed about, and the contents of which would seem utterly ludicrous in the wrong context. But which has given them a lot of fun and many pleasurable moments. The box with the French maid's costume, a vibrator and a few videos.

Tamara had left a note in the box. She had thrown the other things away. Even now, Tamara can't bear to think about what exactly she wrote in that note. She can't quite remember. The words were so mean, so hurtful. But the message was certainly clear. Tamara intended never to have any physical contact with Håvard again, nor should he for a moment think that she had derived any pleasure from the contact they had had. The very fact that he believed that Tamara wanted to make love to him, that he had allowed himself to be fooled and was now standing with an erection between his legs as he read the note in his hand, was yet more proof of his smallness. Or something to that effect. Tamara can't quite remember. He didn't look at her when he came back downstairs. But Tamara saw his eyes, his averted eyes, and she still sees them sometimes.

Tamara was so desperate, so helpless. And so angry. But it just wasn't possible to be angry with the person she was really angry with. So she was angry with Håvard instead. Yet again. Just as she had been too many times in the course of their short marriage.

Sara is frightened of cats. Sara has hated cats ever since that day in the woods. Tamara knows that Sara is terrified of them. Maybe it was Sara who started? Tamara can't remember. Sara and Tamara have never really spoken about that day. But Tamara has let Sara believe that it was Sara who started it. It was Sara who got the hammer, it was Sara who found the box of nails. And maybe it was? Tamara can't remember. But the other thing that happened was definitely not Sara's fault. Tamara knows that. It was Tamara's father who was on top. He was the one doing it. He was moving. Repetitive, aggressive movements. Tamara saw that. Sara's mother was still. Sara's mother was nearly hidden by Daddy's big body. She was just lying there, wasn't she? Sara's mother did nothing wrong. And nor did Sara. Sara is without blame. Sara is so thin and fragile. Sara needs Tamara. And it's good to be needed.

Tamara let Sara know about the rumours that were going round about Sara's mum. Tamara thought it was only fair. That her mother was pretty loose with her favours, as they said. Tamara had heard a few people say it. Sara didn't know what the expression meant, so Tamara had to explain to her. It means that your mother is a woman who lets lots of men sleep with her, Tamara had to say in the end. Even though she didn't want to say something like that about Sara's mum to Sara. Maybe it was the girl with the freckles who worked at the Coop, or had Tamara heard it from some of Philip's friends? Tamara couldn't quite remember. Sara looked at her with her dark eyes and Tamara stroked her hand.

Sara is so beautiful. Tamara wants to be Sara. An angel. White and without shame. Not like him. Not like Daddy. Tamara does not want to be like her father.

Tamara is going to see Jakob again on Thursday. And then she'll be Sara and Jakob will be Tamara's. He's booking a suite at the Grand Hotel. Tamara and Jakob will drink champagne from glasses that look like Sara's small, pointy breasts. Maybe Tamara will ask him to order Russian caviar as well, even though she doesn't really think it tastes of anything other than salt. But it's expensive. On Thursday Tamara will smooth herself with oil and let her body polish his. Tamara will be smooth and soft like Sara. She wants to be Sara. Helpless, pure and completely without shame. Jakob will whisper the same things in Tamara's ear that he whispers to Sara. And Tamara will unlock Sara and Jakob's secret box and in that way become Sara. White and pure and without shame. Someone that everyone has to help.

Jakob is not a good lover. But he is Sara's husband.

Chapter 7

Sewing Circle at Liss',
Tuesday 19 December

Menu
Tomato soup with prawns
Roast reindeer with Waldorf salad and blue Congo potatoes
Lemon mousse

It's raining and they're playing Christmas carols non-stop on the radio. Liss has her period. Her lower back aches. But the fluffy, light yellow mixture that Liss is transferring from the mixing bowl into another bowl with the help of a spatula, reminds her of bed linen. Light yellow silk sheets on a four-poster bed with bedposts turned in mahogany. The four-poster bed is on the second floor of a castle in a vineyard in Normandy. Liss lies down on the bed, her back aching from the long, tiring journey by horse and carriage. Welcome, Mademoiselle Liss, bienvenue, he had said and given her a firm handshake. She had come to the castle to work as a governess. She herself came from a poor, but dignified family, and both her parents had died recently in tragic circumstances. Her employer, the master of the castle, is a young, dark baron. Bitter and closed. A widower. No, no, harrowed by grief after his wife left him and the children for another man. His two young daughters have nearly wasted away through neglect and lack of love and are both so in need of all the knowledge and love that Liss can give them. If only it wasn't for the evil housekeeper. Liss pours out the cream (Here, children, drink this freshly strained milk. It will do you good) and whips it until it's firm. Things get so bad that the housekeeper, wild with jealousy, tries to push Liss over the edge of a cliff. Add the gelatine. Mercifully the baron rides by at that very moment. And miraculously, just at the point when the lemon mousse is ready to be put in the fridge to chill, Mademoiselle Liss is happily married to the master and the evil housekeeper has been exposed as a fraud, and the girls are once more harmonious, healthy and happy.

Tamara called Eva the Queen of Oxo the last time the sewing circle was there. It was a joke, of course, and everyone laughed. Eva too. But Liss doesn't want to risk it. She has nothing against being a queen, but she doesn't want them to judge her because she makes things from packets. So Liss has made the lemon mousse from scratch and now she is skinning the tomatoes. She cuts them into small pieces and takes out the seeds before putting the flesh, onion rings, some bacon and stock into a pan. She's making tomato soup with prawns for the starter. The heroine of the book that Liss is reading (Hot Nights in the Tropics) ate something similar for supper a few chapters back, lovingly prepared for her by her broad-shouldered cooking officer: plump, blushing prawns in a deep red tomato soup, with a rising aroma of delightful, exotic spices and the promise of yet another night with the officer for our heroine. Now that would be something for the sewing circle, thought Liss when she read it. But the only recipe she has found for tomato soup doesn't use any spices apart from salt and pepper, and it has no prawns in it either. Liss has no idea what to add in order to make the soup exotic and doesn't have the courage to deviate from a recipe anyway. So salt and pepper it is, but she intends to add a daring prawn or two at the last minute. And Liss believes that the soup will be a great success, even though it perhaps doesn't taste as exotic and delightful and hot as the one the tropical heroine had. Liss leaves the soup to simmer, as it should according to the recipe, and goes out to the full-length mirror in the hall. There is some eyeliner in the top drawer of the chest of drawers and after a couple of strokes, a pair of dark, slanting eyes stare back at her from the mirror. Liss stands and watches her blonde hair slowly change, getting thicker and darker. Her round face narrows. She loves the feeling of the golden velvet tightening over her swelling breasts and feels her ears beginning to prick up.

Once again she is the Famous Leopard Woman. The Famous Leopard Woman has, of course, a rich and varied wardrobe, but her favourite is the tight-fitting, spotted velvet suit with a long tail. The suit is made from golden, shiny, stretch velvet with black spots. The Leopard Woman also usually wears a black velvet hood with ears and high, black boots in soft kid leather. The whole outfit was specially made for the Leopard Woman by a renowned Parisian tailor. When the Leopard Woman holds her soft, velvet tail in her slim hands with long, oval varnished nails and strokes it over her face, it drives more than one man insane with desire. Counts from myriad countries, a duke here and there and a host of millionaires. And firemen. A whole brigade of strong firemen.

The doorbell rings. In a matter of nano-seconds the Famous Leopard Woman disappears, and it is Liss who opens the door. Eva is standing outside.

'Hi. I finished my pile of marking a bit earlier than expected. End of term tests, you know. Can I come in?'

'Yes, of course. What a lovely surprise. Come in. But I'm not quite ready yet.'

They go into the kitchen. Liss turns off the radio. Can Eva help with anything? Liss shakes her head. Eva sits down and Liss realises that she is glad that it was Eva who came. She likes Eva. Eva has such lovely dimples. Liss is grateful that Eva joined the sewing circle. Why was she so keen for her to join? Liss has come to the conclusion that, at least to begin with, it wasn't Eva herself who was important, but rather that she wanted to push something through that the other two were against. And Liss isn't ashamed to admit that she also thought it would be fun if one of the sewing circle girls was married to a celebrity, a TV star. And anyway, three is too few in a club. If it was just her, Tamara and Sara, things would never be any different. Sara and Tamara would never be able to see Liss for who she really is. The child she was casts a shadow over the woman she has become. The sound of the words 'casts a shadow over the woman she has become' pleases Liss so much that she has to say the sentence to herself again. And it's true. Sara and Tamara don't see her and before Eva came, Liss often left the sewing circle with the childish feeling of two against one. So even though she is very, very fond of Sara and Tamara and they have been her friends since she was eleven, it's good that Eva is in the sewing circle. Eva will help her to get Sara and Tamara to see Liss. Eva sees her. Because Eva has never met Pissy Lissy. Liss smiles at Eva:

'So, how's work?'

'Oh fine. It's going really well, actually,' Eva replies. 'A lot to do, but I like it. And it's the Christmas holidays soon. And what about you, do you like being at home?'

'Love it.'

'Liss, there's something I wanted to ask you. You know them better than I do.'

'Yes?'

'Is Sara all right these days? I just think she seems so jumpy. And she looks even thinner,' says Eva.

'Sara has always been quite highly strung, typical Gemini,' answers Liss. 'Successful and apparently confident, but actually very nervous. Fragile, is that the right word?'

'So she's always been like that?'

'Yes, I'd say so. Sara is dependent on two things: tranquillisers and Tamara. And she can't cope without rather large doses of each. Gemini is both strong and insecure at the same time.'

'Hmm,' Eva says. 'And you?'

'Me? I'm a Pisces, so I'm solid as an ox. Ox! Of course, you're a Taurus. So you and I are well-suited.'

'Of course,' says Eva and smiles.

'Have you got a new skirt on?' asks Liss.

'No,' Eva replies. 'It's just one I haven't used for a long time.'

'It's really nice. You know, Tamara really is getting a bit too old to wear skirts as tight as she does. Don't you agree?' asks Liss. 'Even though she does have a fabulous figure.'

'Maybe,' Eva hesitates. 'They are perhaps a bit tight sometimes. I'm really looking forward to our trip to Copenhagen!'

'Yes, you must know it well.'

'Yes. I grew up just outside, to the north of the city. My mother still lives there. Oh, I miss my mum. But she's coming over for Christmas. Did I tell you? And I'll visit her when we're over there,' Eva says. 'It's going to be a great trip. I'm so looking forward to it.'

Liss is scared of the dark. She lies in bed and is frightened. She tries to hum loudly, but it only helps for a little while. There's something in her room. Something crawling on its belly, squirming and wriggling its way forward, then suddenly it moves very fast. It's hairy, dressed in greasy rat fur that's parted down the middle of its back. Yes, you have to sleep with the light off, Liss. There's nothing to be frightened of. Good night! I'm going now. Liss cries into Bamse's fur. Something dark fills the doorway. It's Mummy. Maybe she'll let her keep the light on after all? Sometimes Mummy puts the light back on and smiles and says, OK darling. Mummy in the doorway. Liss hears something dragging itself across the floor, something breathing heavily, and Liss starts to cry loudly. Liss looks at Mummy in the doorway. Mummy, turn the light on so it will go away. It's going to get me. Mummy doesn't answer. Mummy? If you don't stop this nonsense now, if I hear another peep from you, I won't love you anymore, do you understand? You won't be my little girl anymore, Liss. I'll leave you, Liss. The door closes. Liss hears Mummy's heels click clack hard on the floor down the hall. She hears Mummy shutting the sitting room door with a bang. No one will hear now if Liss shouts for help. The dragging sounds get louder and Liss feels warm breath on her face.

Liss had more dresses and a bigger house than anyone else in the class. Liss' daddy was the captain of a big ship. Liss could just picture it. The big white ship and her daddy in his uniform, looking out over the endless ocean, longing for Liss, his beloved daughter. The gold buttons and gold stripes on his uniform shining in the sun and his eyes as blue as the sea. Liss' father was rarely at home and Liss used to get so excited every time he came back. Not only did she get nice things (even Tamara and Sara had admired the silk scarf that Daddy bought in China and the doll from America). But Mummy was always nice when Daddy was home. My lovely, lovely daughter, said Mummy, and hugged her tight. She held her out so she could see her, smiled with her shiny lips, hugged her tight again and told her father that Liss was her only consolation when he was away. We help each other. We support each other, her mother said. Daddy patted Liss on the head and said that he was happy to hear that. And the weeks with Daddy were always just long enough for Liss to start thinking that everything would be different now. That everything was better. But then Daddy went away again. You're a big girl now, so if you don't stop wetting the bed, you'll have to go to a children's home. Then Mummy won't love you any more.

Everyone looked up to Liss' mother. She was so beautiful and so clever. Her husband was away so much that she was basically on her own with her daughter. And she had a career. But she was still a good mother and housewife. Home-made jam and a spotless house. Seven sorts of home-made biscuits for Christmas. Crunchy crackling. And she was always so polite. Always so well turned out. Really admirable. A woman who managed everything.

'You may not control the external environment as much as you would like, but you are in control of the internal one.' She was 27 years and one week old and she had definitely seen better days, much better. Later in the same week that Liss woke up with the two English sentences chasing round her head, she decided to break all contact with her mother. Her mother still lives in the big house where Liss grew up, and sometimes Liss and Paul drive past and see the house and garden. Liss puts her hand on Paul's which is resting on the gear stick. He slows down, she looks into the big garden, and then they drive on. She hasn't spoken to her mother for years.

Liss is scared. She doesn't want to go to Copenhagen. She's frightened of the dark and doesn't like sleeping in strange places. At least, not without Paul. But there's something else. And it's not the money, because she's spoken to Paul and he said that they'd manage fine. Liss is scared of something but she can't quite put her finger on it. A trip to Copenhagen with her best friends. There's nothing to be frightened of.

It's now gone seven o'clock and the doorbell rings again. Eva goes to open the door and comes back with Sara. They both sit down at the kitchen table.

'You actually have a very nice kitchen,' Sara says to Liss. 'Quite spacious for a terraced house.'

Liss feels light and happy, she looks around, yes, it really is very nice. It's a bright, nice kitchen. Relatively new white kitchen fittings, a cork-tiled floor with rag rugs, blue walls and flowery curtains. There are some gnomes on the windowsill that Martin and Mona made. Liss puts on some water for the potatoes and checks the roast. She takes the pan of tomato soup and a bowl of prawns out of the fridge. Sara has opened a bottle of wine and the girls are smiling and laughing. A few minutes later, Tamara arrives as well. Eva, Sara and Tamara sit round the kitchen table with its plastic tablecloth. Tamara takes up so much space. She talks loudest and laughs most. Liss finishes the wine in her glass and asks for a refill. Her lower back is aching and she can tell that she needs to change her pad. While she holds out her glass and listens to Tamara talking about some hopeless interior designer that she and Thomas have been in touch with, Liss looks around. The kitchen feels dark and pokey. She sees that it's messy and a bit dirty; there are stains and spots on the worktop, one of the bulbs in the lamp above the table where the girls are sitting needs to be replaced. There's an advent calender on the wall behind Tamara. All the windows are open. The glue didn't work, Martin explained. Liss finishes her wine and then begins to stir the tomato soup, which has started to heat up. Her movements feel heavy and awkward. She has to cross the kitchen to get the prawns and she knows that she looks clumsy.

But in fact she's not really here in the kitchen. She's actually lying on a low bed. Tonight she is the chosen one. Again. She is the sultan's favourite wife. And now she is going to be bathed in ass's milk, massaged and rubbed with sweet-smelling oils. She will have pearls and jewels threaded into her golden hair; fair hair is so rare and therefore so highly prized here in the harem. She raises her body, stretches out her hand and rings a little golden bell. The clapper is a ruby. Her two personal slaves appear immediately, the one darker than the other. They bow their dark heads and ask humbly how they can serve their lady.

'Tamara, could you pass me the pepper mill. It's just there on the table,' Liss says. 'And Sara, could you just stretch over for the salt. Thank you. Oh dear, I'm afraid it's a bit messy here.'

'Not at all. I mean, it's just like it always is,' says Tamara and laughs.

'We had a birthday party here yesterday,' Liss apologises. 'Twelve girls at the giggling age. And right in the middle of Christmas preparations!'

'Did it go well?' asks Eva.

'Oh yes,' Liss says. 'But I have to say that I was very glad when the guests finally left. After three hours of constant running around, shouting and balloons bursting you've had enough.'

'Talking of balloons bursting,' Tamara says, 'I've invented something.'

Sara, Eva and Liss all turn towards Tamara. 'Oh?'

'Last night. I was lying awake thinking about that rape that was in all the papers last week.'

'Oh yes, that was awful,' responds Liss.

'Mm, so I've thought of a way in which we women can protect ourselves against men.'

'Hairspray in your handbag. That's what I have,' Eva says.

'Doesn't work,' Tamara declares.

'Doesn't it?' asks Liss. 'What about self-defence, then?'

'Yes, of course, but my invention is a lot better. Imagine a rubber stopper. And then fixed into the stopper there's a sort of razor blade, but it's not sharp at the edges, only at the end. And the end is sharp as can be.'

'Oh God, Tamara!' Liss says.

'And the protection stopper comes complete with an insertion device, the lot. The woman says no, she shouts, tries to run away, screams. No one hears her. The man pushes her to the ground, rips off her clothes, opens his trousers and thrusts himself into her with great force. Whereupon he is sliced in two down the middle.'

'Good grief,' Eva exclaims. 'That's horrible.'

'Tamara, you're really not right in the head,' Liss says and wonders what's the matter with Tamara these days.

'Good idea. A bit anti-men, perhaps,' Sara muses.

'Do you think I could get a patent?'

'Yes, I'm sure. I'm sure you'll become a millionaire,' Eva replies, adding in an exaggerated, not to be misunderstood voice: 'Are you having problems on the men front at the moment?'

'No,' says Tamara.

'You've always had a bit of a problem with them really, haven't you?' Sara says. Joking and laughing as well.

'Yes,' Tamara concedes.

'And poor judgement in that department too?' Sara adds.

There is silence in Liss' kitchen. Liss realises that she's frightened. Something is happening to the sewing circle. An uneasiness. Eva asked earlier on what was wrong with Sara. And perhaps Sara is more tense than usual? Not right now, to be fair. Now she looks completely relaxed. But Tamara seemed so aggressive when she was talking about her invention. A joke, of course. Something is amiss with the sewing circle. It is silent until Eva says:

'Girls, I heard a joke on the bus today. It was about just this. Men.'

'Let's hear it then,' says Liss, relieved.

'Men are like puppies. When you talk to them, they look as if they understand,' Eva says, opening her big, brown eyes wide.

They all laugh. Liss thinks, it's a good thing Eva is here, and says:

'Good point. Sound just like Paul when I'm trying to discuss star sign constellations or mother-in-laws with him.'

'Mmm, Jakob has such understanding eyes when I try to tell him that, in fact, it is important to me that the toilet seat is left down. But I still find it left up several times a day.'

'Thomas doesn't really understand much, either,' Tamara says. 'Thankfully.'

'I remember when I was single and a student at teaching college,' Eva recalls. 'Some of the men I dated – sweet Jesus. I remember sometimes thinking, dear God can we not just get started. Shut up and fuck me. We've got nothing to talk about anyway, so let's just jump into bed. Let's have a little intimacy at least, do something together.'

'Here's to men and their similarity with immature members of the canine race,' says Sara.

'Cheers!'

'I thought we would be having some mulled wine,' Tamara says. 'But this wine is really good, too.'

'Oh, I didn't think of that,' says Liss. 'But you go on in to the living room, girls, and I'll bring the soup.'

Something is happening to the sewing circle. And Liss is scared of losing Sara and Tamara. The only friends she has. At least, the only good friends whom she can talk to. And Sara is so kind. Sara with her bright, starry eyes. And Eva too. Liss likes Eva. Eva has deep dimples and smiling eyes. But Eva is different. Safer. And less exciting. There's nothing mysterious about the fact that Eva wants to be friends with Liss. Eva is more like Liss. But it is a never-ceasing wonder that Sara and Tamara wanted to be friends with Liss. Sara and Tamara decided everything in the class. They would always be untouchable. Like the girls in books. Like the pictures in film magazines and Photo Love. Jet black hair and magnolia skin. Chestnut hair and golden velvet skin. Sara's beautiful starry eyes. The two dark heads, close together. Pissy girl, they shouted. Pissy Lissy, they whispered and held their noses when Liss went past in the playground. Then suddenly one day they wanted to be her friends, and have been ever since. Liss remembers that day well.

Liss was on her way home from her cousin Anna's, who lived quite far away. Liss liked playing with Anna. Liss' mother didn't like her playing with Anna. But that day, they had been sent home early as one of the teachers was ill and Liss had used the opportunity to visit Anna. Liss had been walking fast to get home at the normal time, so her mother wouldn't realise that she'd been at her cousin's. Then just by the kiosk, where the woods start, Liss met Sara and Tamara. When Liss saw them, she got tummy ache straight away. But Sara and Tamara didn't call her Pissy Lissy, like they normally did. They didn't push her. Tamara didn't pull her hair. They smiled at her and asked her where she'd been. She was so surprised by this unexpected friendliness that she told them about Anna and they didn't say anything horrible. In fact, they even asked questions and were nice and interested. Sara and Tamara wondered where Anna lived. Sara and Tamara asked which way she normally walked to Anna's. Sara and Tamara wondered whether she had cut through the woods. Liss answered as best she could. She hadn't gone through the woods, but something in Sara and Tamara's eyes made her say that she had. Liss wanted so badly to give the right answer and to do the right thing.

The next day, Sara and Tamara had come up to Liss in the first break and each taken her by the arm. We're friends now Liss, they whispered, for always. And they had been ever since. But they still don't see her. They look past her. They look at each other and no one else. Sara and Tamara. We rhyme. But still Liss knows that she has the right to be Sara and Tamara's friend. Bente doesn't have the right, nor does Marianne, nor Karin with the long, shiny plaits and sweets in her rabbit-skin cape pocket. It's Liss who's our friend, say Sara and Tamara. Go away. What shall we play, Liss? But there's something that Liss doesn't understand. For some reason she has a kind of power. Forever.

Sara has never said it, but she's always been good at making things clear without having to say anything. But Tamara's said it. Just in case Liss didn't understand. It is Sara and Tamara now and forever, no other friends. Liss never plays with Bente and Therese any more. She never visits Anna any more. She only plays with the two girls in her class who, up until recently, used to call her Pissy Lissy. Liss plays with the two girls in the class who used to pull her hair. Who used to push her around. Liss plays with the two prettiest girls in the class. The ones who decide everything. The ones who are important. Liss has been chosen. And Bente and Therese haven't. Nor has Marianne, nor has Anna. Not even Karin, with the long, shiny plaits.

After the tomato soup (mmm, lovely, home-made soup, Tamara had said knowingly), there is a reindeer roast with Waldorf salad and blue Congo potatoes.

*

'I used the original recipe for the Waldorf salad,' says Liss, thinking that Sara and Tamara would approve. 'The one that was used at the Waldorf Astoria.'

'Delicious,' Eva says.

'Is it celeriac or celery stick?' asks Tamara.

'Celeriac, cut into thin strips and then blanched for a minute in boiling water. And I put the walnuts in a separate bowl, for you, Sara. We can just take what we want then.'

'Thank you,' Sara says.

'I'm not feeling that great today,' Tamara says. 'I think I'm a bit premenstrual.'

'Talk about premenstrual,' says Eva. 'One of the girls in the class was caught shoplifting today.'

'Was she stealing tampons? Sorry, what is the connection?' asks Sara.

'No, no, it was cigarettes, I think. No, but of course she had a million excuses and explanations, and one of them was that she was premenstrual.'

'Poor thing,' commiserates Liss. She really must change her pad now.

'Tamara, were you not caught for something like that in your wild child days?' asks Sara.

'Yes,' Tamara replies.

'What was that like?' asks Eva.

'Horrible. It was horrible. They wrote my name down in a big book and threatened to call the police. I still feel sick when I think about it,' Tamara says. She laughs, but Liss can tell that Tamara means what she says. That being caught for shoplifting was a nightmare for her.

Tamara's shiny, red mouth. Her lips are moving and praising the food, laughing, asking about Liss' children. But when the shiny, lipstick red lips are shut, they say Pissy Lissy. Sara and Tamara look at me and see Pissy Lissy. They think I'm boring and scared. They think I am like I was before. But I've changed. I'm different from when we went to primary school. And I've never been like they think anyway. They were the only ones who ever called me Pissy Lissy. Bente and Therese, Karin and Anna, they all liked being with me. They wanted to play with me. Look at me. Can't you see? I mix with counts and royalty. I am a princess. I am beautiful. I am interesting. I am desired and renowned. I am the Famous Leopard Woman. Look at me! Listen to me! Help me, Eva!

Plates are passed over the table. Dishes are taken out. The heat from the candles flushes the women's cheeks red. They laugh and talk and eat. Praise the roast, discuss whether a real Waldorf salad should have grapes in it or not. Marvel at the blue potatoes. Discuss Christmas food. Pork versus lamb. Red cabbage or white cabbage. Christmas presents. You haven't got them all already? I don't really think that the decorations children make should be hung up. Almond potatoes. What can you get for dissatisfied mother-in-laws? Do you think it's all right to give away a jacket that you got last year but don't like? No, gravy with pork ribs, pah, that's vulgar, some newfangled thing. New pyjamas, maybe. Tie. The gap between branches is so big on pine trees. Spruce, of course. Yes, we always have a silver fir.

'I really love cats,' Liss blurts out.

Sara and Tamara suddenly look strange. Nearly a bit frightened. Liss sees it, but doesn't understand it. Recently Liss has noticed that Sara and Tamara sometimes stop in their tracks and somehow change when she hums, but she doesn't know why. And it doesn't always work either. Sometimes they just look straight through her as they often do. Sometimes they look terrified. Maybe it's got something to do with different tunes. Liss doesn't know. Liss hums when she is frightened and nervous. She's done it since she was child. Until she was eleven, she had a teddy bear and humming. Now she only has the humming.

She looks at Sara and Tamara's faces. Liss guesses that for a moment she has been close to what she has tried to understand for so long. The sudden friendship. The strange power she has over Sara and Tamara. That always slips out of her hands before she can grasp it. Like a slippery, red beach ball. A beach ball that she has had for many years now, but she has never really known what to do with it, a beach ball that she doesn't really enjoy. She looks at Sara and Tamara's faces. Their beautiful faces. Their dark hair. The eyes looking deep into each other's. She starts to formulate a question, she opens her mouth to ask. But Sara and Tamara won't answer. Liss has dropped the red beach ball in the water. She might as well just tell them what she was going to tell them.

No one says anything. All three of them are still looking at Liss, expecting a continuation.

'Well, not cats really, but leopards,' explains Liss. She is glad that everyone, even Sara and Tamara, are listening to her. That they seem so friendly, so interested. And a bit frightened.

'Right,' says Sara and takes a big gulp of wine.

'Is that a new bracelet?' Tamara asks Sara.

'No,' Sara says. 'I got it from Jakob.'

'Right, Jakob,' Tamara says.

'Sometimes I think that I'm a leopard woman,' starts Liss.

'How exciting! Do tell,' Eva says.

'What strange potatoes,' Tamara exclaims. 'They're completely blue.'

'Do you remember Sverre?' asks Liss.

'They're blue Congo potatoes,' Sara says. 'Aren't they, Liss?'

124

'Yes.'

'Are they from the Congo?' asks Tamara.

'No, or at least, I don't think so. They've got them in the supermarket.'

'Did you say Sverre? Was he in the parallel class? The one with butter yellow hair?' asks Sara.

'Yes, that's him,' Liss says. 'Golden hair and sky blue eyes.'

'Didn't you go out together for a while?' Tamara asks.

'He was my first lover,' says Liss, dramatically.

'You've told us that before,' Tamara says.

'Remember that I don't know all these things,' Eva says. 'I want to know about Sverre and the leopard woman.'

'Well, that's what I'm just about to tell you and I've never told a living soul before,' says Liss and continues in a whisper: 'Sverre used to call me his leopard woman.'

'Hmm,' says Tamara and looks over at Sara. 'And why did he do that, pray tell?'

'Well,' Liss giggles, 'because I get red spots on my face when I'm sexually aroused, and the spots spread over more and more of my body, until I'm completely covered. Sverre used to whisper in my ear: "let's go hunting". And when I come – I come with, well, the growl of a leopard, then the spots gradually disappear.'

'Wow, that's quite something,' says Eva.

'Yes, and the point is that now...'

'I can't get over these amazing potatoes,' interrupts Tamara before Liss has finished. She lifts up a piece of dark blue potato on her fork. 'Just imagine, some potatoes grow in Ringerike, and others grow in the Congo. Talk about diversity. When did you get that bracelet from Jakob? Recently?'

The red beach ball is bobbing about in the waves and the current is pulling it further and further out to sea. Liss will never be able to get hold of it. She closes her eyes, kicks off her tight shoes, puts her hands behind her back, leans back her head and listens to the others' voices in the distance. Eva's laughter, Sara's tapping heels. A faint click from Tamara's lighter.

They walk hand in hand along the beach. Just the two of them. Liss is wearing a long, sapphire blue silk dress and stilettos. The count walks at her side. No, wait a minute. It's not the count. It's a woman, a woman with dark blonde hair and nut brown eyes. And big dimples in her cheeks. She's wearing a long, ruby red velvet dress. She and Liss are walking arm in arm, talking. They are on holiday. Yes, they've gone on holiday together. Away from everything. To a country where they eat goose liver and Daim. They have gin and tonic with their cereal, which is crispy and has lots of raisins in it. In the evening they drink tea in front of the fire. They have travelled to a country where women are not bothered by periods. A country where stilettos don't sink in the sand. They are both wearing shoes with dizzyingly high heels that are as pointed as Samoyed snouts at the toe, but fortunately are as comfortable as Birkenstock sandals. The sun shines all the time (when it's not involved in picturesque sunsets and sunrises), but doesn't cause beads of sweat to glisten on the two women's noses or drip under their arms. The very fair woman and the darker blonde woman. Walking arm in arm on the sand. They have gone to a country where cloudberries grow between the palm trees. A country with great forests full of wild strawberries and orchids in all the colours of the rainbow. Forests where golden brown chanterelle and pink, bursting penises spring up side by side from the dark earth. And the two women are friends. They can talk about anything and everything. They support each other. They help each other. Liss' blue eyes looking into her brown ones.

Chapter 8

Sewing Circle at Sara's,
Tuesday 9 January

Menu
Maki rolls with cucumber and salmon, tuna and avocado, halibut and chilli
Beetroot consommé with water chestnuts and spring onions
Stilton soufflé
Tenderloin of pork with mango sauce
Ginger pears with tamarind coulis

Sara is standing by the worktop in the kitchen. After some years of hesitation, bolstered by Tamara's unwavering taste, Sara has decided that Stilton is, without a doubt, infinitely superior to other blue cheeses. Stilton is both sharper and stronger than Gorgonzola and Roquefort. If you first get a taste for Stilton, other cheeses seem tame by comparison. And as Sara managed to get hold of an exceptionally good piece at the delicatessen yesterday, she is now standing in the kitchen, by the shining white worktop, crumbling the Stilton on a plate with the help of a fork, the first step in the preparation of the third course, a Stilton soufflé, an impulse addition to her meticulously planned menu following her find at the cheese counter yesterday. Most of the work will, of course, have to be done later, as is always the case with soufflés, but she can at least make the béchamel sauce ready and mix in the egg yolks and cheese. The egg whites must, of course, not be added until the oven is just the right temperature and the guests are about halfway through the preceding course: beetroot consommé, which Sara has yet to make.

Sara cracks the first egg, lets the egg white run through her fingers into a porcelain bowl, which for two reasons has just been thoroughly washed. The first is Sara's relentless sense of cleanliness and the second is Sara's knowledge that even the smallest hint of fat can prevent egg whites from getting stiff. The egg yolk is left lying in the palm of Sara's hand. For a short while,

127

she finds the weight against her skin pleasing, certainly in no way displeasing, before allowing the yolk to slip into a white plastic bowl. She takes the next egg, separates the yolk and the white, lets the white run into the carefully washed porcelain bowl, and the yolk drop into the plastic bowl. Sara screams. She screams quite loudly. Because suddenly two yellow eyes are staring up at her. Round, shiny eyes without pupils, accusing and full of pain they look up at Sara from the white plastic bowl. Not leaving hers for a second, without blinking. Sara grips the edge of the worktop, and still manages to think that now some of the egg white on her hands will be left on the worktop, which she had of course washed, more or less disinfected, before starting to make food, only a few minutes ago. She closes her own eyes, counts to seven, but when she opens them again, another pair of eyes, a new pair is staring at her from the bowl. New, yellow eyes, glittering with desire. Or triumph, perhaps? The yellow eyes will not waver from Sara's brown eyes and she fumbles over the worktop with one hand to find something that feels like the fork she crumbled the cheese with, and with it she punctures a hole in the eyeballs, punctures the retina and the cornea. She stabs and stabs at the eyes in pure fear, then gradually calms down and starts to move the fork in circles round the bowl, so that the evil, the pain, the accusation, desire and triumph are all transformed into a yellow, foaming mass.

*

If anyone had asked her (but no one did, because Sara did not mention the yellow eyes to anyone), Sara would not have been able to say how she managed to leave the kitchen. But she must have done, because she finds and swallows three light blue pills in the bathroom before she sits down, still trembling, in front of the computer and starts to play Patience. She stays there while her body and mind slowly return to their natural balance. After seven games of Patience, of which the seventh, fortunately, was successful, Sara is still not ready to go back into the kitchen, but on reflection, she feels that she is able to open the file containing the novel that she is currently translating. This realisation prompts Sara to start whistling quietly. She opens the file, scrolls down to the last page, but is not able to start working. Sara sits there thinking. The two sets of yellow eyes are still glaring at her.

Sara stood close to Tamara. They both stood completely still. They both saw. Sara took a few seconds to make sense of what she was seeing. She remained motionless the whole time her brain was receiving this visual stimulation and the strange images were thrown back and forth between the two parts of her brain, until the cells in a practically unused corner at the bottom of the right hemisphere's parietal lobe finally found a category that fitted and could report back to the central switchboard what it was that Sara was seeing in the dark, warm room. She was numb, dizzy, stunned. At the same time that Sara was trying to understand what she was seeing, something she did not wish to understand, Sara registered a weak, but distinctive smell as she stood there in the doorway with her best friend, looking at what was going on in her parents' marital bed. The scent particles crept into her nose, which was by then already fairly large and hooked, and were swept back into Sara's head by the waving movements of the cilia in her nostrils, to the centre of nasal sensations, the olfactory bulb, where they were registered, but not recognised and so classified as unknown. The smell was then almost immediately linked to the newly interpreted images and as a result, Sara would, for the rest of her life, always associate the smell of sex with something unnerving and frightening.

Despite the fact that Sara sent a message to the muscles in her right hand, which remained motionless on the hammered brass door handle, that they should take action immediately, shut the door and thereby stop the scene that Sara was witnessing, she had to stand, against her will, in the same position for a few more endless seconds. Tamara was standing against the door itself. She seemed to be as paralysed as Sara herself had been but a few seconds ago. Sara's hand on the door handle did not have the strength needed to move the door with Tamara's weight on it.

With a sense of defeat and resignation, Sara felt her hand lose all sense of purpose as it slackly held on to the door handle.

This sense of defeat sank down through her body and had just formed a knot in her stomach, when Sara sees her mother's blue eyes. Her mother's eyes are half-closed, but they are looking straight into her oldest daughter's large, brown eyes, as she continues to move her body, as she continues to clasp her hands tight round the other person's hairy back, as she continues to keep her ankles and calves firmly wrapped around the other person's thighs that are alternately tensing, then relaxing. Her mother's eyes. Normally so big and helpless, often pleading. Now they are shiny. With desire? Triumph? Her mother continues to look at her and now Sara hears the noises, the noises that have been in the room from the start, but that have not reached her ears until now. In order not to see, but with her mother's low, half suppressed moans ringing in her ears, Sara moves her gaze upwards and fixes her eyes on her own smiling face and that of her three-year younger sister, which are suspended in a narrow, white wooden frame above the bed. Sara and Synne smiling beside a picture of her mother with a white veil and her father with a flower in his buttonhole. Powerless, in an attempt not to see, not to hear, to get away from the smell, Sara moves her eyes up even further. Sara looks at the ceiling with its yellow, varnished pine panels with dark knots in them, and she realises in a short rush of joy, that she can in fact shut her eyes, which she immediately does. A pattern of seven knots is fixed on her retina and she starts to count them. One, two, three, four, five, six, seven. Over and over. She is still counting when she feels Tamara stirring beside her and a sense of deep relief washes over her, together with the certainty that now, now it is over. In the space of a few short moments, the door is silently closed and Sara can see, hear and smell again. Sara can look at Tamara's brown hair, hear Tamara's quiet breathing, smell the scent of her hair. Sara's feet start to move and she follows the dark, bent head. She follows it into the woods, where the branches scratch her face. The whole time, she feels Tamara's hand on her upper arm.

But most of all, she remembers the cat's yellow eyes looking straight at her. Half-closed with pain, they looked straight at her. The whole time. Sara is frightened. And her mother's eyes. The black cat against the light birchwood. Like a black cross against a white background.

But Tamara is holding her tight and supporting her, so tight in fact that she has bruises on both sides of her arm for several days, but at the same time so supportive that Sara knows that she would not have coped without that hand. Tamara's grip round Sara's upper arm was so hard and therefore supportive that it takes Sara and Tamara nearly three decades to get over it.

There is an air of weariness about Sara when she gets up from the chair in front of the computer. Her hand knocks into Duden's German dictionary, which is pushed back across the shiny surface of the desk and hits the mouse, which causes the screen saver promptly to disappear from the screen and a page of the novel she is translating to appear. Sara looks down at the black letters on the white, gently flickering screen and recognises the tight cluster of adverbs that earlier on today had caused her to sit staring at the screen for a long time after the screen saver had been activated. But the clock at the bottom of the screen shows that the apparently hopeless, but for that very reason, tempting knot of long adverbs, finishing off with the past participle hinübergegangen, must now, without a doubt, be left in favour of preparations for the sewing club.

The chicken stock for the beetroot soup is simmering on the cooker and Sara peels the cooked beetroots quickly and efficiently with the help of a short handled vegetable knife. Just as she is about to remove the last remains of the thin brown skin, which after cooking almost comes off by itself, from the fourth beetroot, the knife slips and cuts deep into the soft skin between Sara's index finger and her thumb. The knife falls on to the worktop. It lies there, see-sawing, before settling beside the Rosenthal plate, where the already peeled beetroots have been placed in an orderly, elegant triangle. For a long time, with her still bleeding left hand pressed into her mouth like a bridle, her thumb resting against the lower curve of one of her cheekbones, she watches the blood from her hand mixing with the beetroot juice on the white worktop and thinks of Tamara.

A while ago, when Sara had turned to Tamara for comfort because she thought that Jakob was having an affair, Tamara had somehow given the wrong answer and something – Sara could not say what - about the way in which she answered has stayed with Sara ever since, like a fermenting uncertainty. Sara stares at the two red fluids on the worktop, but what she thinks she almost knows, slips away, perhaps falls down into one of the many small folds in the brain or right to the bottom of the sylvian groove and disappears in a pile of unanalysed feelings and other disjointed thoughts. Sara's concentration focuses on the beetroots again. First on the three perfectly peeled, naked beetroots that are resting on the white plate with a thin gold stripe round the edge, two of them darker than the third, which is the roundest and smallest. And then on the fourth, the nearly peeled beetroot that is lying on the worktop. The fall from Sara's hand onto the worktop has left a red mark on the white surface, and a red stripe shows where the beetroot has rolled, with purple-red liquid still seeping out of it, and by the round, red mark from the fall are drops of blood from the cut in her hand. The shapes in two different shades of red on the worktop are trying to tell Sara something. It is a sign. She hears an echo of her own shrill, high girl's voice. With her left hand still in her mouth, she bends down to look closer at the marks on the worktop and sees a flock of flying birds, a man in the background. Or is she mistaken, is it women and not birds that she sees, perhaps? Then Sara sees an old person staggering away, in a black waistcoat and white shirt, with a hunched back who dribbles as he stretches his arms up to Sara, and his nails are crinkled and yellow with age, he smiles at her, and there are scabs in the corners of his mouth. Sara moves her head back, but the old man immediately disappears into the red spots, she bends closer again and hears the signs whisper. She cannot hear what they are saying. Perhaps Tamara can help, thinks Sara. Tamara has always helped me.

Tamara has always been there. Tamara has always supported her.

Sara cannot imagine life without Tamara. Golden brown, slim and beautiful. Sara and Tamara have always been close, almost like sisters. Tamara has always helped her. When Sara had pelvic dysfunction and could barely move. When she was depressed after her father died. Tamara had taken care of all the practicalities in connection with the funeral. Tamara had protected her when they were inter-railing in Paris and were assaulted by some mad Americans. Tamara had helped when Sara completely unexpectedly lost her job as an interpreter. Tamara had always been there. Tamara who reluctantly told her about the rumours going round about her mother and helped her to understand. Tamara is so confident and sure of herself. Tamara always looks after her.

Sara looks at the beetroot on the worktop. She nearly always feels a quiet, calm pleasure in Eva's presence. Eva is happy and kind. And simple. A bit too fond of food. Rather overweight. Eva does not take things too seriously. Tamara did not want Eva to join the sewing circle. Sara had also protested, from force of habit and to support Tamara, who thought that Eva was a silly idea. But now Sara is glad that Eva has joined them. She is a stabilising factor, she will help them stay together. Because they have to stay together. Sara needs Tamara, and perhaps she even needs Liss and Eva. In fact, it is a paradox that the person who joined last will be the one who helps to ensure the sewing circle's longevity, but that is the way it is. They will always be sewing circle friends, the four of them, and Eva will make sure of that. An eternal four-leafed clover. Sara needs Tamara.

Liss has been with them since the start. No, not quite from the start, because it was Sara and Tamara who established the sewing circle. Their mothers were in a sewing circle and suggested that Tamara and Sara could also start one. There were seven of them and only two of Sara and Tamara. Seven mothers who had been meeting since they went to secondary school together. During the war. Both Tamara and Sara had been reared on stories of sewing circle friends who had altered old dresses, saturated with the smell of turnip steaks fried in cod-liver oil, behind blackout curtains. In their own sewing circle, there was only her and Tamara. 'Just the two of us, Sara,' Tamara had said. The others are so stupid. Or perhaps it was Sara who had wanted it that way. Yes, it was in fact Sara who wanted no one else. At least, that is what Tamara says, and you can trust what Tamara says. Tamara and Sara. But then Liss joined the sewing circle. Liss had to be a part of it. They had no choice. Sara could tell that Liss knew. That she must have seen what happened by the hut in the woods. 'Did you go through the woods?' Tamara had asked. Liss had made them wait for her answer. She had looked at them for a long time and then she had finally answered. 'Yes', Liss had replied. And her round, fair face had a knowing look, full of unspoken threats.

A vague feeling of tiredness trickles slowly down Sara's back and seeps into her pelvis, as she stands still bent over the mysterious signs and beetroots on the worktop. But before Sara can allow herself to straighten her back, and thereby relieve her pelvis, she has to count to seven. As soon as that is done, she stretches her back and with some embarrassment laughs at what she has tried to read in to the worktop's Rorschach figures, which she now wipes away with the snow-white, chlorine-scented dishcloth. She lifts up the fourth beetroot, which is to blame for everything. Her reason battles with the strong urge to throw them all away, buy new beetroots, or make another soup, saying that none of the beetroots came into direct contact with the blood. Sara closes her eyes. She feels the two emotions sloshing against each other inside her, like some great sea battle. It makes her feel nauseous, seasick, dizzy. But when she opens her eyes again, it is with the crystal clear conviction that all she needs to do is rinse the fourth beetroot thoroughly and then put all four in the pot so that they can be mashed, sieved and then mixed with the chicken stock. The joy that she feels in knowing that her rational side has won so easily, so swiftly and so totally over her irrational desire to throw away the beetroots, which Sara has known all along are not contaminated, makes her whistle cheerfully. It is a habit. Sara whistles when she has won over herself, and today she has conquered two egg yolks in a white plastic bowl and a rebellious beetroot and so has every reason to whistle. But to stop herself from getting carried away in a laughable, light funfair feeling with whirring merry-go-rounds, candyfloss, children's laughter and hurdy-gurdy music, Sara runs her right index finger along her nose bone. As expected, as soon as her finger touches her deformed, monstrous nose, she is pulled out of this fairground fantasy and into a more sober state, far more appropriate for preparing the tenderloin of pork with mango sauce.

When all the food has been made – the maki has been rolled and cut, the wasabi, soy sauce and pickled ginger put in three porcelain dishes, the beetroot soup has been sieved, the pork is in the oven, the mangoes pureed and the sauce thickened with cornflour, the pears have been cooked tender in ginger and the tamarind coulis is cooling in a crystal glass jug – there are only ten minutes left until the guests arrive. Despite having such a limited amount of time, Sara makes the heroic decision to try to untangle the knotted adverbs in the German translation, which is starting to be urgent, something that the publisher has not failed to remind her of in the past few days. But not today. Today Sara has purchased (that is to say asked Jakob to buy, which he immediately did) a phone like the one Tamara suggested that shows the number of the caller on a grey display screen in clear black digits. Today Sara has only answered the phone once. When it rang at lunch time. No number appeared on the granite-grey display field, only the message that the person calling Sara at that very moment had an undisclosed number. But when Sara lifted the receiver and said 'hallo', no one answered. In the course of the day, the phone has rung at least a dozen times more, and each time it was either an undisclosed number or the publisher's by now familiar number.

*

On the way over to the computer, which Sara has to admit does not look particularly tempting now, standing on the antique desk, full of complicated, unsolved linguistic problems, Sara goes over to the mirror that hangs between the windows. She inherited it from her great-aunt and it has a heavy gold frame with bunches of

135

grapes, chubby cherubs and vine leaves. Sara just wants to confirm quickly that nothing other than the usual is at fault with her appearance. She just wants to check that her hair is as it should be, that she does not have beetroot juice on her forehead or mango sauce on her cheeks. But in the cool shiny surface of the mirror, Sara can only see something huge, covered in pale, opened-pored winter skin rising out from the middle of her face like a pyramid. It takes a fraction of a second before Sara realises that it is herself she sees in the mirror, but then she notices the dark eyes on each side of the grotesquely large body part. She also recognises her own mouth, even though it is no more than a tightly-shut dark stripe under the imposing monstrosity. How could this have happened without her noticing it, completely unaware as she whistled and prepared a carefully composed menu, consisting of five courses, for her sewing circle friends?

Her heart starts to pound, her pulse starts to race. Sara is almost immediately overcome by doubt. It is a doubt that has plagued her many times before, the doubt that a muscle really can contract 75 times a minute, day in and day out, year after year, without even taking the tiniest break. Sara does not think that it is possible, she suspects that the striated muscle that is her heart is starting to wear out, burn out. She has the distinct feeling that her heart needs a break, a short pause, to catch breath, and she knows only too well what will happen the moment her heart decides to give up. Throw in the towel, as Tamara would have perhaps described it in her jaunty journalist jargon. Tamara has said that you have to take heart problems seriously. Maybe you should contact a heart specialist, Sara? Sara can feel that her heart muscle needs a rest right now, at this precise moment, that her heart, after many years, well over thirty, of loyal work has finally decided to take the holiday it undoubtedly deserves. That the coronary arteries around Sara's heart are starting to get blocked and when they collapse, the heart will have no fresh blood supply and then the end is unavoidable. As if in response to this realisation, Sara feels her heart beating faster and faster, her pulse must be well over 200 now. This must be what they call the final cramps, she thinks, and clearly feels the upper auricle on the left side of her heart is full and cannot take any more blood, whereas the left ventricle is pumping on empty. Her cardiac valves are flapping futilely in the uncontrolled flow of blood, her heart is hammering against her ribcage, which she can hear is about to break, collapse under the strain, and she knows that then it will be over. And when she realises that her time has come, that she will live no longer, the gold frame of the mirror from her great aunt starts to swell and the frame becomes pocked. Boils and tumours start to grow under the gold leaf that get bigger and bigger until they finally burst and something forces its way up from under the thin layer of gold, first in one place, and then in several, until the whole frame is covered in burst, overflowing tumours. With disgust, Sara sees something furry emerging from the gold leaf, something that she soon recognises as heads with bristling fur, more and more, sharp triangular ears that unfold and half-closed eyes, yellow and spiteful that stare at Sara. The mouths are open, but not a sound is to be heard. The sitting room is as quiet as it has been all day. The only thing Sara can hear is the faint humming of her computer, but otherwise all is still. Then the doorbell rings.

'Thank goodness, I hoped it was you,' Sara says, practically throwing herself round Tamara's neck, trembling in a cold sweat, but at least her heart is still pounding. She has been saved by Tamara. Yet again. Sara cannot survive without Tamara.

'Oh sweetie,' says Tamara. 'What's the matter? Smells delicious in here, by the way. Don't cry, Sara, I'll look after you. I'll always look after you. Sorry, what was that? Cats? Where? No, pull yourself together now. I'm here now. Everything will be fine. Where have you been all day? I've been trying to phone you to see whether I should bring red or white wine, but there was no answer.'

Long before the other guests come, Sara has regained complete control. The quiet, confidential chat that she and Tamara managed to squeeze in before the other two girls arrived, a light blue pill and a large glass of wine, have all had the desirable effect. Tamara has helped her. Tamara has saved her. And there are lots of people with ex-directory numbers. Sara does not want to think about it now. And Emma couldn't know that Sara was scared of cats. Of course she had only meant well when she gave her the picture of a cat. And as for Jakob and Tamara, that was no doubt only her imagination. Sara has always had an overactive imagination. Sara does not want to think about Jakob and Tamara now.

All three kinds of sushi tasted delicious. Tamara praised Sara's sushi and asked why Sara had not pickled the ginger herself. It was quite a simple process, Tamara said, and kindly explained to Sara the basics of Japanese ginger pickling. Sara listened, nodded and smiled. Then Tamara gave a detailed account of an article she had just written for the Saturday paper. About Zen architecture. Liss, Eva and Sara listened and nodded and smiled. Tamara told them about Emma who is exceptionally good at writing essays. 'Must run in the family,' says Tamara. Emma is very good. She is the editor of the school magazine now. Liss, Eva and Sara listen, nod and smile. Sara is fully aware that Tamara can be quite domineering, that she takes up a lot of space, talks a bit too much about herself, interrupts others a bit too often. At least, when there are more people there than just Tamara and herself. But Tamara is not really like that. Tamara is kind and soft and agreeable and Sara needs her. Sara must listen and smile. Over the years, Sara has had to do quite a lot to keep hold of Tamara.

Liss helps Sara to clear away the chopsticks, the small dishes and the wooden Japanese boards. Liss carries in the soup bowls and Sara carries in the large soup tureen. Sara serves the beetroot soup in the white soup tureen she inherited from her mother. Sara visits her mother every Thursday. She does it out of duty.

'Bon appetit, ladies,' Sara says, when everyone has been served.
    'What a fantastic colour,' Tamara says. Sara knows that Tamara loves red.

As soon as Sara touches the handle, the door opens. Her mother is standing just inside the door. Her mother stretches out her arms, she looks like a dark cross in the doorway, against the light from the sitting room. Like a dark cross against a white background. 'Sara, where have you been? It's past eight o'clock.' Her mother's voice is low, but it is trembling slightly. 'Mother,' says Sara. 'It's only two minutes past and I'm here now,' says Sara and goes straight into her mother's arms. Sara could see that her mother had been crying. Her eyes had been red and wet. Mother has such helpless eyes. They are so big and blue. Sara's mother is very small and thin. Her skin is strawberries and cream, like a porcelain doll. 'I promise I'll be on time next time,' says Sara and gives her mother another hug.

*

No one else has to be home as early as Sara and Synne. They are always the last ones in the class to start wearing sandals in spring and the first to wear tights in autumn. Sara and her little sister are given cod liver oil every evening and they are not allowed to do downhill skiing, because it is too dangerous.

Right after the winter break, in class three, Sara, Tamara and the rest of the class are going to go to a camp. They are going to visit the Children's Farm and the whole class is looking forward to it. Sara loves animals so much, all kinds of animals, and she is sure that no one is more excited about it than her. She is looking forward to trying to milk a cow, she is looking forward to riding. She's going to collect eggs and play with the cats and rabbits. But then in the middle of the winter break, her mother says that she can't go after all. It is too dangerous. 'I'm scared that something might happen to you, Sara. You might have an accident in the barn. You might be bitten or gored. You can't go, Sara,' says Mother. Sara's mother's big blue eyes fill up with tears and soon they are silently overflowing. 'I won't have a moment's peace, Sara.' Sara strokes her mother's hair. Sara's mother carefully dries her tears with her hand. 'Please Mother, please let me go.' But her mother only cries. 'I'll be so worried, Sara.' Sara wants to go so much, but she does not want her mother to suffer either. They sit close together on the sofa and hold each other. Finally they agree that Sara's mother will go too. 'Isn't that a good solution, Sara?' Her mother rings the teacher and Sara goes to the camp with her mother. 'Mother has come to help the teacher,' says Sara. Not that anyone would dare to tease Sara, but she and her mother have agreed that that is what they can say. Mother and Sara have a secret. The week at the Children's Farm is over far too fast.

But then the autumn that Sara turned eleven, Sara suddenly stopped listening to her mother. She looked pleadingly at Sara with her big, blue doll's eyes, but to no effect, and tears ran down her strawberries and cream porcelain skin in vain. Sara's mother opened her arms and stood like a black cross against the light in the doorway, but Sara did not run into her mother's arms. Sara stopped liking animals as well. It was good that Sara had Tamara. Sara needs Tamara more than ever now.

'I bought some new skis yesterday,' Liss says. 'What a delicious soup, Sara!'

'I didn't know you were a keen skier, Liss,' Tamara remarks, immediately.

'I'm not really, but Mona and Martin want me to go skiing with them sometime. And for some reason, the shop assistant asked...'

'Was he young and handsome?' Tamara wants to know.

'Of course,' Liss says. 'Blond hair, pink cheeks and about 2 metres tall. Well, for some reason, he asked me how much I weighed.'

'Why on earth did he do that?' exclaims Eva. 'I'm never going to buy skis in that shop.'

'Something to do with the bindings, apparently,' Liss replies. 'Where they go and things like that. I was a bit embarrassed so I whispered how many kilos.'

'And he repeated it in a loud voice,' Tamara guesses.

'No, no. He was a polite young man,' answers Liss. 'But I did feel pretty stupid all the same. So, to cheer myself up a bit, I jokingly asked him if he'd like to know my age as well.'

'What did he say?' Sara asks.

'He laughed and said no. And then he said – as a joke too – that I was of course 29, because that's what you say, isn't it. At first I smiled, but then I thought it was awful. It wasn't funny at all that he obviously thought that I was nowhere near 29. In fact that I was old enough to make 29 amusing.'

'You have my deepest sympathy,' Eva says. 'Fantastic beetroot soup, Sara. What are the small round things?'

'Water chestnuts,' Tamara says.

'Girls! We are ageing. We are on the decline. We just have to accept that we are old,' Sara says.

'Yes,' Tamara agrees. 'We've reached that age when all compliments are modified. Before they said, "you're so beautiful", now they say "you look fantastic for your age". Or imply that you're doing well for your age. Or that you've got a great body, considering that you've had x number of children.'

'And in a few years, we will see men we went to school with turning round to look at our daughters, but not even gracing us with a glance,' Sara laments.

'What a thought,' Liss says.

'Yes, and when you stop being young, you suddenly become youthful, have you ever noticed that?' asks Eva.

'Oh yes,' sighs Tamara. 'That happens when your age is roughly the same as your body temperature.'

Sara is lying on her stomach beside Jakob in their double bed, on the white sheets that she bought in a well-known shop in Dresden, famous for its bed linen. She searches every part of her body desperately trying to find that overwhelming tiredness she felt when the alarm clock rang this morning, when she sat up in bed, half dead. She tries in vain to recall the wish that she had the last time she was in this bed, the desire to sleep forever, but even though she searches in every nook and cranny of her body, she can find no tiredness and she knows that she will lie there, sleepless. Jakob is lying with his back to her. She can hear from his breathing that he is not asleep either, even though he is pretending that he is. Sara counts to seven before stretching out the arm that has been squashed under the weight of her body, towards him, towards Jakob, but before she touches his lower back, in a flash she knows that he is thinking about his lover. Jakob is thinking about Tamara. Because that is the truth. Tamara is Jakob's lover. Sara is swept from her double bed and Jakob by a tidal wave of grief and impotence, she closes her eyes, paddles with her arms, careful not to disturb Jakob with her splashing, Sara feels the water running down her cheeks and suddenly tastes salt in her mouth. She lies there like this for a while, thinking, as her face gets wetter and wetter. Sara thinks about many things. Who is it who keeps phoning Sara and then hanging up? Sara thinks about Tamara. She thinks about Kristian. She remembers Kristian well. He had such a lovely smile, almost naïve. Sara remembers that Kristian carried on smiling, even though his eyes were unbearably sad, after she had told him that it was over. Kristian had a sailing boat and he loved taking his girlfriends – not that he had had many before – out onto the fjord. He loved wild flowers and once he had picked a big bunch, written down the names of all the flowers on small cardboard labels and attached them to the right stems. Kristian had a real sweet tooth, like Sara. He loved sweet desserts, chocolate and rich cakes. White bread and honey. 'You pigs, you two had better watch out or you'll end up looking like one,' said Tamara to Sara and Kristian. Kristian loved white wine and shellfish. And so does Sara. It is a shame that it had to finish. They had so much fun together, all three of them. Tamara, my best friend, thinks Sara. I need Tamara.

With a corner of the sheet that she knows Tamara has tumbled with pleasure on, Sara dries her face. She does not want to cry any more. The whole thing with Kristian was a long time ago. And she is probably just imagining everything with Jakob and Tamara. Sara knows that she has an unfortunate tendency to imagine things, to see things that do not exist. Tamara has said that it is not normal. Sara dries her tears. She decides to stop imagining things. Of course there is nothing going on between Jakob and Tamara.

*

In Sara's beside table drawer, right at the back, is a half-eaten bag of peanuts. Sara loves nuts. She eats a lot of nuts. But always in secret.

Sara does a lot to keep hold of Tamara.

142

Chapter 9

Sewing Circle Weekend in Copenhagen, Friday 9 February

The four ladies have just been shown to their table by the maître d'hôtel and now a black and white-clad waiter heads over to them. Lovely ladies, all four of them. A couple of them are even quite beautiful, as far as he can see, though his eyesight is not what it used to be. Nice clothes. Probably thirty something. Pleasant voices. Obviously a sophisticated party. The tall blonde caught his attention first. He noticed her fine posture as she walked over to the table. Looks like she has fabulous breasts too, and he certainly knows how to appreciate them. And then there are two dark-haired women and a bubbly darker blonde. Was it Swedish they were speaking?

'Good evening, ladies,' he says, bowing slightly, and when the ladies return his greeting and order their drinks, he hears that they are Norwegian. The darker blonde talks to him in Danish, but speaks Norwegian to the ladies round the table. He places a menu, in a large leather folder, in front of each of them, then he looks at the very blonde one as he says:

'We have an à la carte menu. We also have a set three-course meal. However, I would like to recommend our eight-course dinner.'

The ladies discuss it. The waiter runs through all the courses in the eight-course menu, gets the drinks the ladies have ordered, lights a cigarette for one of the dark ones. Beautiful eyes, but far too thin for his liking. He leaves the menus on the table and withdraws to let the ladies decide in peace. When he approaches the table again, it sounds like they have agreed:

'I think the eight-course dinner sounds tempting,' the darkest one says, the one with almost black hair and big eyes.

'Won't it be too expensive?' asks the blonde one.

'But we're here to enjoy ourselves,' the slightly chubby darker blonde replies.

'We'll take the eight-course dinner, all of us,' says the other dark one and nods at the waiter.

'Excellent,' the waiter says. 'And drinks? Should I choose what I think is most suitable? In the mid-price range?'

'Yes please,' the black-haired one replies.

'Thank you,' the waiter says. 'May I recommend a champagne with the halibut?'

'Yes, champagne sounds delightful, don't you think, girls?'

'Yes, yes. We have to have champagne. We're here to celebrate, after all.'

'You ladies are celebrating?' enquires the waiter. 'May I ask what you are celebrating?'

'Friendship! Girl power!' the darker blonde explains, the one who answers in Danish.

'We are celebrating ourselves,' says one of the dark ones.

'The twenty-fifth anniversary of our sewing circle!' the blonde, beautiful one says. 'Could I have another gin and tonic, please.'

The restaurant is tastefully decorated, with nougat-coloured walls, cream tablecloths and lots of spotlights on the ceiling. And when she turns in her chair to look around, Liss sees smiles and well-groomed heads everywhere. She hears people chatting, laughing, eating and raising their glasses at all the tables, like an even, comforting blanket of sound. But Liss needs an extra gin and tonic.

First course: Quails' eggs in port jelly

Liss has a miniature white plate in front of her. On it are two small eggs, like a couple of round, noble testicles. They are surrounded by brown, diced port jelly. Liss has to smile.

'What a sweet plate, girls. It reminds me of a doll's tea set I had when I was little,' she says. 'And the cute little eggs. They taste good too. I've never had quails' eggs before.'

'Really? Never?' Tamara says.

'Yes, it is a bit like being at a doll's tea party,' Sara says. 'It is a while since I was at the last one.'

'I remember I had one of those lovely sleeping dolls with curly hair and painted-on shoes,' says Eva.

'I had a teddy bear that I loved. A grey-blue teddy bear,' Liss says and pops another bit of egg in her mouth.

'Did you?' asks Tamara in a kind voice.

'Mm,' Liss answers. 'A teddy bear with practically no fur. I'd more or less worn it out. It went everywhere with me.'

'Lovely wine,' Tamara says. 'Very fruity.'

'And have your children got it now?' Eva asks. 'Tastes good with this sherry jelly.'

'Port jelly,' corrects Tamara.

'No, sadly it just disappeared one day,' Liss says. 'I came home from school and it was gone.'

'That is sad,' Sara says.

*

Liss thought the quail eggs were delicious, even though there was only a mouthful – an 'amuse-gueule' as the waiter had said. And the wine was lovely. Eva was sitting beside Liss and Liss couldn't remember seeing her like this before. Eva sat straight in her chair without leaning back and beamed liked a hostess. She talked and laughed, pointed and gesticulated. Eva has such lovely dimples. She told them about Copenhagen, curiosities and funny stories, shopping, sightseeing and the history of the town. It all just flowed out of her, sometimes she switched to Danish when repeating something that someone had said. Sara and Tamara were sitting beside each other as always. Confident and beautiful, side by side, generally listening to Eva. Sara leans in towards Tamara, a white cigarette between her lips. Sara with the starry eyes. Tamara immediately picks up Sara's elegant silver lighter from the table and lights her cigarette. Sara and Tamara smile. The smile that excludes everyone else, the smile that Liss has seen Sara and Tamara smile at each other for more than 25 years. Thousands upon thousands of knowing, private smiles, only for each other. For those in the know, those who are different from the others. Darker and prettier.

Liss looks around the restaurant. People dressed up in nice clothes everywhere, glittering and sparkling necklaces in one corner, an expensive bracelet catching the light in another. The men's shirtfronts were blinding white, the ladies had colourful tops in silk and velvet. There were candles and tempting beautifully prepared food, red nail varnish and big cigars. Gleaming wineglasses, green bottles. Busy waiters with steaming plates on outstretched arms, held high in the air. The restaurant was full of sounds and smells, colour and movement. It was full of anticipation and joy, comfort and pleasure. It should feel like reading a romantic novel or dreaming a dream, thinks Liss. Liss likes books and dreams, but she can't let go. She hears Sara's laughter in her ear, but she doesn't catch what the girls are laughing at. Is Liss the only one who feels a bit nervous, almost frightened? She looks down at the tiny plate, which is now empty. Just like the doll's tea set she had when she was little, she thinks again. She is in the sitting room at home. It's summer. Liss is sitting on Mummy's lap on the green velvet sofa. The smell of freshly baked bread wafts in from the kitchen. Fantastic mother, fantastic housewife. Everyone admires Liss' mother. Liss feels her lips against her crown, moving, whispering pet names. 'Little Liss, my treasure. Mummy's little girl.' But Liss knows that it's coming, no matter what. She gets scared. The sun streams in through the newly cleaned windows, marking out a square on the floor. Liss is frightened. Liss doesn't dare to turn round and look at Mummy. Because what if it isn't Mummy? What if it's the lady with the red, angry mouth and the black shoes? Bamse is in her bedroom. Liss hums to herself. 'Little Liss, Mummy's little girl. You and me, Liss. You and me.' Liss hums and doesn't dare, can't turn round.

And then came the day when Bamse wasn't there waiting for her when she got home from school. Mummy's big, red mouth comforted her, said they were sure to find him again, and that maybe Liss was too big to have a teddy bear in bed.

'Here's to the sewing circle,' Eva says. 'And here's to wonderful Copenhagen!'

'Cheers,' responds Sara and raises her glass.

'Cheers,' Tamara and Liss say at the same time. No one looks at Liss.

Tamara hears her own and Liss' voice say cheers at the same time and she thinks of Liss' grey-blue teddy bear. For some reason or another, Tamara feels a faint twinge, a mild irritation in her diaphragm. But it vanishes before she's able to grasp what it is. Does she feel sorry for Liss? Eva is telling a funny story about someone who went to school with her and who now lives in Kristiania. Everyone laughs. Liss' teddy bear disappears from Tamara's mind again.

Second course: Thai consommé with Kamchatka crab

Tamara sips her wine. Sara is sitting beside her. All their lives, Sara has sat beside Tamara. Sara is wearing a white sweater. Definitely expensive. She looks like an angel. A white angel in a fitted designer sweater with a plunging neckline. Tamara sees Sara in another white sweater. Sara with dark pigtails in toggles. Tamara is in her room. She is sitting on her desk looking out of the window. Her doll is lying on the floor. And beside her is a suitcase of doll's clothes. The case is open and the clothes are spread out all over the floor. Earlier in the day, Sara and Tamara had played families. Sara wanted to be mother, as usual, so Tamara had to be the father. Sara has such big, dark eyes. 'I don't like being the father,' says Sara. Every time. And Sara knows what she wants.

Tamara is sitting on her desk looking down into the garden. She's not allowed to sit up there, but does it all the same. Sometimes Tamara likes doing things she's not supposed to do. Philip is in the garden. He's asleep in his pram. It's made of dark red corduroy and was Tamara's when she was little. A long time ago. The pram is standing in the shade and there is a kind of net over it. Mummy has explained that it's there to stop wasps getting in and stinging Philip. At the bottom of the garden, under the tree with wild cherries that Daddy says even the birds don't want, sits a girl. She looks small from up here, but she's big. It's Sara, and Tamara and Sara are the same age. They are six and half. Sara has black pigtails with new toggles. Tamara has brown plaits with ordinary red hairbands. Sara is all huddled up, crouching. A thin back in a white sweater. It's shaking a little. Tamara knows that it's because Sara is crying. Tamara knows that Sara is crying because of Tamara. It's me who made Sara cry, thinks Tamara. She hides behind the curtains with butterflies on.

'Tamara?' Sara touches Tamara's shoulder and leaves her hand there. Tamara tilts her head, for a brief moment she presses her cheek against Sara's slim hand. Sara and Tamara get up and Tamara follows Sara's dark head upstairs to the toilet. A beautiful room with grey tiles and white cala lilies in high vases. They each disappear into a cubicle. Tamara hears that they start to pee at exactly the same time. Sara finishes just after, but Tamara waits to leave the cubicle until Sara has flushed. Suddenly Tamara feels a rush of warmth and goodwill towards Sara. The tinkle in the neighbouring toilet bowl sounded so innocent and childish, almost pathetic. Just like Emma when she was little, thinks Tamara. The sound of that little stream the first times Emma sat solemnly on the big, cold grown-up toilet and her potty had been carried down into the cellar forever. Sara, my best friend. Sara has small feet with a high instep. She has a slim back and big eyes. The skin over her temples is delicate and transparent and her blood vessels make an elegant pattern, reminiscent of a faded tattoo. When she is frightened or stressed by something, one of the blood vessels on her left temple swells up. Tamara likes to see Sara's blood vessels swell with fear.

They stand side by side and wash their hands. The taps are sensory-activated and the water starts automatically when you put your hands under them. Lavender soap. No paper towels, of course, but soft, folded cloths to dry your hands on. The lighting is discreetly low. This is not a place for young people. This is a restaurant for people who have been earning good money for many years. Tamara applies some lipstick. She looks at the faces in the mirror. We're beautiful. We look the same. Sara's hair curls nicely behind her ears. Sara takes out an eyeliner and makes a new, thin black line across the bottom lid of her eyes. Tamara waits. We look like each other, she thinks. Like sisters. We are more than just friends, Sara and I.

Sara leans in towards the mirror and outlines her lips with a pencil before finding her lipstick and painting her lips dark red. She bought the dark red lipstick at Gardermoen earlier on today. But she didn't pay for the perfume. Tamara saw her slipping it into her bag. Tamara remembers when they were sixteen and three serious men in suits came towards them. When they found the eyeshadow in Sara's pocket, Sara looked at Tamara and made her say that it was her who had stolen it. But Tamara hadn't even known about it. Later, Tamara couldn't say anything and just had to accept the serious men's contempt for her for blaming her friend and putting the stolen goods in her pocket. Tamara said nothing. When Sara looks at Tamara, she can never say no. And the men didn't for a moment believe that it was Sara, with her big eyes and fair skin, who was the thief. Of course they didn't think that. Sara always looks so white and innocent. Like an angel. And afterwards, Tamara greedily savoured Sara's admiration and Sara's gratitude. Gobbled it down. Just as she swallowed Sara's certainty that Tamara would always help. But on Sara's sheets, Tamara swallows other things. Greedily in large mouthfuls.

Sara is still not finished with her lips and is now applying lipgloss with a small brush. Tamara waits. Tamara looks at one of Sara's ears. The left one that is turned towards Tamara. There's a plaited gold earring in her earlobe. It looks like the earrings Tamara got from Håvard just before they split up. Just before they separated. Tamara loved Håvard.

Sara powders her nose. Her beautiful, straight nose with the fine curving nostrils. Sara's ear is still facing Tamara. That earring. She got it from Jakob. Suddenly Tamara has the urge to rip it out of her ear, rip it so the skin tears. Ripe it off so that the earlobe splits and opens out to each side, like Tamara opens her legs for Jakob. Tamara smiles. If only you knew, Sara, but you haven't got a clue. I'm the one fooling you now, Sara. I'm smarter than you. Jakob lies between my thighs, Sara. That clumsy man of yours shoots his sperm into my vagina on your sheets. Into my mouth. Drunk with desire he groans ridiculous rubbish in my ear. Rubbish that I swallow greedily. And you know nothing. Tamara smiles at her best friend and together they walk down the stairs. Shoulder to shoulder. Tamara's brown hair mixing with Sara's black hair. Now it's me who decides, Sara.

'You have returned at just the right moment, ladies. A spicy delight awaits you,' says the waiter when Sara and Tamara arrive at the table. He gives them a friendly smile and points at the steaming, scented faience bowls.

'Crab consommé. With red and green chilli, fresh ginger and a hint of garlic. Bon apetit!'

They eat the soup. Tamara is silent and hungry. She loves spicy food. Tamara is in a good mood. And in her bag is the thick little book with the black velvet cover.

Sara normally likes Thai food and she admires the golden colour of the soup and the large pieces of red and white crab meat. But the soup will be too spicy for her. She can see that. Is it only her bowl that has so much chilli? There are lots of pieces of red and green chilli and masses of chilli seeds floating in Sara's soup. Sara counts. One, two, three, four. She can see nine seeds floating on the surface. Nine. That is not a lucky sign. Cautiously she lifts her spoon to her mouth to test. The soup feels like a corroding agent as it slips down her oesophagus. She knew it. It is far too spicy. Sara does not feel comfortable. She checks her pulse. It is alarmingly high.

Palate cleanser: Thyme sorbet

No, Sara is not happy. Ever since she walked under the awnings and through the solid wooden double doors into the restaurant, Chez Jean Pierre, on one of the wide boulevards in Fredriksberg, Sara has been conscious of a feeling of discomfort sneaking round her body. Sara knows that the room they are sitting in is large and very elegant, but she thinks it is so in a dismissive and arrogant way. The walls are dirty brown with some innocuous, abstract black and white lithographs. The waiter is always creeping around their table, which is covered in a light, patterned damask tablecloth and set with glass cover plates and heavy silver cutlery. He is short with a disproportionately large torso, bow legs, dressed in black trousers with a sharp crease and patent leather shoes which, on the basis of the man's stealthy approach, Sara assumes have rubber soles. He must be heading for retirement from the Danish restaurant business. His thin hair is combed over his liver-spotted crown and his piercing eyes look unnaturally large behind the thick, concave lenses of his glasses. Sara does not like him.

Nor did Sara like the two quails' eggs that were served as the first course. She simply cannot stomach eggs any more. She knows that all eggs conceal yellow eyes. But Sara chewed and swallowed bravely and the yellow eyes made their way down into Sara's digestive system. While Sara talked to Eva, who is unusually chatty this evening, the quails' eyes reached the heaving muscles of her stomach and Sara used both her hands to try to smooth the sensation of undergoing a bizarre gastroscopic examination. Then Liss started to hum on the other side of the table. Liss was humming. Liss sometimes does that and Sara does not like it. The old, hunchbacked man, the yellow eyes making their way through her body, Eva's incessant chatter, Tamara's unusual silence and now Liss' humming. It is almost unbearable. But Sara says nothing.

The women eat the palate cleanser, a small scoop of thyme sorbet, served in a high stemmed metal bowl, with a sprig of thyme on top. To cleanse the palate and allow the taste buds to rest after the spicy Thai soup with two types of chilli, explained the waiter. 'Now you can rest for while, ladies,' he said as he left the table with what was probably supposed to be a joking and cheerful smile on his thin-lipped, old-man's mouth.

Tamara, as always, is sitting beside Sara. Sara can feel the warmth of Tamara's body, she can smell the lavender soap from her newly washed hands, she feels the ripple in the air when Tamara shakes her shiny brown hair. Sara feels the sofa cushion moulding to Tamara's movements when she changes position, when she crosses one leg over the other.

Suddenly Liss' voice pierces through the dense noise that fills the restaurant, the noise of strange voices, Eva's loud stories, grating laughter, the scraping of cutlery on porcelain. Despite the fact that Sara is certain that Liss has uttered a grammatically correct Norwegian sentence, she is unable to decode Liss' words so that they make up a comprehensible unit. Sara has registered the nouns astrology and personality type, both frequently used words in Liss' vocabulary, but the verb and the rest of the sentence must have got lost. Perhaps the missing words are still making their way past the anvil in her ear, or have got caught on the stirrup bones or are still beating on one of Sara's ear drums.

Sara sees that Tamara almost imperceptibly glances over at her and winks, she feels Tamara's warm breath on her cheek and hears her whispering something. Sara hears nothing. But this time, despite the fact that she cannot catch the words, Sara is still able to interpret what is being said. More than thirty years' experience of talking behind people's backs and the character assassination of friends means that Sara can easily reconstruct Tamara's poisonous barbs about how childish Liss is. But Sara does not answer Tamara. Sara wants to sit quietly at the restaurant table and think. Sara wants to eat her sorbet.

Sara thinks about Tamara. Sara thinks about Kristian. As so often before. And recently, more often than before. When Sara thinks about Kristian, she feels sad. Sara moves a few centimetres to the left on the restaurant sofa. Away from Tamara. Kristian with his sailing boat and wild flowers. Kristian who loved sweet things, desserts and cakes. Sara remembers Kristian well. He had such a lovely smile, almost naïve. Sara remembers how Kristian carried on smiling, even though his eyes were vulnerable and sad when she told him it was over. They had thought of getting married. It's a shame it had to end. They had so much fun together, all three of them. Tamara, my best friend, thinks Sara. I need Tamara.

Kristian had some very positive sides that were apparent to all, but only Sara saw the less favourable sides as well. Kristian was possessive, he was jealous and could be quite domineering. And he was not the most faithful man, either.

In the end, Sara felt compelled to tell Tamara about these sides of Kristian. 'I know that you think that Kristian is perfect, but there is no one I care about as much as you, Tamara,' Sara said. 'There is something I have to tell you,' Sara said.

It was only a few months before the wedding and Sara was round at Tamara's to help with the guest list. Sara was, of course, going to be chief bridesmaid. 'He's actually made a pass at me on several occasions,' Sara said. She tried to be as gentle as possible. 'I've thought about it and gone over it again and again, and I thought you should know before it was too late. Before you get married.' Sara offered to tell Kristian, if Tamara could not face it. Tamara could not face talking to Kristian. So it was Sara who had to tell him that there would be no wedding for him and Tamara.

Tamara had broken down completely. Was he really like that, she sobbed. 'Oh sweetheart,' Sara had said and hugged her tight.

Sara started to think about Carlos. Tamara met Carlos when she was studying journalism at college. Carlos was clever, always gallant and polite to Sara. The dream man. He used to invite both of them out. Carlos had an old black bicycle and when they had finished their meal or been for a drink or to the cinema, or perhaps an exhibition, Carlos would kiss Sara's hand, Tamara would give her a hug and Sara would be left alone on the pavement while Carlos cycled off with Tamara sitting on the rack. Tamara would hold her legs out to each side and point her toes like a ballet dancer, her dark hair flowing in the wind behind her. They looked so happy. It was a shame that Carlos and Tamara had to split up. Carlos had his faults too. It was such a shame that Tamara was always so blind when it came to men. Tamara had been very upset by the break-up with Carlos. Just as Tamara had been upset when it finished with Lars and with Henrik. And that time with Harald. Long ago. Tamara was heartbroken every time. It was good thing that Sara was there to comfort her. Tamara has never been very good at keeping hold of her men. It ends after only a few months. Every time. It's too close, too intense, there is no room for anyone else. Sara has to step in. Put her right, point out her boyfriend's bad sides. Sara has to do it every time. It is a shame that Tamara is always so blind. But it is a good thing that Sara is there to help her.

Tamara and Håvard. Tamara took the divorce very badly. Sara rubs her nose, her big nose, against the skin of her forearm and thinks about Håvard. Tamara's ex-husband. Emma's father. Tamara and Håvard had a good marriage. At least, to begin with. She saw that they were very close. Far too close. There was nearly no room for anyone else. There was nearly no room for Sara. It was a good thing that Sara could tell Tamara what Håvard was really like. It is a good thing that Sara is there to help sometimes. Because Tamara is so blind when it comes to men. It is terrible that it had to end in separation and divorce. Sara had tried to step in earlier. Before they went as far as getting married. But Tamara would not listen to her. It was the first time Tamara did not listen to Sara. And later Tamara admitted that she should have listened to her. Sara had comforted and forgiven her.

Sara knows that she could not manage without Tamara. She has always been there. She has always taken care of Sara. Sara cannot manage without Tamara. Tamara must always be there.

*

Over the years, Sara has had to go to great lengths to keep hold of Tamara.

Sara looks down. Her sorbet is finished now. Only a stiff, small twig of thyme remains in the metal dish. Dry and inedible.

At exactly the same time, on the other side of the table, Eva also looks down into her dessert bowl. Nearly empty. She runs her spoon around the edges and licks off the last remains of ice. It was so good. Imagine coming up with the idea of using herbs to make a sorbet, she thinks enthusiastically. Eva looks around. Looks like the others have finished too, with only a small sprig of thyme sticking up from all the bowls. A sweet little twig with small, green, round leaves. Maybe she should gather them together, make a small bunch and pop it in her bag. A souvenir from this evening. She should make a crown of thyme. Like a crown of laurels. She could wear it round her neck, lift her arms above her head and walk around with the applause thundering in the background.

The waiter comes and clears away the dishes and spoons. Eva smiles at him. She doesn't need the sprigs of thyme. And anyway, they're far too small.

Third course: Tomato, herb and two cheese millefeuille

Eva is happy. She is pleased with the choice of restaurant. Chez Jean Pierre is just as she'd imagined. And Eva has imagined this evening many, many times. The interior is light, with beautiful brown walls and warm tones. Stylish and sophisticated, but not a minimalist wasteland. Light-coloured tablecloths, happy people. Eva wants to embrace them all. There are large appealing black and white prints on the walls. There are spotlights in the ceiling. It's full of small, bright points. Like stars, thinks Eva. I want to swim in the stars. I want to eat the sweet air. Eva wants to fly between small white clouds, as light and sweet as candyfloss. She wants to swim in the soft, dark warm night air, parting the shining stars like phosphorescence.

Eva looks at Tamara. Tamara is as beautiful as ever. No, even more beautiful. Eva thinks that Tamara keeps looking over at her. That she is waiting for her, Eva, to say something. All the girls look happy and satisfied. This is the start of a successful evening. And this evening is the start of Eva and Tamara.

'Here you are, ladies,' says the waiter. The charming old waiter. 'Course number three. A tomato, herb and two cheese millefeuille. Mozzarella and chèvre. I hope that you enjoy it. Bon appetit,' he says and Eva thinks that he winks at her as he puts down her plate.

In front of Eva is a tall, artistic construction. It's a pleasure to look at. There are three layers, built up with crispy, golden puff pastry. On the bottom layer of pastry, there are tiny pieces of tomato and herbs, the next is covered with a white, creamy cheese, which Eva assumes is the white goat's cheese and on the top layer are small pieces of something that must be mozzarella. Then right on top balances another thin, almost transparent sheet of the same crispy, golden puff pastry. The whole tower has been showered in herbs.

Eva is delighted by the sight. It looks delicious, but the moment she reaches out her fork to start eating, the tower crashes down into a pile of cheese and pastry flakes.

*

Eva lets the girls eat for a few minutes, but she can't contain herself any longer. She taps her glass, half stands up and then sits down again.

'Well, as we are all here in Copenhagen, my childhood home, I have something to tell you.'

'Oh,' Sara looks up in surprise.

'You see, there is a very special reason why I wanted us to come here.'

'You wanted? I thought we all agreed,' Tamara says.

'Because it was here, in Royal Copenhagen, that it all started. A man and a woman met. It was the middle of the Swinging Sixties. They were both Norwegian. She was visiting a sister who was married in Denmark and he was on a six-week exchange programme with work. They fell madly in love.'

'How romantic,' sighs Liss.

'The sharp taste of that chèvre is divine,' Tamara says.

'And just before the man went back to Norway, they discovered that their relationship had had consequences, as they say. The problem was that the man was already married in Norway. He loved the woman he had met in Copenhagen with all his heart and he was willing to leave his wife to start a new life with her and the baby they were expecting.'

'How wonderful! If people love each other, they should get each other in the end,' Liss says. 'Did the wife in Norway have any children?'

'No. The man went back to Norway to tell his wife that it was over. That their marriage was nothing more than formality and habit, as he put it. But when he got home, his wife told him that she was pregnant. He chose to stay with the woman he was married to, out of duty. And some months later, he became the father of two little girls. One born in Copenhagen to the woman he loved, and one born in Oslo to the woman who was his legal wife. Two small girls with the same father grew up in two different cities. Only, one never saw her father. Not until she was an adult. But she longed for him all the time. And for her sister, when she discovered that she had a sister who was the same age. No, before she even knew, she longed for her sister. Always. She had always longed for a sister.'

'Yes,' Liss said. 'I know what it's like to be an only child.'

'But now I have met both my father and my sister,' Eva announces.

'Oh, it was you, you were talking about!' exclaims Liss in surprise.

157

'Tamara, I have become very fond of you in the time that we've known each other and I feel deeply connected to you. I know that you feel the same. And it's not just friendship that binds us, but also blood. You are my sister, Tamara. I am the baby that was born in Copenhagen and you are the girl who was born in Oslo. We're sisters, you and I.'

Eva feels intense joy at being able to say that sentence out loud, a sentence she has repeated to herself so many times. We're sisters, you and I. You and I are sisters.

'Is everything to your satisfaction, ladies?' asks the waiter. He has come over to the table without anyone noticing and starts to clear away the empty plates.

'Yes, lovely, thank you,' Eva says and smiles at him.

While the waiter clears the table, images flood into Eva's mind. Tamara and Eva picking flowers in a meadow. Tamara and Eva in an inflatable paddling pool, naked and glistening wet, with pot bellies and chubby creased thighs. Tamara and Eva in front of a snowman. On skis. On a sledge. On the beach in bikinis. Tamara and Eva with new bikes. Each with an ice cream. On the day they finished school. Close together, smiling, whispering.

*

Later on tonight in the hotel bar. Tamara leaning forward to say something to Eva. Eva feels Tamara's dark hair brushing her cheek. That's how it will be. Eva can see it quite clearly.

She has arrived. Now she is where she wants to be. Eva is swimming in the stars. She is eating the sweet air. Now they are sisters, Tamara and Eva. All is quiet round the table. A peaceful quiet. The waiter tidies and smiles.
Sara watches the waiter clearing the table, removing the used, oily plates, the dirty glasses, the cutlery with scraps of white cheese on. It is not obvious on the outside, but Eva's words have

surprised Sara deeply. A surprise that crept up from behind. She had been listening intently to Eva's story, had been with her in Copenhagen in the Sixties, followed the unhappy man home and suddenly, without any warning, as is always the case with surprises, it hit her from behind, hard, because it was a huge surprise, and Sara had jumped at the unexpected pain. Eva was Tamara's sister. Sara does not like surprises. Sara likes to know what is happening. Sara likes to be in control. Tamara did not do as she was told when she married Håvard. That was the first time. Sara forgave her. But now Tamara has done it again. Tamara has to look after Sara. Sara cannot manage without her. Therefore Tamara has to be Sara's sister, not Eva's.

It's just like a novel, Liss thinks. Two sisters, separated at birth, but who've found each other again. And she's happy for Eva. Because even though Eva has never said so directly, Liss knows that Eva has missed having siblings. Eva has always been so interested in Synne, Sara's sister, and she often asks about Tamara's brother. But it must be a shock for Tamara. That her father was unfaithful to her mother. Liss smiles a bit hesitantly at Tamara. But Tamara does not smile back. She neither looks at Liss' interested, well-meaning face or Eva's blindly expectant face. She looks at Sara's white face.

It is absurd. Of course Eva is not Tamara's sister. Tamara has one sister. She doesn't want any more.

Fourth course: Duck breast carpaccio with herb salad, spicy dressing and warm foie gras sauce

Eva sits trustingly with her head on one side looking at Tamara. The waiter has finally finished clearing the table. Tamara waits until he is a few metres away before leaning forwards and saying, with her eyes on Sara:

'Eva is not my sister. You are, Sara, you are my sister.'
'What do you mean?' Eva asks in disbelief. Still smiling.

'I said you are not my sister.'

'Yes I am,' Eva says. She can hear that her voice is far too loud and cheerful. She feels that her face muscles have frozen and that she is still smiling.

'No,' Tamara practically shouts. 'Sara is my sister. It's no secret, or is it, Sara, that my father is Sara's father too? Sara's mother and my father had a relationship.'

'What?' Liss exclaims.

'What are you saying?' Eva says.

'We saw it ourselves,' continues Tamara. Calmer. Did one of the men at the neighbouring table just turn round and look at her? 'We've known it since the day we saw them together. We're sisters, Sara and I.'

'I am your sister,' Eva repeats. Lower and with less force than before.

'No,' Tamara says. 'Sara is my sister.'

'But I've...,' starts Eva.

'Sara and I are more than friends,' Tamara continues. Her voice is not raised, but insistent, as if she were talking in italics. 'We've grown up together. We went to school together. We started the sewing circle together. We were each other's chief bridesmaid when we got married. We are best friends. And sisters. We saw them together. That day 25 years ago. And we realised that it had been going on for a long time. Everything fell into place.'

Eva's hands lie listlessly in her lap. They feel heavy and alien. She tries to move them, but she can't. She can't, doesn't manage, can't bear to say any more. And Tamara is her sister. Eva knows that. We are sisters. She has known that all her life. Eva has longed for Tamara all her life. She has imagined this evening all her life. But there are no stars, no sweet air, and Eva never imagined it would be like this.

Liss looks at the others. She looks at the two dark, beautiful women whom she has always admired, always looked up to. Are they really sisters? And she looks at Eva. Her brown, kind eyes under a bleached fringe. Eva, whom she has really come to appreciate. Liss wants to help, but doesn't know what to do. In a well-meaning, inadequate gesture, she stretches out her hand and puts it on Eva's, which is lying in her lap. Eva's hand is ice cold and Liss doesn't even know if Eva notices Liss stroking it carefully.

Sara has to say something, thinks Tamara. Sara has to confirm that we're sisters. Because now Tamara is frightened. She may have wanted to hurt Sara. Have her revenge, perhaps. Tamara admits it. Tamara and Jakob. Jakob's red face and shiny big lips. But Tamara does not want to lose Sara. Tamara can't lose her little sister. Sara, say something! Say that you're my sister, Sara. But Sara says nothing. Sara is thinking.

Tamara has to help Sara. She has always helped Sara. Tamara must do what Sara wants, because Sara needs Tamara. And Tamara did not do as Sara said: she married Håvard. That was the first time. But when Tamara wept and said that she should have listened to her, Sara had forgiven her. Forgiven and comforted her. But now Tamara has done it again. Tamara has done it a second time. She has defied Sara. She has gone behind Sara's back. Jakob and Tamara. Sara has looked at Tamara with her big, brown helpless eyes and Tamara has helped her every time. And that is how it should be. But now everything is ruined. Broken. Destroyed. Because Sara knows about Jakob. Sara sees, even though she does not want to, even though she has tried to turn a blind eye for a long time, tried not to see that things around her, things that have always been the same and that she has therefore taken to be written in stone, eternal, immutable, impervious to change, are falling apart. Everything is falling apart. The pattern is shattered, words do not make sense any more, familiar gestures are suddenly without meaning. Sara cannot trust Tamara any more. Sara has to manage without Tamara. Will she manage?

'I have never been your sister,' Sara says and launches herself into the dark abyss. The cold air whistles past her ears.

161

'What? Of course you have,' says Tamara. 'We saw them.'

'Yes,' Sara says. 'But we are not sisters.'

Liss looks at her friends, the only two friends she has from childhood. They look equally upset. And equally angry. The waiter has arrived with the duck breast. It lies in pink slices beside some basil and parsley leaves and something else that Liss doesn't know the name of. He returns with another bottle of wine. A light Rhône wine, he tells them. He pours some into the glass in front of Liss and asks her to taste it. Yes, it's lovely, smiles Liss. Eva, Sara and Tamara have all bent over to eat their food and are cutting it into pieces, putting it on their forks, which they then guide to their mouths. Lovely. Delicious. So tender and good. They nod at the waiter who has come back to fill their water glasses. Thank you. They sip the wine. The waiter bows and leaves the table.

'I neither am nor have ever been your sister,' Sara says, her eyes fixed on the black and white back of the waiter. 'It is true that we imagined it to be so for a while. But we were very young. And I have known for many years that we were wrong.'

'That's not true, Sara,' Tamara says.

'We are sisters,' Eva says.

No one answers Eva. Sara does not reply to Tamara, but she lifts her handbag up onto her knee, takes out her purse and searches for a photograph. Liss can't see who the photo is of, but she sees that the picture is very small, possibly a passport photo, and that it's in black and white. Sara gives the picture to Tamara, who looks at it for a few seconds before handing it back to Sara.

'Now can you see?' asks Sara. 'That is my father. My mother's husband. My father. I have looked on you as a sister, Tamara. As a dear sister, but now I have discovered your true colours. I know that you phone me and then put down the receiver.'

'Sara,' says Tamara.

'I said nothing when I discovered that we were not sisters, because I did not want to hurt you,' Sara says. 'But now I know what you are doing to me.'

'Sara, can I see?' asks Liss, without much hope that Sara will even notice her. Sara and Tamara don't always hear Liss. Sara continues to look at Tamara, but hands Liss the photo across the table. Liss has known Sara's father since she was little and she sees instantly that it's him. But it's a picture of him when he was young, maybe his confirmation. His hair has been combed down with water and he's wearing a white shirt and spotty bowtie. He is so young that he nearly looks feminine and you can't fail to see the similarity between him and Sara. The same black hair and pale skin. The big, sad-looking eyes and nose. The same hooked, unusually refined nose.

'Can you see it?' Sara asks again.

'No,' answers Tamara.

But Tamara has seen it. She has seen that the man in the photo looks like Sara and she has seen that he is the man who was married to Sara's mother. Sara's father? But she and Sara saw them! That time, and everything fell into place. You're so alike. You're so beautiful. No one else has such dark hair as you two.

'And you think I don't know that you are having an affair with my husband?' Sara says. 'Do you really think I don't know that you and Jakob are deceiving me?'

'We are sisters,' Eva says.

Liss' eyes are focused on Sara. She can only see her profile. Her black hair that curls at the neck. Her long eye lashes. Her beautiful nose, exactly like her father's in the photograph. Sara is looking at Tamara. Tamara looks down, but then she lifts her head.

*

Sara has filled pages and pages in Tamara's memory book and there are so many that Tamara doesn't dare to open. Lars, Kristian, Carlos. Håvard. Tamara really loved Håvard. Tamara lifts her chin

163

even more and looks straight at Sara. One of Tamara's arms is resting in her lap. The other is lying along the back of the sofa, golden brown, slim and elegant and completely still.

'I have seen you,' says Sara. Her voice is monotonous, it sounds like she is reading something out loud. 'I have seen you, Tamara. Several times. I saw you last Monday. You came out of my house, from my and Jakob's house. You walked down my steps and you put your hand on my banister. There was strong sunshine. Your hair was shining in the bright light. Your eyes were glittering like amber. You leant back your head. You leant back your head and licked my husband's semen from your lips. Just like a cat that has cleaned a bowl of cream and savours those final drops. Your tongue was pink, slowly and pleasurably moving round your mouth. Several times. You closed your eyes and smiled. Then you held out your arms and stretched. Like a cat that has just got up after rolling in the softest velvet cushions. Disgustingly self-satisfied.'

'And then I raised my tail like a flag and tripped home on soft paws?' asks Tamara. Her voice is low and full of derision. 'Or did I catch a mouse on the way, perhaps, which I then marinated and ate for dinner?'

'I know that you are having an affair with Jakob. I saw you on Monday,' Sara repeats.

Tamara laughs quietly and says:

'Last Monday, my dear Sara, I was working in Bergen. I interviewed that playwright from Hordaland. You read the interview yourself, in the paper, on the plane earlier today. You know that fine well, just think about it. My hair shone in the sun and my eyes glittered like amber. Poetic, Sara, very poetic. Reminds me of Solomon's Song. I quote: thy nose is as the tower of Lebanon which looketh towards Damascus.'

Sara touches her nose.

'It was raining in Oslo on Monday,' Eva says.

'Exactly. Hence no shining and no glittering. It was raining, Sara,' Tamara says. 'Wasn't it, Liss?'

'Yes,' Liss echoes. It's always been difficult not to answer Tamara.

'Do you hear, Sara? Everyone knows, so there's no point in hiding it any more, Sara, you see things that other people don't see,' says Tamara. She talks slowly and clearly, as if talking to someone who might not understand. 'You are quite simply a bit mad,' Tamara says and smiles at Sara.

'But,' Eva says and draws breath to continue. She doesn't know what to say and before she can get any further, Tamara turns to her:

'And you,' Tamara says to Eva, her voice trembling. Only Sara has heard Tamara's voice tremble before. 'You know that what you're saying isn't true. It is utterly absurd. That my father had a relationship with your mother! That my father loved your mother! I may not have met your mother, but I can certainly imagine what she's like.'

'But it's true, Tamara,' Eva says. 'Mummy told me everything.'

'Mummy,' sneers Tamara. 'Your mummy is just as full of lies as her daughter. I know that my father never loved anyone other than my mother. Sara's mother was a hussy and he has never met your mother.'

'It is fairly obvious who was to blame when it comes to your father and my mother,' says Sara calmly. 'Your father has obviously had plenty of skirt on the side. And you fall from the same tree. My poor mother was fooled by your father. That is plain to see.'

'Rubbish,' hisses Tamara.

'Keep your voice down,' says Sara in a friendly manner. 'Think of the other guests.'

Tamara raises her glass of red wine and for a moment, Eva thinks that she's going to throw the contents over Sara or herself. But Tamara takes a few sips, then puts the glass down again carefully.

'Tamara,' Eva says. 'I've met and spoken to our father many times. I've visited him at the home regularly over the past few years and he...'

'I know nothing about *your* father, Eva,' Tamara snaps. 'But if it's *my* father you've met, you should know that he is a loveable, but senile man. Alzheimer's. He often talks rubbish. He doesn't know what he's saying.'

'But look,' Eva says and produces a faded colour photograph from her bag. T and P summer '79. 'Look, I found this when I was thirteen. This picture has meant so much to me. Since I found it...'

'A picture of me and Philip! What the hell does that prove? Jesus, do you all go round with old photos in your handbags, or what?'

'Shh,' says Sara gently.

'...since I found it, I've been looking for you, because then I knew who to look for,' Eva continues.

'Dear God, Eva. You have known nothing whatsoever,' Tamara says.

'Not only have I spoken to our father, Tamara,' Eva tries to explain. 'I've also seen the letters he wrote to Mum, I've seen the pictures. I've seen my birth certificate, Tamara. He really is my father. We are sisters. I...'

'He talks rubbish,' Tamara says again. 'Alzheimer's. And it looks like one of his daughters has inherited the genes. And when I say one of his daughters, I mean you, Sara. What a tragedy that someone who is only in her thirties has such a useless brain. I feel sorry for you, Sara.'

'Tamara, darling,' Sara says. 'I share no genes with either you or your father.'

'I got to know our father before he got Alzheimer's. And he's not as senile as you make out,' Eva says. 'We've talked together a lot. He's sorry that he didn't get to know me before I was an adult and he was an old man. But his greatest sorrow is that he never really got to know his other daughter. You, Tamara. Dad...'

'Do not call him Dad.'

'Dad said that you never really talked properly to him, that you weren't that old when you started to hold him at a distance.'

'Now, ladies, are you finished?' asks the waiter, standing behind Eva and Liss.

'What? Finished? Yes, I think we've had enough,' says Tamara.

'Lovely duck,' says Sara at the same time.

'Well, I'm sure you can manage another two or three courses,' smiles the waiter and winks at Liss.

Eva and Liss nod and smile. Eva is unable to say anything. She should never have said what she did about her father. What his greatest sorrow was. It's true, but she should never have told Tamara. She and her father have talked about Tamara, and their father has said several times that Tamara behaved differently towards him, was almost hostile, from around the age of eleven. He thought it was just puberty, but it never passed. And he doesn't really understand it. Eva should never have told Tamara. Eva regrets it. She doesn't want to hurt Tamara, does she? Eva feels sick.

The waiter continues:

'Perhaps some of you have had enough already. That was, after all, the fourth course. I will just clear the table and then bring the halibut in a minute. I'll be back with the champagne.'

'Thank you,' Tamara says.

No one says anything until the waiter returns with a wine cooler and a dark green bottle of champagne. He smiles at them all, looks at Sara and asks jovially:

'Perhaps the beautiful, dark-haired lady would like me to open the bottle of champagne with a sword?'

'Well,' Sara hesitates. 'I don't know.'

'Have no fear, madam. The true art of cutting a champagne bottle with a sword lies in getting the spray to take away any splinters, so there is no danger. And I am a master of the art.'

'Oh,' Sara says.

'But I do not have a sword.'

'No,' Sara says.

'And how are you ladies enjoying your celebration?' the waiter then asks. 'Your sewing club anniversary?'

'Fine, thank you,' Tamara says.

'Yes,' Liss echoes.

'Did you know that the most common injury on New Year's Eve in France is getting a champagne cork in the eye? Parisian eye specialists always work overtime that night. So careful now, ladies, so that no one gets hurt. We want you to get back to Oslo in one piece, don't we?'

'Yes,' Tamara says weakly.

*

The waiter smiles and a few seconds later he holds the cork in his hands and it only released a suitable, small sigh when it slipped out of the bottle.

'Well, now you can really celebrate, ladies,' he says and pours champagne into the tall, thin glasses. Liss is served first.

'Excuse me a moment,' Tamara says and nods to Liss, Eva and the waiter. Sara is wearing a white sweater with a plunging neckline. White like an angel. The gold earrings that remind Tamara of the ones she got from Håvard, blink at her. They grow. They glitter and sparkle. They blind her. Tamara squints in the sharp light, bends over to Sara's ear:

'Bloody bitch,' she whispers.

Then she leaves the restaurant. In her hand she's holding a plaited gold earring.

Fifth course: Halibut on a bed of truffle risotto

It's cold outside, far too cold to be out without a coat. Tamara puts Sara's earring in her mouth. It tastes of blood. Cloying and sweet. Sara's blood. Tamara sucks on the earring, she presses it so hard against the roof of her mouth with her tongue that it hurts. Tamara doesn't need a sister. And Sara doesn't want to be her sister anyway. So what, thinks Tamara. And Tamara's father thinks she's let him down. Fair enough, thinks Tamara and kicks a pile of dirty snow. He has no right to accuse her of anything. The mole on the white backside. The half-open mouth. The sharp teeth and the red tongue.

And Sara knows that Tamara is having an affair with Jakob. So what, thinks Tamara again. God knows I didn't need to put much effort into getting him where I wanted. Sara must know that it's her own fault. She's an intelligent and gifted woman who must realise that there could be no other grounds for choosing Jakob as a lover. And if she doesn't understand that, well, Tamara can explain. Jakob is a hopeless lover. The book with the velvet cover is still nestling in Tamara's bag, by the table inside. There's a lot that Sara should know. There's a lot that Sara doesn't understand.

Lars, Kristian, Carlos. And then Håvard. Tamara had to believe Sara when she told Tamara what they were like. Harald, Henrik. Tamara had to believe that Sara only wanted the best for her. That Sara only wanted to help Tamara. Just as Tamara had always helped her. Tamara paces up and down on the pavement, sucking hard on the earring, feeling the sharp edges cutting the roof of her mouth and the taste of blood intensifies. Sara's blood. Tamara's blood. Tamara crosses her arms as she walks. She walks over to the corner and back again, backwards and forwards. She walks fast. They have been friends since before they were born, sisters from the autumn they turned eleven. The autumn she gained a sister and lost a father. And Philip. Tamara practically never thinks about Philip. She quickly turns those pages. The taste of blood is very strong now, black and bitter.

Tamara sits on her desk, behind the butterfly curtains, looking down into the garden. Philip is sleeping in his pram. Sara is sitting under the cherry tree. Sara is crying and it's Tamara who made her cry. 'Do you really love your brother?' Sara had asked. 'Yes,' replied Tamara. 'But you love me more,' Sara had said and looked at Tamara with her big dark eyes. 'Yes,' Tamara said. 'We'll see,' Sara says and pulls off the netting that protects the pram. Philip is asleep. 'Don't,' Tamara says. 'A wasp might get in and sting him.' 'I'll go then,' Sara says. Sara leaves. Tamara doesn't run after her, like she normally does. Philip has fair, thin eyebrows and soft, smooth skin. Tamara runs her finger over his cheek. Then she puts the net back on again and makes sure that it's secured round the edges. When she has finished and turns round, Sara is standing there again. She has a stick in her hand. Tamara knows where she's been. She's been into the neighbours'. They have a big garden with tall grass and pine trees. Sara and Tamara call it the jungle. Behind the compost heap is a small ant heap. Sara's stick is crawling with ants. Small, red ants. One climbs up her arm and Tamara knows that they have a nasty bite so she pinches it off Sara's thin, white arm. Tamara takes care of Sara. Sara mustn't get hurt. Sara looks at Tamara and takes off the netting and puts the stick in. 'Don't,' Tamara says. Sara holds the stick above Philip's head. 'Don't,' Tamara says. Two ants fall into the pram and one races down Philip's cheek and then disappears behind his ear. Sara smiles.

Tamara hit Sara hard right in the middle of her smile and Sara started to cry. Sara ran away and Tamara did not run after her. Tamara found the two small ants under Philip's pillow. She dropped them on to the paving and crushed them with her heel. First one, then the other. Then she pulled the netting back into place and went in. At first, Tamara stood behind the butterfly curtains to keep watch on Philip. Now Tamara is standing behind the curtains feeling sorry for Sara. Tamara jumps down from the desk. She goes down into the garden again, past the pram and over to Sara. Tamara puts her arm round Sara. Sara is Tamara's bestest friend. Tamara takes care of Sara. Sara needs Tamara. Sara is thin and white and she has such big eyes.

Philip doesn't sleep well that night. Nor does Tamara. She is woken by Philip's crying several times. The next morning, Daddy phones the doctor. Mummy sits beside him with Philip in her arms, Tamara strokes Philip's back and neck. Poor Philip. His skin is covered in sore red bumps. And some of them have started to leak.

*

Tamara takes the earring out of her mouth and puts it in her pocket, then opens the door to the restaurant and goes back in. There is silence around the table when Tamara comes back. The food is standing untouched in front of them. Their glasses are full. It is so quiet that Tamara imagines that she can hear the champagne bubbles bursting in the glasses. Tamara sits down, picks up the fish cutlery and starts to eat. Eventually Eva starts too, then Liss and finally Sara. Tamara looks at Sara. She has a small white plaster on one of her earlobes. Sara does not want to look at Tamara.

Why won't Sara look at Tamara? Tamara has always been there for her. She has always helped Sara. Quietly and without protest, she has always helped Sara. My dearest friend, my sister. Sara has looked at Tamara with her big, dark eyes and Tamara has done whatever Sara wants. It's always been like that, all Tamara's life. From long before they started school. Philip had to put up with a good deal more than ant bites. Tamara had to hit Andrea and Liv Torunn with her spade because Sara didn't like them. The black fur and nails through the pink paws, the pink arse. Tamara had to say to the men in suits that she had stolen the eyeshadow. Tamara had to lie. To others and to herself. Sara told Tamara to take it. Tamara took it and threw it away in the neighbours' bin. It was a grey-blue colour and nearly bare and it had kind button eyes. Lars. Henrik and Harald. Sara has filled many pages in Tamara's memory book and there are far too many that Tamara does not dare to open. Kristian, Carlos. Håvard. Tamara really loved Håvard.

Tamara looks down at the white halibut. Lame and colourless. White fish on white rice with small shavings of truffle. Tamara regrets not having eaten more of the previous course. The bloody, juicy duck breast. She still has the taste of blood in her mouth. Her diary is in her handbag. Tamara clutches the velvet cover with one hand. Should she take it out? Should she give it to Sara? There's a lot that Sara should know. Jakob is hopeless in bed. Kristian and Tamara would have been happy together. Tamara and Håvard were happy together. Tamara loved Håvard. Tamara realises what

Sara has done to her over the years. And Sara can read about it in the book. The small, thick book with velvet covers. Tamara drops the book into Sara's rather big handbag. Tamara does not want to be Sara's sister. She does not even want to be Sara's friend.

Tamara suddenly feels happy. Bizarrely happy and light and free. After all, they are in Copenhagen to celebrate.

'Cheers,' Tamara says, turning towards Sara and raising her champagne glass.
    'Cheers,' responds Eva.

Why does only Eva reply? She doesn't look at Eva. Chubby and insignificant. Tamara quickly looks into Liss' round face instead. She's actually started to get used to her. But then again, Tamara has had to drag her around for 25 years, so it's not that strange really. She looks at Sara again.

Sara knows fine well that Tamara is looking at her, but Sara does not want to look at Tamara. Sara's ear is hurting. The ear closest to Tamara.

Then suddenly Sara starts to speak. She repeats that she has seen Tamara leaving their house, sneaking out like a cat. The same words as before. The same well-formulated sentences. The same monotonous voice, the same far-away look. Everyone listens to Sara's rush of words. No one tries to stop her. Her voice is quiet and controlled.
    'Because that is what she is like,' Sara concludes. 'As crafty as a cat. Fickle. Purring one minute, then scratching you the next.'
    'Is everything all right? Are you enjoying the food?' asks the waiter. His voice makes everyone sit up straight, as if they were little girls again and the head teacher had just come in.
    'Yes, thank you. Everything is fine,' replies one.
    'Mmm, perfect,' answers another.
    'Delicious fish.'
    'And fantastic risotto,' adds the last one.

'More champagne? How are your celebrations coming along?'

'Thank you.'

'A little more for me, please.'

'Yes, this one too.'

'Thank you.'

'Cheers, girls,' says one of them and raises her glass.

'Cheers,' the three others reply.

'Excellent,' says the waiter.

'You obviously want to talk about cats today, Sara,' Tamara says as soon as the waiter has disappeared again, 'which is fine by me. I'll tell the others about the cat in the woods.'

Sara is obviously startled by Tamara's unexpected words. Surely Tamara cannot mean what she says. Surely not! Sara jumps and Tamara's elbow comes into close contact with Sara's upper arm. For a moment, Tamara feels Sara's soft upper arm. It feels so soft and helpless. It feels so white against her elbow. Tamara focuses on Sara's nose, because she cannot look her in the eyes when she says what she is going to say. Something they have never spoken about before.

'You see, I remember another cat,' Tamara says quietly. Then she continues in a slightly louder voice. 'A black cat. Quite a young cat. Do you remember it too, Sara? Why don't you tell the girls why you're so hysterically frightened of cats? What no reply? Don't tell me you've forgotten who hammered in the first nail? And the next? And the next again?'

When Sara jumped, her right arm was flung away from her body and collided with Tamara's elbow. Tamara's hard, sharp elbow banged into Sara's upper arm at precisely the same point where Tamara had gripped it so firmly 25 years earlier and steered her away from her parents' bedroom, down the street and out into the woods. The slight bump from Tamara's elbow, which was not really hard enough to cause any pain, must, however, have activated the nerves in Sara's upper arm because now that spot feels exactly as it did 25 years ago when it was black and blue, ice cold, naked, skinless and sore. Sara puts her left hand over her

173

right arm and holds it tight, and keeping her hand on her arm, she stretches her right hand out and grasps her champagne glass.

Tamara talks for a long time. She tells Liss and Eva about what happened in the woods that day. Tamara tells them about the hut that the boys in third year were building, about the hammer and the box of nails. She tells them about the cat and the crucifixion. About the sharp claws, the gaping mouth and all the blood.

'Sara crucified a cat. She nailed up a sweet, little kitten, because that's what she's like.'

Tamara been speaking quietly and quickly. She says the last sentence in a louder voice, with her eyes fixed on the two couples in their fifties sitting at the next table.

While Tamara has been speaking, Sara has been leaning forwards over her champagne glass. Eva and Liss have kept their eyes on Tamara and every now and then looked over at Sara's bent, black head. Did Sara and Tamara really do something like that? But why? thinks Eva. What made them do that? And did Tamara actually do anything? If Eva had heard the story only a few hours ago, she would never have believed it. Now she believes it. Because nothing is what Eva thought it was.

'But why?' she asks when Tamara has finished. 'Why did you do that? There must have been a reason?'

Tamara draws her breath to answer.

'No,' says Sara. It is the first thing she has said. 'There was no reason.'

'Then it was just for fun?' Eva asks again.

'Yes,' answers Sara.

Eva shakes her head. Of course, everyone knows that children can be indescribably cruel. And perhaps Tamara and Sara have sides that Eva has never seen, never wants to see. But the story about the cat is not Eva's story. Eva did not grow up with Sara and Tamara. Eva has never heard about the crucified cat in the woods, not until this evening. And children sometimes do terrible things.

It is Tamara she is thinking about, not what she just heard about the cat.

But beside Eva, sits Liss with her fair hair and round face. Liss remembers standing in the playground and feeling absolute horror when she heard about the cat in the woods. In her eleven-year old mind she envisaged the cat writhing, she thought she could hear it screeching. She remembered evenings in her room with the closed door and no Bamse. She remembers Sara and Tamara in light summer dresses and sandals. Pissy Lissy. And Liss is filled with disgust. She straightens up, as if she wants to get as far away as possible from the two dark-haired women on the other side of the table. Tamara sees this, and her facial expression, and says:

'You don't need to look so bloody innocent. Hypocrite.'

'What d'you mean?' Liss asks. 'You think it's wrong to react? I remember the boys in third year finding the cat and then the police came to school and questioned people. I remember I thought it was horrific just to hear about the poor cat. And now I find out it was you...'

'Don't play the innocent,' hisses Tamara. 'Don't pretend you didn't know! For years you have driven us mad, always reminding us about what happened in the woods that day. What you saw in the woods that day. Humming, saying things. You love it!'

'I didn't see anything,' Liss says and suddenly it dawns on her that the day Tamara has just told them about is the same day in late summer that she visited her cousin and later met Sara and Tamara by the edge of the woods. The next day Sara and Tamara had asked her to be their friend. Sara and Tamara had not chosen her for her own sake. But because of the slow agony of a crucified cat. Liss sits still as stone.

But most of all, because of the shame, because of all that was forbidden and dirty. Liss doesn't know that. They chose her because of the smells and the sounds from earlier that day, which for Tamara and Sara will now always be inextricably linked to the cat. To the cat's randy miaow, its quivering tail and shameless, pink hole. But Liss doesn't know that. They did not choose her for her own sake. They had chosen her because they thought that Liss had seen what they did to the cat in the woods and therefore all the rest. They had chosen her because they believed that if Liss had seen the tortured cat, she had also seen the rest. It was as if Liss had been with them in the doorway that day.

Well, well, thinks Tamara. So it could possibly have been just Sara and Tamara all along. Always. They hadn't needed to include Liss. Pissy Lissy. Tamara can tell when someone is lying and Liss is not lying. Liss didn't see anything. And if they'd known that they might not be here right now. Tamara doesn't like being here. She doesn't like Copenhagen. But nothing would have been different, anyway. It doesn't matter any more.

Sara told Eva what she wanted to know and has now sunk back into the same trance-like state she was in when Tamara was talking about the cat. No, there was no reason. Eva and Liss did not need to know about the cat in the woods and the other thing that she and Tamara saw, that happened the same day. And Tamara did not need to know about her mother's eyes. Mother's big, blue eyes that had looked straight at Sara. Mother's arms and legs wrapped round a hairy body, and her big, blue eyes looking straight at Sara.

Eva is staring rigidly at a point to the right of Sara. Eva is looking at Tamara. Sara notices that Eva looks old, she looks like she has aged about a decade over the first five courses. This observation unleashes a powerful, irrepressible urge to comment, to verbalise the visual impression that is so firmly imprinted on her chiasma opticum. The urge to say something, combined with the wish to be polite, means that Sara surprises all three and herself by suddenly saying:

'You are looking really good, Eva.'

No one says anything. The couples at the next table turn round and look at Sara, smile a bit and then continue eating. Sara does not allow herself to be disconcerted by the silence that followed her comment or the fact that Eva has not answered. After all, it was a pointless remark. But then she sees Eva nodding weakly. Tamara looks almost concerned.

*

Why did Sara say that? She must be completely out of it. Poor Sara. Maybe she'll break down completely soon. I don't want to feel sorry for her, thinks Tamara. But Tamara sees the vein throbbing in Sara's temple, the one that is facing her. The skin on Sara's face is even whiter than usual. As white as the plaster on her ear. She's so thin. So thin she almost looks ill, pinched in the face. Her eyes are even bigger and darker than normal. Tamara can see Sara putting her hand to her heart under her jacket and that she then checks her pulse by pressing her middle and index fingers to her slim wrist.

And Tamara feels sorry for her. Tamara doesn't want to, but she feels terribly sorry for Sara. Tamara has always helped her. Made sure that nothing upset her. Who will look after Sara now? And who will Tamara look after? Won't they always be sisters, Sara and her? Sara and Tamara. It even rhymes. It's a sign. That's what Sara said.

Tamara suddenly wants food. She picks up her knife and fork and eats the rest of the fish. It might be white and colourless, but it tastes incredible. The small, dark truffle shavings give the dish flavour and character, just as the waiter said. The truffles are from Périgord, he explained. They are the black diamonds of cooking. Tamara washes the diamonds down with some champagne.

Sixth course: Platter of seasonal cheeses

The waiter clears away what is left of the fish course and comes back with the cheese. The empty champagne bottle and cooler are carried out. An Italian red is opened. Bon appetit! The four women nod and smile. Nearly nothing is said during the sixth course. The cheese is eaten and the Valpolicella drunk in silence. It is as if, given what they have eaten and heard, the women already have enough to digest.

Sara leans back and looks at her friends on the other side of the table. Eva glances at her briefly before her eyes once again slide to the right and fix on Tamara. Liss' fair head is bent over her cheese platter, which consists of two small pieces of cheese and a little, apparently arbitrarily arranged pile of caramelised nuts. She sits like a robot automatically putting the food in her mouth. Perhaps she is thinking about that day in the woods. Or perhaps she is thinking about something completely different. Liss' thoughts mean nothing to Sara. And beside Sara sits Tamara. Dark and beautiful, and as always, enviously calm, Tamara sits, obviously enjoying the cheese and when she notices Sara looking at her, she says contentedly, without Sara being able to detect the slightest irony in her voice:

'Delicious cheese, isn't it?'

'Lovely,' Sara replies, partly because she now discovers that the soft, creamy unpasturised brie, the Münster cheese, which is almost liquid inside the red rind and the dark, slightly sweet bread does indeed taste delicious and partly because it is Tamara who says it. And Sara needs Tamara. Doesn't she? Or maybe she can manage without her.

But as Sara sits on the sofa, she is overwhelmed by a great fear. It washes over her as if in answer to the question she has just asked herself. A flock of monstrous creatures flies through the air towards her, beating her with their wings, whipping her with their tails and pushing her down. She curls up and lies shaking on the soft velvet of the restaurant sofa, listening to the beating of black wings above her head and she stretches out an arm out to Tamara who, unaffected, like the others round the table, continues to eat cheese and drink wine. Sara's heart first starts to beat too fast in her chest, then it starts to miss a beat. An obvious case of extrasystoli, released by the auricle of Sara's heart. How will she cope without

Tamara? And if she loses Jakob as well? Who will protect her then? Sara turns and appeals to Eva and Liss, but sees immediately that not even they, neither Pissy Lissy nor Mrs Mousy Nothing, want anything to do with her, not after this evening.

The beasts have flown away. The plate is nearly empty. Just one small reddish-yellow piece of Münster rind and an untouched heap of caramelised nuts are left. A shining silver fork enters from the right and carefully scoops up the nuts. Some fall off and are left lying on the plate. Sara lifts her head in time to see Tamara putting the forkful of nuts into her mouth.

'You can't eat them, Sara. You're allergic to nuts, you know,' says Tamara.

'Thank you,' says Sara.

That is nearly all that is said during the cheese course. The women sit like strangers around the table. Each of them caught up in her own thoughts. They were full long ago, but continue to eat.

The minute Sara puts her hand on the door handle, the door opens from inside. Sara's mother is standing in the hall. 'Sara, where have you been? I've been so worried about you.' Her mother opens her arms, she looks like a dark cross against the doorway into the bright sitting room. Like a black cross against a white background. Like black fur against light birch bark. It was her mother she had crucified in the woods that day. It was her she thought of as she hammered the nails in one by one. Her mother's eyes looking straight at her. Never again can she let herself go in her mother's protective arms.

But now it is I who have Mother's eyes, thinks Sara. Sara's mother was artless and gentle. Like a small doll. With huge helpless eyes. Eyes that get everyone to do exactly as she wants. Sara will manage on her own. Sara does not need anyone to look after her. Not Mother, not Jakob. Not Tamara. I am strong. Sara puckers her mouth as if to whistle, but immediately stops when she sees the old, hunchbacked waiter approaching the table.

Under the black silk waistcoat, his shirt is snow white, but his nails are ridged and yellow with age. He smiles at them, there are scabs in the corners of his mouth and his teeth, when revealed, are completely brown. He pours wine into their glasses, asks if everything is all right. Sara feels a shiver down her spine. Three of the black beasts that flew her down are sitting on one of the lithographs. Their tails are beating against the frame.

Sara was the next first person in the class to get a colour TV. Only Liss' family had a colour TV before Sara's. Tamara often went round to Sara's to watch TV. To begin with they even watched the entire skating championships. It was so strange to see that the skaters had red and blue outfits and not black and white. There is a table beside the TV. On the table is a vase of flowers and a photograph. Quite a large photograph in a big silver frame. On either side of the picture are candlesticks with white candles that are always burning. No one is allowed near the table. No one is allowed to touch the picture. Mother polishes the silver frame every day.

Sara did not say anything when she discovered that she and Tamara were not sisters after all. She had been sitting looking through some old albums and there she had found a small picture of her father when he was young. She had seen pictures of him before, including photos from when he was young, but this particular picture was different, something to do with the profile, something to do with the eyes. Something that made him different. And she saw it. It was so obvious that she had to see it, cutting through the belief that Tamara's father was also her father. Tamara and Sara had never said to each other that they were sisters, but they both knew and thought that that was the case. They had seen it. And it explained so many things. Tamara was Sara's big sister. Sisters help each other. Big sisters help little sisters. Sara did not say anything. She wanted to continue being Tamara's little sister. It was more convenient that way. Over the years, Sara has had to do quite a lot to keep hold of Tamara.

Sara and Synne shared a room. They had a desk with two sets of drawers along the one wall and bunk beds against the other. Sara's name, embroidered in red cross-stitch with small birds around it, hung above her bunk. It was her mother who had made it. Above her sister's bed hung a frame with Synne in green cross-stitch and ladybirds. Sara and Synne each had their side of the wardrobe and their own shelves in the bookcase.

Between Sara's parents' room and Sara and Synne's room is another room. A room with a locked door. Only Mother is allowed in there. But Sara goes in as often as she can. There is a completely new bed in there. Sara knows that her mother changes the sheets once a week. There are books on the shelves. GGP, Miss Detective and the Bobsey Children. Up on the top shelf, three Barbie dolls sit in a row. There are clothes in the cupboard. A party dress just like the one Sara wants. Sometimes new clothes appear in the cupboard in bigger sizes and the old ones disappear. Sara does not know where and she cannot ask. Pictures of ponies and puppies hang on the walls. Above the bed is a cross-stitch embroidery with birds. Mother has embroidered Bitte in light blue letters. Bitte died when Sara was only two years old and before Synne was born. Bitte was found just lying dead in her cot, eight months old. Maybe it was something to do with her heart, the doctors said.

Sara's mother is frightened that something will happen to Sara and Synne. They are barely allowed to do anything at all. Let me feel your heart, Sara. I think it is beating a bit too fast, I do. Sara's mother was artless and gentle. Like a small doll. With huge blue eyes. Blue eyes that made everyone do exactly as she wanted. Tamara's father too. No doubt Mother had got Tamara's father where she wanted. Sara knows exactly what her mother is like, because she is like that herself. Sara's eyes also get people exactly where she wants them. Håvard. Tamara had been away at a seminar. Keep an eye on Håvard for me, will you, Tamara had said to Sara as a joke before she left. Håvard and Tamara were so happy together. They had got far too close in the time that they were married. The same day that Tamara left for the seminar, Sara had problems with her car. Fortunately it happened just by the street where Tamara and Håvard lived. Håvard was so practical, at least for a poet. Sara rang the doorbell. 'Isn't Tamara at home?' Sara had asked in surprise. Then she had looked at him with big, misty eyes and unbuttoned his trousers. Håvard had cried afterwards. 'Sara, we should never have done that,' he said. He more or less threw himself at me, Sara told Tamara and stroked her hand. Sara comforts and forgives. No, of course I'm not angry, Tamara. No Tamara, it is not your fault. Poor Tamara. She has always been blind when it comes to men. Yes Tamara, you should have listened to me. You should not have married him. Sara comforts and forgives.

Over the years, Sara has had to do a lot to keep hold of Tamara. And has managed every time.

But now Sara does not need her any longer. Sara simply cannot use her any more. Tamara is not to be trusted. The three women around this restaurant table are useless. One who cannot be trusted and two who know too much. I have Mother's eyes, thinks Sara. I have eyes that make everyone do exactly what I want. I can manage on my own. I do not need any one to look after me. Not Mother, not Tamara. Not Jakob. I am strong. And if I do not manage, I can always phone Synne. We have not spoken for several years, but she will come if I ask her to.

Sara holds her wrist to check her pulse. It is completely normal. Her heartbeat is slow and regular. Well protected by her ribs. Sara lifts her fork from the table. The three black beasts immediately take off and fly away. Sara whistles inside herself.

Tamara's fork is approaching the rest of the nuts on Sara's plate. But Sara's fork is faster. Sara pops the nuts in her mouth, chews them and swallows. Sara has always loved nuts. But for a long time now she has refrained from enjoying them in public. Sara is not allergic to nuts. Her heart is young and healthy. Her pelvis is in perfect order.

'But Sara,' Liss says. 'You shouldn't...'

'I know what I'm doing,' says Sara before Liss has a chance to finish. And Sara is right about that. Sara has always known what she is doing.

Seventh course: Honey and passion fruit mousse

Sara smiles at Tamara as she slowly chews the nuts. Is she smiling disdainfully? Tamara feels her heart beating wildly and uncontrollably. Tamara has never noticed anything wrong with her heart before. It has lived in her chest for nearly 37 years and has never given her cause for concern. But now it feels like her ribcage is about to burst. And isn't it missing some beats? What does that mean? Is it dangerous? Tamara gasps for breath, tries to breathe slowly, but it's as if she can't get enough air to her lungs. She opens her mouth to say something, but her tongue gets in the way. It fills her mouth. There is no room for words. Tamara is dizzy. The people around her are blurred. Maybe she's drunk too much? The waiter's white shirt hurts her eyes and the clattering of the cheese plates as he clears them away, hurts her ears.

Eva sits with her eyes closed while the waiter clears the table. She doesn't feel particularly well either, and for some reason she starts to think about another party. A party Eva went to when she was seven. She is wearing her best frock and she's at Lotte's birthday party. Eva wants to swim in the soft air. She wants to fly between the small white clouds, light and sweet as candyfloss. And Lotte's father smiles and nods and lifts Eva up high. Eva flies. Just as she has dreamed of doing. His hands hold tight around Eva's tummy, which is full of birthday food.

Eva opens her eyes again. She feels slightly sick. The waiter has arrived with the first of the two desserts. Quite a light dessert, he explains and with an exaggerated, elegant hand movement he puts the small glass bowls with dark yellow cream down in front of the ladies. 'Honey and passion fruit mousse,' he says. 'Lovely,' say the four ladies. And it does look lovely. Eva is looking forward to it. Despite everything. She loves food.

'Tomorrow I wouldn't mind...' starts Liss.

'Lovely taste, isn't it?' Tamara says and looks at Sara. Her voice is different. Unclear and woolly. Loud and uncontrolled.

'Absolutely lovely,' Liss answers. 'I wouldn't mind going down to Nyhavn.'

'Passion fruit, isn't it?' Sara asks, looking at Liss' fair head. 'Or was it pomegranate?'

'Passion fruit,' Tamara answers, in the same strange, loud voice.

'Yes, that's correct, madam. Passion fruit. And how do you like it?' asks the waiter. He has returned with a bottle of Sauternes.

'Absolutely divine,' Sara says.

'Delicious,' Tamara says, like a helpful echo.

Eva looks down and continues to eat. Yes, it tastes delicious, she says to herself. Over and over. Delicious food. Think about the food. Don't think about Tamara. My childhood home. A man and a woman. The relationship had consequences. Loved with all his heart. Two little girls. Longed for. Don't think that. Think about the food. Spoon into dessert bowl, spoon to mouth, mouth open. Chew, swallow. Again and again. The passion fruit mousse tastes sweet and intense, with rich honey undertones. Overwhelmingly sweet. You barely feel the mousse. It melts and dissolves the minute it touches your tongue and the moist walls of your mouth. All taste and no substance. Tamara. Eva suddenly realises that she's going to throw up. She gets up, but then it comes. Six courses in yellow honey and passion fruit mousse are vomited up on to the damask tablecloth. A yellow, sour mass of half-digested bits of food. Eva stands there and watches the bubbles burst and turn into craters before disappearing. She is astonished by the colour, size and shape of a piece of duck breast that lies on the table like a pink, rather large oblong sponge. The pungent smell fills her nostrils and she gets a sour taste in her mouth. She watches the vomit run down the wineglass and drip slowly from the edge of the dessert bowl.

She hears Tamara's repeated, monosyllabic explosions of disgust. 'Yuck, ugh.' Two silent waiters run over with a bucket and cloth. Another comes with a new tablecloth, new serviettes and a large glass of water. The two middle-aged couples at the next table do not look over, but continue to eat and drink. In the space of a few minutes, Eva's place is as it was. Eva nods in thanks to the waiters. She sits down and drinks some water. The horrible taste in her mouth is rinsed away. The other three look at her. Liss with sympathy and understanding, Tamara with obvious disgust and Sara with indifference.

'How are you feeling?' Liss asks. She is the first person to say anything.

'OK thanks,' Eva says. 'It was too much for me. Sorry.'

'Yes, that's fairly obvious. How disgusting. God,' Tamara says sharply. 'Shall we take a taxi back to the hotel afterwards?'

'Is it too far to walk?' asks Liss and looks at Eva again.

'No, it's fine to walk,' Eva replies, glad that Liss is concerned about her. 'But it might be a bit chilly.'

'I think it would be good to have some fresh air,' Liss says. 'After all this food.'

'I can't face walking,' Sara says. 'I feel a bit tired. I think it's my pelvis playing up.'

'I'm sure a short walk will do you good,' Liss says. In that high, happy voice that Eva has started to grow so fond of.

'Of course she can't walk. We'll get a taxi,' Tamara says rather loudly.

'I'll walk,' says Sara. 'Mind your own business. I don't need a nurse.'

Tamara breathes in. Her heart is thumping so hard that it must mean she's got heart problems. Sara leans over the table and says in a friendly voice.

'By the way, Liss. It was Tamara who took your old teddy bear.'

Sara gets up and walks over to the stairs. I am the queen, she thinks. I can cope with everything. I do not need anyone. And should I need anyone, I know where to find her.

Eighth course: Vanilla parfait in warm kirsch sauce

Bamse. The cat in the woods. Twenty-five years of secrets and lies. Backstabbing. Subtle humiliation. The day they met her by the edge of the woods. Pissy Lissy. Liss' own shortcomings. For these two! Liss looks at Tamara's red painted lips. She hears Sara's heels clicking on the way back from the toilet. Liss realises that she is happy. She realises that she feels relieved, the incredible relief, the day she decided not to visit her mother any more, to break off all contact. And these two. Everyone admires Sara and Tamara. They're so clever, so well groomed, so beautiful. The one darker than the other. Look, Sara has just dropped her napkin on the floor. A young, smiling waiter immediately places a new one on her plate. Sara doesn't even notice, she studies her eyeliner in the mirror. And beside Sara sits Tamara, as always. She doesn't really look herself though. Her face is far too pale in contrast to her blood-red lips.

'I'd like to come to Nyhavn with you tomorrow,' Eva says suddenly.

Liss nods to Eva, who gives a fragile smile back, a smile that could easily break. At the table furthest in to the wall sits a man whom Liss has not noticed all evening. He is masculine and broad-shouldered. In a well-fitted, charcoal grey double-breasted suit. And when he smiles, his pearl-white, no snow-white teeth flash at her. He looks like an Italian count. And he is too. Liss recognises him when he raises his glass to her.

'He's rather good looking,' says Eva.

'Is he looking at you or me, Sara?' asks Tamara.

'Who is it?' asks Sara with curiosity and leans over the table to Liss.

Liss laughs out loud. Then she raises her glass to the count. One of the waiters comes over with a silver tray. On the tray is a vase with a single, deep red rose, and beside it an ice-blue envelope.

The envelope is lying so that the family coat of arms with crossed swords and two leopards is facing up. He puts the vase down by Liss. For you. From the gentleman over there, he says and nods discreetly at the man in the corner. Liss met the count at a conference. She is a very successful business woman. But before she can concentrate on the next million-dollar transaction, she has to get rid of two secretaries. Two dark-haired, completely useless secretaries. They are not even good enough to make her coffee, let alone answer the telephone, or polish her shoes. Liss smells the rose and opens the envelope. The others watch her. As she takes out the thick, ice-blue card, something white falls on to the floor. What was that? I thought I saw some eggshell, says Sara. Liss pretends not to hear. You're fired, Liss says to the two dark-haired women.

Just then, before they have a chance to ask any more questions, their usual waiter arrives carrying a tray with four high-stemmed glasses. In each glass is a scoop of white ice cream and around the ice cream a red sauce. Out of the ice cream sticks a sparkler that has been lit and is joyfully spitting silver-blue sparks in four small fountains.

'And now, mes dames, you have reached the final course for this evening,' says the waiter, 'which is vanilla parfait with warm kirsch sauce, made from fresh cherries and Peter Heering, our famous Danish cherry wine.'
He lifts up the tray on the palm of his hand and clicks his heels before placing a portion in front of each of the ladies.

Sara, Liss and Eva eat the ice cream. The white ice cream in the red sauce. No one says anything. Tamara digs around in the ice cream with her spoon, but she eats nothing. Sara waves over the waiter and asks for the bill, which is brought immediately and put in front of Liss on a small dish.

'Cheers. It was certainly delicious food,' Liss says and empties her glass of Sauternes.

'Yes, fabulous,' Sara says. 'I think I liked the pastry with the herbs and tomato best. And the truffle risotto was just divine.'

'Shall we split the bill four ways? I actually had two drinks before the meal, whereas you all only had one,' Liss says and bends over the bill.

'Split it four ways,' Eva says. 'That's easiest.'

'Absolutely,' Sara says.

'No problem,' says Tamara. Far too loud.

They pay, give a good tip, stand up. They nod to the two couples at the nearest table and leave. Liss first. She holds her head high. In one hand she has a long-stemmed red rose. In her handbag is an ice-blue envelope. Eva walks beside Liss. Liss stretches out her arm and puts it around Eva's shoulders for a moment before it slips down around Eva's waist. Eva smiles. 'Nyhavn?' she says. 'Nyhavn,' answers Liss. The blonde and the darker blonde heads close together. Liss' blue eyes in Eva's brown eyes. Behind them come Sara and Tamara. They look straight ahead. They say nothing to each other in the short distance from the table to the cloakroom. Tamara's hand touches Sara's, maybe unintentionally, maybe on purpose. This touch makes both of them pull back their hands. In Eva's bag is a faded photograph of two dark-haired children. Soon it will lie in one of Copenhagen's municipal rubbish bins. In Sara's bag is Tamara's small, thick book. Sara will discover it and read it tomorrow.

The ladies retrieve their outer garments and leave. The waiter stands in the doorway to the restaurant. He stands and watches his Norwegian guests as they walk out into the cold January night. Then he closes the door behind him and we see no more of the four ladies.

Chapter 9

Breakfast, Thursday 5 July

In a hotel room in Germany, a woman with nearly black hair wakes up. She yawns, stretches her arms above her head. The blanket and sheet she has had over her fall to the floor. She opens her beautiful big eyes and looks at her slim, silk-clad body with satisfaction. The room is big. Light walls, light wall-to-wall carpet. Light, blond wood. A laptop sits on the desk beside the table. Beside the computer is a pile of dictionaries. In the other bed, a woman lies sleeping. She has pulled the blanket up so that it nearly covers her face. She moves restlessly in her sleep, mumbles something, pulls at the blanket.

The black-haired woman goes whistling into the bathroom, showers, puts on her eye make-up and gets dressed. Then she wakes the other woman. Sits on the edge of the bed and lets her hands slide gently through the other woman's brown hair.

'Guten morgen. Did you sleep well?'

'Yes, thank you,' answers the other woman after a few seconds. 'I was having such strange dreams.'

'I feel exhausted today,' says the black-haired woman. She looks at her companion in the bed with big, frightened eyes. 'I can't understand why, but my pelvis is hurting today.'

'Oh no,' says the other.

'I don't think I can face going to the exhibition this morning. I know that you were looking forward to it so much, but I am just too tired.'

'Oh you poor thing. Forget about the exhibition. It's not a problem. I can go another day.'

'But the opening's today and you know the artist and all that.'

'It's not a problem, Sara,' says the brown-haired woman.

'Maybe we could wander round the shops a bit instead,' suggests Sara.

The other woman nods. Sara starts to put up her hair and follows what the other woman is doing in the mirror. Sara pulls a lock of hair loose in front of one of her ears. She does not like people to see the scar, even though it is almost invisible. Just a thin, white stripe on her earlobe. She has new earrings. Small, glittering diamonds. Sara got them from Tamara. I cannot accept them, Sara said. Yes, they are for you, Tamara said repeatedly. Sara turns and meets the eyes of the brown-haired woman. We are sisters, thinks Sara. We are sisters forever.

'I feel a bit better already,' Sara says and smiles.

'That's good, Sara,' Synne replies.

The two dark-haired sisters go down to the dining room. Sara's black hair against Synne's brown. Breakfast. Walnut bread with apricot jam. No, don't touch the orange marmalade, Sara, you know you're allergic to citrus fruit. Thank you, Synne. Strong coffee. White milk in glasses. White as an angel.

Sara is in Germany with her sister. Evidently they are going to be away for a whole month. Before she went on holiday herself, Liss talked to one of her neighbours who had met Sara and Synne on the ferry between Rødby and Puttgarten.

And what about Tamara, then?

Well, at the same time that Sara and Synne are sitting eating walnut bread in Germany, Tamara is sitting somewhere else in Europe eating breakfast. She is sitting at a formica table and she is naked. Or perhaps she has a red, open kimono on. In any case, she is now leaning forwards over the table with a cigarette between her lips. A good-looking man with a moustache lights her cigarette and looks at her breasts that are brushing the crumbs from the table. The man is wearing boxer shorts and a vest with holes in it. In one corner of the room is a portable keyboard. Over the back of a chair hang the clothes he is going to wear to work tonight: an azure blue tuxedo with sequins. Liss giggles. But quietly. She mustn't wake Paul.

Tamara has finished her cigarette and is about to eat breakfast. But what do they actually eat for breakfast in Hungary? Or was it Bulgaria? White bread, surely. Dripping with sweet honey. And maybe some olives. Liss had never been to Bulgaria or Hungary. Liss gets into a more comfortable position, closer to Paul's warm body. She closes her eyes again. No one else is up yet. It is completely quiet in the cabin.

Liss knows very well that Tamara is not eating breakfast with a dance band musician somewhere in southern Europe. Tamara has never been to Bulgaria, or Hungary, for that matter. But she is eating breakfast. Right now Tamara is eating small pieces of bread. They have been cut up for her. Because where Tamara is, she is not allowed to have knives. One slice of bread with cheese and another with ham. The same every day. Tamara is wearing a white tunic. She has a name tag in clear plastic round her wrist. There is an obvious dent in the soft plastic where Tamara holds her middle and index fingers to check her pulse. Tamara eats slowly. She has no appetite. But she obediently swallows two light blue pills with some apple juice.

Not many people visit Tamara. She has lost them all. Kristian, Carlos, Håvard. And now Thomas. Sara had found Tamara's thick little book in her bag and read it. She ripped out a few pages and sent them to Thomas with love to Emma. Liss knows where Tamara is, because Eva visits her regularly once a week. But Liss prefers to think of Tamara in a red kimono in a dining room where the windows can be opened. Eva says that Tamara has become terribly thin and that her skin is nearly as white as the clothes she has to wear.

Liss gives a little sigh, turns over and enjoys the warmth of the bed. She is tired.

A blonde woman walks slowly down a shaded avenue. Beside her walks an Italian count. He is wearing a black cape and... No, not today. The blonde woman buttons up her emerald green Yves Saint Laurent suit and picks up the folder with the coded pages. No, Liss frowns. No, no counts today. No secret mission either. Something else. I want to dream about a breakfast table.

Yes, a breakfast table with a blue checked tablecloth. Liss shuts her eyes. A basket of fresh toast. A table set with seven – at least three of them different – flowery patterned plates. A chipped jam jar full of wild flowers. Soft-boiled eggs in a home-made egg warmer. Liverpaté, salami, goat's cheese and cervalat. In among all the spreads, some pink knitting. The door is open and it is a warm summer's day outside.

*

There are only two people at the table. A very blonde woman and a darker blonde woman with big brown eyes and dimples. The darker blonde has large arms, but when she gets up to stretch over for the teapot, we see that her stomach is not all fat.

'Here comes the whole gang back from fishing,' says the blonde woman, with a round happy face. 'I think I'd better start washing up.'
    'I'll dry,' says the darker blonde woman.

The two women start to clear the table. For a brief moment their hands touch over the bread basket. They smile at each other.

Liss wakes up with a start. Paul is not lying in bed beside her any more. She pads over the wooden floor in bare feet and out into the small kitchen. It's a warm summer's day outside.

'Good morning! Sit yourself down,' Eva says cheerfully. 'Paul and Erik have taken the children out fishing. I didn't want to wake you. Would you like some tea?'
    'Yes please,' says Liss.

Eva drinks tea and picks up her soft pink knitting.

'She's going to be a brave little Sagittarius,' Liss says and pats Eva on the stomach. Eva takes her hand and squeezes it in her own.